TABOO

When Alex met Sally... 'I wasn't all that crazy about meeting her. It wasn't that I didn't like her painting. I guess I was afraid she wouldn't meet my expectations. Then she walked in. Sally French was the sexiest woman I'd ever seen.'

When Sally met Alex... 'I had to crane my head to look up. How old was he anyway? Twenty, twenty-two? Much too young. I shouldn't be here, drinking Scotch with Alex Langley, wanting to touch his face. I should be at home, alone, making love to a canvas...'

TABOO

TABOO

Taboo

by

Ellen Archer

Black Satin Romance
Long Preston, North Yorkshire,
England.

British Library Cataloguing in Publication Data.

Archer, Ellen
   Taboo.

   A catalogue record for this book is
   available from the British Library

   ISBN 1-86110-013-2

Published in Large Print November, 1996 by arrangement with
Kensington Publishing Corporation.

Black Satin Romance is an imprint of
Library Magna Books Ltd.
Printed and bound in Great Britain by
T.J. Press (Padstow) Ltd., Cornwall, PL28 8RW.

Acknowledgements

Thanks to Martin Brown, my cousin the pharmacist, for the New York directions and the sleeping pill research (are you awake yet, Marty?); to Maureen Mitchell, therapist, and Roy Hedrick, M.F.C.C, Sexual Trauma Expert, for their insights on survivors and perpetrators of child abuse; to Pamela Dean, spinner of fantasies and all-around neat lady, for filling in the Minneapolis weather details that time and distance had scrubbed out of my head; to Sandra, at the Rose Petaler in Scottsdale, for going well out of her way to get me the scoop on Sonia roses; and last, but certainly not least, to my agent, Oscar Collier, and my editor, Beth Lieberman, for their guidance, faith, and humour.

1

Sally

When the doorbell rang, I was upstairs, working to the rhythm of Rachmaninoff and rain.

The last warm cloudburst of the season charged the air, rattled the studio windows, fanned undulating curtains of water across the skylight. The storm was a beauty, the kind I love: all gale and roar and gush. The kind that goes with Russian symphonies.

The bell jarred again, failing to harmonize with either the thunder or Rachmaninoff. Usually, I don't answer the door. Nine times out of ten, it's the Avon Lady or a Jehovah's Witness or a couple of those stark little Mormon missionary boys who are just aching to tell you all about Joseph Smith and The Other Testament of Jesus Christ. Either that, or somebody selling light bulbs.

But this time I knew who it was, and she knew I was home. I was stuck.

I put down my brush, rubbed most of the cadmium red off my hands with a stray paper towel, and started for the front stair. The studio perfumes—turpentine, alkyd, varnish, rain—were diluted, then overtaken, by the downstairs scents: lemon polish, sandalwood, more rain. I opened the door to a humid rush of undisciplined

9

currents and invisible sparks and more of that wonderful rain smell, like green electricity. It prickled my skin, tickled my nose.

Ardith was out there, too. Behind her, the sky had gone from grey streaked with black to black streaked with pink.

'What the hell's wrong with you?' She shook her turquoise umbrella, spattering the porch.

'What?' I stared past her into the rain. It bent the yellowing locust branches, beat down the fresh-mowed, raw-tipped grass, streamed over Ardith's little red Mercedes, scrubbed the pavement on its way downhill. There would be a small lake in the intersection by now. I had a sudden yen to walk down the street and go wading.

Rachmaninoff drifted down from the studio, but for some reason I thought of snake charmers' flutes and East Indian drums and Lord Byron. And colours. Aunt Mariah always said I had an undisciplined mind, for somebody who was supposed to be so smart.

'Sally, wake up! Are you going to ask me in, or what?' Ardith waved her umbrella angrily, and I moved aside. 'it took you forever to answer the bell.' She shot the umbrella into the stand, nose-down, and tugged at the belt of her raincoat. Like everything Ardith Crawford owned, it was expensive. 'It's not like you didn't know I was coming,' she growled through bright red Elizabeth-Ardened lips.

'Sorry,' I said. 'I was working. Guess I didn't hear you right away.'

'Right away? I've been leaning on the damn

10

thing for fifteen minutes.'

I lifted an eyebrow.

'Oh, all right. Five minutes. Well, you *did* take your sweet time.' She hung her coat on the hall tree, kicked off her shoes, walked past me into the front parlour, and lowered her fashionably emaciated frame into an armchair. The rain streaming the windows cast wonderfully eerie half-shadows across the room to give everything, Ardith included, the look of watered silk. I poured us both a Glenlivet, and she inhaled hers before I had time to fetch her a coaster.

'Better,' she said. She clinked her ice, in sharp contrast to the flat plop of raindrops on windowpanes. I refilled her glass quickly, more to make her stop than to be hospitable. This time, she took just a sip before she set the tumbler aside.

'I must be a mess,' she said. A manicured hand patted her auburn hair. The twist was perfect, as always. Not a hair out of place. Ardith was close to sixty, but she barely looked forty-five.

'You're never a mess.'

She ignored me. 'I want to talk about this exhibition—'

'Ardith, I told you—'

'I know what you told me, and you're being obtuse. I've been carrying your work for more than seven years. And every September I give you a one-woman show. And every damn time you stand me up.'

'You know I don't like to—'

'I don't care. Do you realize your collectors

11

are beginning to think you don't exist? Last week I heard a rumour that "Sally French" is really five collaborating Hungarians. My Lord, Sally, do you *ever* go out of this house?' She had leaned back a little, and she didn't look so angry anymore. Maybe she'd remembered that frowning gives you wrinkles.

'Of course I go out. I go to the market. I go to the post office. I go to...' I had to stop and think. I stared at my Scotch, watched the melting ice diffuse its colour. Swirls, sensuous eddies, like clear oil flowing thickly over tanned skin...

Thunder rumbled outside. A black shape, like a large, half-cooled droplet of wax, pressed behind my navel to vibrate with dark, thick sound. I love thunder.

'Sally, you're drifting on me.'

I made myself pay attention. 'I go see Chips every now and then. Every few weeks. And she's here all the time.' Chippewa Quincannon is my best friend, and a sculptress of the Native American variety. She does these amazing, crazy bronzes, really huge, of war ponies and buffalo and war ponies and Indian braves and more war ponies. She's part Crow and part Chippewa and mostly Irish, and if she has a real first name, she's not telling. Ardith's gallery carries her work, too. My work is what they call 'hot' on the East Coast. Chips is just as hot in the West.

Ardith cleared her throat. 'Chips says she hasn't actually seen you since February, Sally.' She just let it hang there in the air.

I took a cigarette from the box on the table and lit it. It was stale, but I dragged on it anyway and tried to look blasé. Had it really been seven months?

'Well, I talk to her nearly every day. And I've been busy,' I said with a shrug. When she didn't answer, I added, 'You *know* I've been busy. I just sent you a van-load of new stuff last week.'

'That's not the point.' She twisted in her chair and tucked an immaculately hosed leg under her fanny. 'The point is that you're turning into a goddamn hermit. Hermitess. Whatever. When's the last time you got laid?'

No preface of *If you don't mind my asking,* or *I know it's none of my business, but...*

'You're so subtle, Ardith.' I wished she'd go. I wanted to carry my Scotch upstairs and paint those seductive incursions of clear, cold water into amber whiskey. I wanted to paint the feel of it, and of that black-thunder shape in my stomach.

She laughed and lit one of her long brown cigarettes. 'The velvet glove's for clients, Sally. I've known you too long to pussyfoot. Fact is, I'm worried about you.'

'Well, thanks, I guess, but you really don't—'

'Yes, I do. I can't help it. It's my nature. For God's sake, Sally, look at yourself!'

I stared down my bluejeanned legs to my bare feet. I wiggled them. I twisted them into the rug. I'd always liked my feet. Nice shape. Great toes. Toes were a good colour, an interesting form. Mine fit together quite wonderfully, I thought.

13

Toes and Scotch. Scotch-coloured toes. Scotch *on* toes...

'Sally!' Ardith was staring at me, one eyebrow hoisted like Mr Spock's.

'Oh. Sorry. What should I look at? My nose on crooked, or something? What's wrong with me?'

She shook her head, drained her glass. 'Aside from the fact that you've got the attention span of a gnat, nothing. Which is my point. How old are you, anyway?' The room lit bright with lightning for a half-second, but she didn't seem to notice.

'Thirty-nine.' The number sounded strange when I said it. What had happened to thirty-one through thirty-eight?

There was another low roll of thunder before she said, 'Well, then.'

'Well, then *what?*'

She sighed. 'Honestly, for someone as bright as you are...'

I thought of Aunt Mariah. The Rachmaninoff disk finished and Paganini kicked in, reminding me of the temporarily jilted painting waiting on my easel. Outside, the storm was lessening, moving away, taking the last of the afternoon with it. I considered turning on a lamp.

In the fading light, Ardith's stencilled lips moved. 'If you're going to make me spell it out, I will. You're attractive, Sally.'

'What does that have to do with anything? Besides, I'm not—'

'Shut up. You're practically gorgeous. All that blond hair and those big grey eyes. And you're

14

smart. *And* talented. And rich, by the way—or at least, upper-middle. I should know. I write your cheques. Which reminds me...'

She opened her bag and brought out a familiar pale lilac envelope. *Ardith Crawford Gallery,* read the trendy logo above the return address. 'Your August cheque came in from New York. Oh, and I sold the big red thing last Wednesday. Statement's in there, too. And the inventory sheets for the new pieces.'

I accepted the envelope and laid it on the end table, unopened. 'How come you always call them "the big red thing" or "the big green thing" or "the little purple thing"? They have titles, you know.'

She ground out her cigarette. 'Titles are for art-history books. And don't try to change the subject. Honestly, how can someone who paints with such passion live the way you do? Those canvases of yours are so overripe I've practically had people orgasm on the gallery floor.'

'Oh, Ardith—'

'Don't "Oh, Ardith" me. All I'm saying is that you need to get out of this house, and that—more important, my dear—you need to get laid.'

That black glob of thunder behind my navel lurched to the side. Damn her, anyway. Why do some people think sex fixes everything? I took another sip of my Scotch, this time without studying the colour. It was getting too dark to see much colour, anyhow.

Ardith reached across and clasped my wrist. Her nails were perfect, and she was wearing

15

a diamond the size of Nicaragua. 'Look at it this way, Sally. If your paintings are this provocative now, just imagine where they might go if you...well, it's not healthy, living the way you do.'

I pulled my arm away, a little rudely, perhaps. I was no longer accustomed to human touch. 'I'm perfectly happy, thank you.'

She stood up, smoothed her skirt, and patted at her hair again. 'All right. But you *are* coming to this next opening if I have to drive over here and dress you up and drag you downtown. And you're going to smile and shake hands and make nice with the people. Got it?'

I became a painter because my mother had been one. Well, I probably would have become one anyway, once I'd figured out I had some talent; but finding out about Mother was what got me started.

Nobody told me about her, of course, let alone that she'd been, in a small way, famous. To my face, the Aunts spoke of Mother only if pressed, and even then they rarely had anything kind to say. To them, my mother was the hussy who'd stolen away their brother Michael. It was bad enough that she'd come from New York, far worse that she'd been a beatnik.

This last was told to me, in hushed tones, when I was about eight and had no idea what a beatnik might be. I later concluded that the Aunts had no idea, either. To Aunts Mariah, Little Meg, Millie, and Mavis, New York plus artist equaled beatnik, which meant nothing less than a never-ending naked, drunken, cross-country spree with Jack Kerouac.

Not that they knew much about Jack Kerouac, either. I think that part must have come from my cousin, Norman French Gilchrist, who was four years my senior.

Norman's father had departed this mortal coil during the Korean War, when Norman was barely two, and he was always referred to by Aunt Mariah as a war hero, although I later found out he had died at Fort Dix of a burst appendix. But he'd left behind a 640-acre farm, just outside town, that Mariah rented out; and that, combined with a little government money and a smallish trust my parents had left me, supported me. Years later, after I left home and farmland prices skyrocketed, Mariah sold the farm and stuck the money in the bank, and she and Norman lived off the interest in a tidy but far from fancy way.

Back then, when we were kids, Norman spent most of his time lurking in our earth-floored cellar (which he dubbed the Cave of Mysteries and Science), where he cooked up chemistry experiments that exploded or smelled like rotten eggs or both. He also invented useless gadgets, and read everything he could get his hands on. Mostly he was skimming for the dirty parts, but he had a mind like a deep-sea sponge and picked up a good bit of information by osmosis.

Mariah called Norman her 'little genius' and told everybody that one day he'd be rich and famous and support her in the style to which she'd like to become accustomed. And then, no

17

matter how many times they'd heard that line, everyone would have to laugh.

If They Knew What Was Good For Them.

Norman surfaced from the cave only for meals, for school, and to make my life a misery. When I was four or five, he'd chase me with snakes or bugs, or hold me down while he chanted, 'Fuckshitdamnpee!' By the time I was seven and he was eleven, the game had changed. He called me Little Orphan Annie while he yanked my hair or kicked me or tried to pull my panties down. By then, I'd given up telling Aunt Mariah. She always believed Norman, and I always ended up spanked or supperless or both.

When we were both a little older—and Norman had discovered the joys of *National Geographic* and a locked bathroom door—the taunts shifted focus. He still tried to pull my panties down, but now he had a singular purpose. My mother had been a rope-smoking whore, Norman assured me, and I was bound to be the same.

Hey, Sal, here's a quarter, might's well start practisin' that last part.

How those little titties growin', Orphan Annie? Lemme see, Sal. Lemme pinch your nips or you'll be sorry...

I had my hiding places. Until I grew too big to fit, there was the old woodbin in the storage shed. I remember that it smelled of ancient dust and cobwebs and what I assumed were rat faeces. It was a terrible place to hide away in the dark, but it was better than being caught by Norman.

18

Later, I sought refuge in the big oak that grew outside my bedroom window and towered above our house. From my perch I could see most of Brigston—from the old Creamery at the north end to Beedle Road and the last line of houses at the other—and the barely rolling yellow-green patchwork of corn- and wheatfields beyond.

Even now, thirty years later, I still dream of this tree: the feel and musty earth-scent of its ancient bark; the damp traces its leaves would leave on my face and arms when I scurried up through its branches, dark and slick, after a rain; the way the light came through each unshaded leaf, glowing green, just short of translucent. You could hold one up against the summer sky and the green would fairly blaze. How many times in the years since had I painted that particular green, struck with the liquid butter-yellow of a hot Kansas sun?

Norman suffered from acute vertigo and never followed me into the oak, although he'd sometimes sit below and wait for an hour, if he had nothing better to do.

Gotta come down and pee sometime, Sally. And when you do, I'm gonna getcha...

I learned to hold my water for a very long time.

Norman was one of those people who, by rights, should have been big-nosed, pimply faced, and lumbering. That he was clear-skinned and rather handsome in a rock-jawed way and tested on the Stanford-Binet with an IQ of 156 has always been strong proof to me that God is not paying attention.

19

We both did well in school, but neither of us was popular. The girls thought Norman was handsome—and he could be very nice when he wanted to be—but seldom did any girl take up his offer of a second date. This surprised me not at all. I had few friends, and the ones I had I kept at arms' length. Or thought I did. Perhaps it was the other way around.

Norman was Aunt Mariah's world, whereas I was merely her burden. Norman, his life and times, was also the centre of focus for the rest of the Aunts, since Mariah and my father had been the only two of the French siblings to marry and produce offspring.

Around Brigston, the Aunts were known collectively as 'the French girls' long after the youngest had shouted a distant goodbye to middle age. Every Sunday they met at the Methodist church for nine o'clock service. After, they gathered at our house for fried chicken, canasta, and an update on the wonders of Norman.

'What did you invent this week, Norman?' Aunt Little Meg would mumble brightly around a mouthful of chicken skin. Little Meg, like all the French girls, was possessed of a rather tiny, moist mouth centered in a jowly face. Like Norman and my late father, they were dark-haired and tall: Little Meg was the shortest at five-feet-nine. Aunt Mariah was 6 feet tall in her stocking feet.

They were top-heavy, with huge bosoms and thick waists and double chins, but each and every one had long, shapely, slender legs—not

20

a varicose vein in sight—and, whenever possible, wore shorts from spring thaw right through to the first snowfall. The French girls preferred White Shoulders cologne and were not stingy in its application; when the four of them were together in a small room, it was like drowning in the stuff.

To this day, the smallest whiff of White Shoulders instinctively inspires me to avail myself of the nearest exit.

After Sunday dinner, Norman would have to speak for a few minutes about his current project. I think he often made it up as he went along. No one could prove him a liar, since no one was ever allowed into his padlocked lair, although he did, on occasion, actually produce some gadget or other he'd made. I remember a pretzel-dough twister, an alarm clock that woke you with a squirt of water, a battery-powered apple peeler. There were more things, although I don't remember most of them, not even the gizmo that won him a prize in the state science fair. I do remember the trophy, though, mainly because I had to dust it.

The fried chicken and the Amazing Norman Show were followed by canasta. I'd clear off the dishes and, dinner having been served on card tables set up in the living room, the Aunts would get right down to business. Norman disappeared into his cave, I washed up, Mariah brought out the plastic card tray and two decks of Bicycle cards—one red, one blue—and, over the fading odours of friend chicken, gravy, green beans with bacon, and White Shoulders cologne, the

Aunts would commence to shuffle and talk.

I don't suppose it ever occurred to them that since I was only a room away, I could hear every word. I probably could have heard them from out on the porch.

The gabbing pretty much followed the same pattern: a rehash of The Norman Show; a discussion of what a fine young man he was getting to be ('Oh, he'll make hearts flutter!' Aunt Mavis said every single week, without fail); general town gossip; and then me.

Sally doesn't look like a French. Sally doesn't act like a French. Goes around slouched and stoop-shouldered, with that awful yellow hair hanging in her eyes; if her grades didn't say otherwise, why, a body'd think she was stupid. Maybe she is stupid. Maybe she cheats—she used to lie all the time. Likely, still does, even if I can't catch her at it. Oh, the stories she used to make up about my Norman!

Probably can't help it, poor thing. Bad blood. Such a shame about her father, her mother. Such a shame about Sally. If only Michael had married that nice Schoonover girl. If only Michael hadn't been so hasty. If only Michael hadn't married at all and hadn't had that woman hammering at him to better himself, he never would have changed jobs, never would have pushed for that promotion, never would have gone off to Kansas City, never would have died. Why, if it weren't for that woman—that beatnik—he'd still be working at the Coöp and living right here in Brigston, in this very house with Mariah—what could be better than that?—and providing a father figure for poor, brilliant Norman.

How cheated they had been to have lost their brother. How cursed to have been burdened with his odd-looking, odd-acting, ill-pedigreed child, who did noting but remind them, by her presence, that they had been jilted.

At this point, at least one of them would get a little weepy, and the conversation would turn back toward Norman's luminous future. I'd be putting away the last of the dishes and wiping off the counters by then, and most times I'd get clear of the kitchen and safely up to my room or into the arms of my oak before Aunt Mariah came to fetch the brownies or cake she'd saved back for the game's midpoint.

I liked to tell myself that I was used to it, that it didn't hurt any more. But it did. I had just stopped crying over it, that was all.

Norman and the Aunts aside, I had, by the time I'd reached the age of twelve, formed a wishful mental picture of my mother: her face was something like mine; her figure was slender in a black pullover and black stretch pants like the ones Laura Petrie wore on the *Dick Van Dyke Show*. I imagined my mother wearing a black beret and little black slippers with no heels, and smoking endless cigarettes over endless cups of espresso in smoke-fogged coffeehouses, all of which were in Greenwich Village, while she passed the reefer and quoted Ginsburg and Ferlinghetti.

And then one humid summer evening I went to babysit with Dickie Kleister, and everything changed. I hadn't wanted to go. I'd wanted to stay home and watch *Bonanza;* I had the most terrible crush on Michael Landon. But Aunt Mariah had already told them I'd be there at seven sharp.

Dickie was a brat of the first water, but the Kleisters had air conditioning and a colour television, which made up for nearly all of Dickie's sins. And at least I wouldn't have to put up with dear cousin Norman, who would sometimes surface during my favourite TV shows to sit beside me on the couch and try to cop a feel if Aunt Mariah should leave the room for a minute or two.

Tell and I'll hurt you, Orphan Annie. I'll hurt you bad...

He didn't need to threaten me. I'd learned by then that at our house Norman was golden, Norman could do no wrong. Mariah would pretend not to see him hastily jerk his hand out of my pants or from under my blouse when she came back from the kitchen or the bathroom.

So I went to the Kleisters'. I put Dickie to bed, made popcorn, poured myself a tall Pepsi over ice, and settled in to watch Little Joe keep Virginia City safe in living colour.

And in peace.

But Dickie wouldn't stay in bed. 'Read me!' he insisted, waving a battered book as he climbed into my lap and spilled Pepsi all over his Doctor Dentons and my jeans.

I got him cleaned up and changed, got myself sponged off, all the while trying to catch glimpses of the TV screen. I consoled myself that at least Little Joe wasn't in this episode very much.

24

'There,' I said at last, tucking Dickie back into bed. 'Stay put.'

'Read!' he shouted, as I reached for the light switch. He still had the book. He waved it at me as he tugged back his covers and sat up.

A commercial drifted down the hallway. *See the USA in your Chevrolet...*

I sat on the edge of the mattress. 'Three minutes.'

And then I looked at the cover. *The Blue Elf*, written and illustrated by Rosalyn Mitchell French.

My breath caught in my throat. I turned to the inside back cover. No coincidence. There it was: a photograph of my mother. She had her arm around a tricoloured collie, and she was laughing. The sun sparkled through her straw-coloured hair, washed over her freckled cheeks.

Below, a small block of copy told me that Rosalyn Mitchell French had written and/or illustrated several other Big Books for Little People, and that she was a native of upstate New York and currently lived in Kansas with her husband and brand new daughter, Sally.

From the living room drifted the music announcing the next act of *Bonanza*. Ben Cartwright said something wise, although I registered only the tone, not the words. I was too busy looking at the pictures—soft, enchanting, misty watercolours—my mother had painted.

Dickie kicked me in the leg. 'Read me the story!'

I did.

Dickie didn't have anymore of my mother's books, but the grade school library had two. I went there several times, surrounded by a sea of smaller children, just to sit and look at her handiwork, to run my fingers across the printers' inks that had reproduced her art. I never checked them out and brought them home, though. The result would have been unpleasant. But I did start to paint.

I loved it from the beginning.

I signed up for what our county school system optimistically called their All-Age Summer Arts and Crafts Cornucopia: ten weeks of classes in everything from drawing to leather crafts to flower-arranging. And when school started again in the fall, I signed up for every available art course, bought or borrowed every 'how-to' art book and artist's biography I could get my hands on, and began to spend all my spare time sequestered in my room, painting or drawing or reading about it, or lazing, eyes closed, dreaming of colours.

I had expected some flack from Aunt Mariah, what with her considering anything to do with the arts bohemian and therefore nasty and decidedly 'un-French,' but she didn't make much fuss. She even let me install a little slide lock on my bedroom door so that nothing could disturb me while I painted.

It was a mystery at the time, but looking back, I guess she did it because of Norman. Giving me that locked door was the closest she'd ever come to an admission.

In the twenty-two years since I'd left Brigston

behind, I'd seen Mariah only once, when she and Little Meg had won round trip tickets to the Twin Cities in some radio giveaway. They'd stayed not with me, but with an old school friend of Little Meg's, and had visited me for only one very long, uncomfortable afternoon during which I discovered that our feelings towards one another had been softened neither by time nor age.

She continued to phone me every other month of so, but those calls came more from her sense of duty than from any real interest in what I was doing or how I felt about it. After forty years, she still resented me, and I was still intimidated by her. And we, neither one of us, found anything even slightly likeable about the other.

I called Chips Quincannon the afternoon after Ardith's visit.

'Good for her,' Chips said. She sounded just a little too pleased. 'I knew the old bat had to be good for something besides sucking thirty-five percent off the top. When's she got you scheduled, anyhow?' I heard papers rustling. 'Saturday, right?'

'I sighed. It was too soon, just two days away.

'You got anything to wear?'

I hadn't thought about that.

'I'll be there in twenty minutes,' she said, and hung up before I had a chance to answer.

She showed up on my doorstep with what must have been half her wardrobe piled over

27

her arms. I humoured her, and tried most of it on, but nothing worked. Her things were bright, theatrical: dripping with feathers or beads or leather fringe or chain mail. On Chips, with her straight blue-black hair, strong chiselled face, and startling Irish blue eyes, they were stunning. On me, they were ludicrous.

'They're not me, Chips,' I said. I was sitting on the bed in a jumbled nest of leather and lamé. 'They're not *anybody* except you. And maybe Cher.' A tiny pink feather shed by some skirt or cape drifted on the air and landed on my nose. I swatted at it.

'Well, crap.' She plopped down on the windowseat and propped her legs in front of her. A stick of Juicy Fruit (her fifth or sixth since she'd arrived) went into her mouth, the wrappers into her shirt pocket. 'I s'pose we'd better go shopping.'

'No. I'll come up with something.' I hated stores, hated piped-in music, hated crowds and the brush of strangers. Too many voices, too many lights, too much ill-choreographed confusion. Too many people saying 'Have a nice day' from behind the Genuine Faux Pearl counter.

Chips dragged herself off the windowseat and threw open my closet doors. There wasn't much to look at. 'And just what do you figure to come up with?'

I moved her out of the way and yanked open a dresser drawer. '*This* is what I'm wearing.' I tossed a pair of jeans, an eggshell cable-knit, and a pair of boots on top of her spangles.

28

There was a pause before she said, 'You're kidding, right?'

'Nope. You're forgetting. We're goddamn *artistes*, Chips. People *expect* us to look...unique. You do it your way, I'll do it mine. And on second thought...' I scooped up the jeans, threw them in their drawer, and rummaged at the back.

'Here,' I said, when I'd found the pair I wanted. I shook them out and smiled. They were ripped and full of holes. Spatters of paint decorated the thighs. My own smeary handprint, in cadmium yellow, decorated the right back pocket. Aunt Mariah would hate them.

'Perfect,' I said.

Chips was laughing. 'Ardith's gonna stake you out on an anthill.'

I dropped the Levis on the bed and, smirking, lit a cigarette. Chips is totally crazed, and one of the few people who can hold my attention for more than five minutes. 'No way,' I said with a grin. 'I make her too much money. She rakes forty percent off me, you know, not that measly thirty-five *you* pay her...'

I jabbed her with that little gem whenever I got a chance. Chips works in bronze, which costs more to produce than works on canvas. Ardith, like most galleries, made an allowance for that.

'Aw, jeez,' she began. 'Are we gonna have to go through this *again?*' She looked terribly long-suffering, and I took pity on her.

'Relax,' I said, and chuckled before I took another drag on the Salem. Chips would be at

29

the opening, too. She'd volunteered to be my 'date.' Maybe I could brave it out. 'So. How many people come to these things, anyway?'

She waved her hand. 'I dunno. I guess at my last show there were two, maybe three hundred.'

I slumped against the dresser.

'Well, not all at one *time*, Sally. They kind of drift in and out all evening. Course, there might not be so many at your show. I'm *much* more famous than you.' She was back on the windowseat. Sweeping the heavy lace curtains to one side, she struck what she thought was an artistic pose.

'Very funny.'

'Thanks. But honest, it's not that awful. There won't be any wackos or anything. I'll protect you from the big bad public.'

I tried to smile. Ardith thought I was just being stubborn. Chips knew I was terrified.

'Really, don't worry about it. Ardith's got all kinds of people to channel off the riffraff. She'll want you rubbing elbows with the high rollers, anyway, not the tourists. She's got all new staffers since the last time you were in, too. Which was probably sometime around the Italian Renaissance, right? Coupla cute guys. Heterosexual, I might add.'

I hopped up to sit on the edge of the dresser, then leaned forward, propping my elbows on my knees. 'Doesn't sound like you're going to spend much time looking at my paintings.'

She yawned, dug out another stick of Juicy Fruit, and peeled away the wrapper. 'Already had one of them,' she said matter-of-factly.

'My paintings?'

She shook her head, then spat out a grey wad and jammed the fresh stick in her mouth. 'The staff. Guy named Darryl. I can't afford your damn paintings.'

I laughed. 'Uh-huh. Aren't you the one who just sold a bronze for a hundred and fifty grand?'

'Oh, sure. Before expenses. And before the LA gallery hacked off their thirty-five percent and Ardith sliced off another ten and the IRS...and then there's Frank. And Pops.'

She stared out the window for a second. If she was thinking about Frank, her ex, I could count on a half-hour tirade about lazy bums who took alimony from their ex-wives when they had MBAs and were perfectly capable of working.

If she was thinking about her father, and if he'd been in bad shape during her last visit, then we'd be in for a few tears. Pops had been in a nursing home for something close to seven years and hadn't lived anywhere near the present tense, mentally speaking, for the last five. Chips went to see him twice a week, even though he'd stopped recognizing her years ago.

Me, I don't remember my father. Or my mother. They were on their way to Kansas City: it was a convention, I think—my father had something to do with farm equipment—and they were going to make a second honeymoon of it. I was just ten months old, and they left me with Aunt Mariah for a long weekend. Somewhere along highway 50, a cattle truck

31

wandered into the wrong lane and collided with them, head-on. They were both killed instantly, and my long weekend with Aunt Mariah turned into forever.

Sometimes, when Chips was having a rough patch and I was getting a little weary of repeating the same hollow, consoling phrases over and over, it'd be on the tip of my tongue to remind her that at least she'd had parents who'd loved her and a childhood she remembered as all summers and sunshine, when all I had was Mariah and the rest of the Aunts, and a youth that seemed a grey and endless winter. But I always held my tongue, and I always hated myself for even thinking of mentioning it.

I supposed we all get the families we get for a reason. I just wish I could figure out why I got Aunt Mariah. Not to mention Norman.

Chips was still staring out the window, and I waited to see who she was thinking about: Frank or Pops. Luckily for me, it was Ardith.

'Jesus Christ,' she spat. 'I wish *I* had a business where I never had to pay a damn cent for the inventory until *after* it was sold. And I swear to God, all she does for the agent's fee is wander over to the studio every six months or so and point at stuff and say, "I believe we should send this piece to Santa Fe, Chips, dear." *Plus* which—'

Grinning, I held up my hand. Chips is at her best when she's in her curmudgeon mode. I laughed and said, 'I'll get the violin.'

'Oh, shut up.'

'So how was he?'

'Who?'

'Your friend from Ardith's What's-his-name. Darryl?'

She shrugged noncommittally and spat the latest gum into a bit of paper before she burrowed into her pocket for the pack. 'Oh, him. Not bad, but too starstruck. I wouldn't've been surprised if he'd asked for my autograph mid-screw. Jeez, I'm gonna have to start smoking again. Damn gum's costing me a fortune.'

'Wouldn't if you didn't chain-chew it. What about the other one?'

She folded the newest victim in two and stuck it in her mouth. 'Huh? Oh. No, not him. Not my type. Way too young. Pretty, though. Very pretty. Sharp, too.' She jabbed a finger at her temple. 'Ardith's got him practically running the place. Alex Something-or-other. Don't suppose you've got any booze around here, do you?'

'Early for you, isn't it?'

'Yeah, but we're gonna have to chop at least a foot off that hair of yours, and—'

I grabbed my head and slid off the dresser. 'What?'

'It's all scraggly. Needs some evening up.' She got to her feet. 'Can't expect me to do that sober. Plus which, I haven't seen you in person for light years. I wanna gab. Seems to me we used to actually get together and talk. In person. You know, like this? Two actual people in the same actual room?'

'Chips—'

'Seems to me I used to come over here practically every week or so. And if memory serves, I think you've seen the inside of *my* house, too. I mean, I know you're a hermit, Sal, but lately you're dug in like you're waiting for the mushroom cloud. You got a stockpile of canned food and ammo I don't know about?' She started for the door, then stopped. 'Oh, yeah. Langley.'

'What?'

'Alex Langley. The other guy at Ardith's. I knew I'd remember it.' She gestured at me to follow. 'C'mon, Sal. Let's crack open the Wild Turkey.'

'If you think for one minute that I'm going to let you anywhere near my hair with a sharp instrument—'

She waited in the doorway. 'C'mon, White Eyes. Me needum new scalp for war lance. And let's do it in the studio. I wanna see what you're workin' on.'

2

Alex

I can't say I was happy when Ardith told me Sally French was coming to opening night.

It wasn't that I didn't like her paintings: when the gallery was slow, I used to stand in front of them and stare. They hypnotized you, bored into your groin, and you could tell right away which buyers were wired into their own guts by the way they reacted when they saw a French for the first time.

I was fairly used to the effect by now, but there were still days when I couldn't catch one out of the corner of my eye without getting hard.

Anyway, I wasn't all that crazy about meeting her. I'd worked her shows the last couple of years, and we got along fine without her. It sounds stupid now, but I honestly hoped she'd skip out on us. I guess I was afraid she wouldn't meet my expectations. Or anybody else's, for that matter. I didn't figure anyone could live up to the emotions she wrenched out of those canvases.

Maybe she was pulling all our chains. Maybe she was some brainless ditz who didn't have the slightest idea what she was putting across in her paintings. I've seen that happen.

I'd worked for Ardith for a little over two years, since the tail end of my sophomore year at the Institute. I was a painting major, but after a couple years I knew I didn't have what it took. Oh, I suppose I could have been a decent illustrator, but I didn't have *it*, whatever *it* is. I guess if I knew, I'd have it. So I decided that if I couldn't be a painter, the kind I wanted to be, I'd at least stay in the business of art.

I quit school—imagine how thrilled my folks were about *that*—and went to work for Ardith, and she and I hit it off right away. After about a year and a half she made me manager. That really pissed off Betty and Darryl. Betty'd been with Ardith four years and she still hadn't

35

figured out the consignment sheets. Darryl hired on about the same time I did, but he's got ten years on me and he hated taking orders from a kid. That's what they called me behind my back—the Kid. Or the Asshole.

But as I was saying, I wasn't looking forward to meeting Sally French. I was curious, sure, but it wasn't the kind of curiosity you really wanted satisfied. I suppose I was a little scared to meet her, but not because I was in awe of her: I'd met some big names working for Ardith, and I was already pretty jaded. I just didn't want to find out that the woman whose paintings had been psychically sucking my cock for two years was anything less than I wanted her to be.

The paintings were enough. Sally French, in person, could only be a letdown. I even asked Ardith if I could take the night off.

'Are you crazy, Alex?' She was waving a fan of brochures at me with one hand, one of those brown cigarettes with the other. 'You know what kind of a madhouse this place turns into. I've already got Mary out with the flu. You *have* to stay!'

I snatched the brochures away from her before she bent them up too much. The day of an opening, Ardith always ran around like somebody had just severed her brain stem. But come seven o'clock, the champagne would start to bubble, the caterers would lift the lids off the hors d'oeuvre steamers, the doors would reopen, and Ardith would unfailingly metamorphose into the Princess Royale. It happened every time. You couldn't get more gracious (or more persuasive) than Ardith Crawford.

But right then she was still in panic mode. 'The lights!' she was shouting at Darryl. 'Did you double-check the lights? I can't have a spot go out tonight. I have people flying in from New York and Toronto and goddamn *Miami*, for Christ's sake!'

I shook my head and straightened out those brochures. And tried to keep my mind off Sally French.

3

Sally

In my freshman year of high school, Aunt Mariah allowed me to convert the old storage shed into a summer studio.

By then it had nothing to do with keeping me away from Norman, who was miles away at Kansas State. No, nothing to do with Norman, but perhaps quite a bit to do with the boys who walked me home from school and brought me home too late from dates. Perhaps Aunt Mariah viewed both my artistic bent and my appeal to the opposite sex as creeping symptoms of bad beatnik blood, and figured she couldn't fight both, so she'd fight the more sinful. And giving me a place to work and a seemingly endless list of things to paint was the most Christian way to keep my dance card filled.

37

At least, that's what I thought at the time.

'Little Meg has that new gold and avocado davenport, and nothing to hang over it, Sally. Don't you think you could paint her some nice flowers?'

So I painted flowers and fruit and puppies, and, late in the evening, when the downstairs lights went off and Aunt Mariah's bedroom light went on, I'd let Bobby Daws into the studio for a little beatnik bebop. Bobby wouldn't have known a beatnik from a broom handle, and I didn't love him; but he wanted me, and I was needy enough that his want was sufficient. Free love was the coming thing, and San Francisco was the place Bobby was going as soon as he saved up some money, he'd say.

After we'd finish humping on the paint-spattered studio floor, I'd pull my jeans back on and Bobby'd offer me another hit of the grass he'd grown down along the drainage ditch west of his daddy's northernmost wheatfield.

I viewed myself as fashionably decadent. If I closed my eyes, I could imagine that I was on the art world's cutting edge and that I had just made love to a famous movie star or writer in my Paris studio. But every time Bobby went home and left me sitting alone—stupid from the dope and empty and staring at rough-boarded walls lined with paintings barely one step up in their subject matter from bullfighters on black velvet—I'd be thinking that maybe old tit-tweaking Norman had been right, after all: rope-smoking whore.

Like Bobby Daws, I felt San Francisco's pull;

not so much for the city, but for what it represented. Sex, drugs, and rock and roll aside, there was something intoxicatingly exotic—and erotic—in the atmosphere surrounding the flower people. And if any of them had an Aunt Mariah, they didn't seem to be swayed in the slightest by what she said.

Honestly, Sally, do you have *to go around looking like that? You have perfectly good dresses. Sally, are you listening to me?*

Sally, you're so thick! *You'll never amount to anything, but that shouldn't surprise me, should it? Sally! Listen when I talk to you!*

Sally, pay attention. And get that hair out of your eyes. Just like your mother...

Not that Mariah was constantly in my face. I do have good memories of my childhood, like the time Mariah rented a pony for my sixth birthday party and Norman dressed up as a clown and turned somersaults on the lawn while everyone cheered and waved balloons; and later, after the guests were gone, Norman taught me how to ride my new bicycle. Three months later, when I rode my bike off the road and down into a ditch, Norman was the one who patiently straightened the frame and replaced the chain.

He was about ten then, and those were the days before the bad things happened between Norman and me and when I still thought he was a minor god. Even later, when our relationship developed into a game of cat-and-mouse—with Norman in the continuing role of cat—he always fixed stuff for me, often without being asked, and always cheerfully. Sometimes I almost liked him.

Our kitchen always smelled like Betty Crocker lived there, except that Mariah never 'baked from a box,' and looked down upon those who did. Everything she made was from scratch, and she, like her sisters, was a good cook: a trait I did not inherit, to her everlasting exasperation. Of food and warmth and shelter I had a plenty, and, as the fads came and went, Mariah saw to it that I had my own Davy Crockett cap or Dale Evans cowgirl skirt or hula hoop. Once, as a reward for achieving my first (and last, as it turned out) 'A' in algebra, she drove me to the county seat and bought me the new Beatles album, my first real lipstick (Yardley frost, of course), and a pleated skirt with knee socks to match.

I do remember being hugged and comforted by Mariah when I was small and prone to suffer skinned elbows and scraped knees. When I was eight and had chicken pox, she cared for me tenderly and made up games to keep me from scratching at the rash. But well before I got to junior high, we didn't touch much, she and I. I guess Norman was taking up the slack.

Mariah and I never engaged in any knock-down, drag-out battles, but by the beginning of my high school years we had, at least, an armed truce in a very cold war all our own.

The fall of my sophomore year, Bobby Daws drew his 4-H cattle money out of the bank and went to San Francisco without a goodbye. Bill Oerbach took his place as my late-night caller until he found Jesus at a camp meeting and forsook sins of the flesh. He was succeeded by Delbert Foster, whose father was the town druggist. Del supplied me with bootleg birth control pills. After Del came Jimmy Lightfoot, son of our chief of police. Like the others, Jimmy met the unspoken qualifications: he didn't pretend to love me, and he kept his mouth shut about our trysts.

I kept on painting. I became obsessed with the process and the colour and the way it came off my brush. If that process had to result in apples and daisies for Aunt Millie's bathroom or Aunt Mavis's breakfast nook in order to keep the peace, so be it.

Dear, perfect, panty-yanking Norman finished college the same week I finished high school; since he was coming home to his mother's loving arms, I packed up my brushes and left.

The Aunts came to see me off at the depot, and Mariah cried. I was almost touched until I heard her say to Little Meg and Millie, 'Thank God, thank God.'

I didn't wave when the bus pulled out.

I never went to San Francisco, but I did assume the lifestyle. I moved to Kansas City and took a job on a factory assembly line. I was terrified of the city and the crowds and the noise and the strangeness, but I made myself do it. It was either that, or go back to Norman and the French girls. Days, I fitted the same little green piece of plastic over the same little metal nub over and over and over again, all the while painting glorious pictures in my head. Nights, I painted or made love or both.

Norman visited me once, uninvited and unannounced, about two years after I left home. It was brief and highly unpleasant, and once the unpleasantness was over, he went back to Brigston. I moved out of state.

My work had already begun to change, to take me toward some indefinite, cloudy destination. The years passed and the cities changed, along with the jobs that supported my painting.

I lost count of my lovers. Their faces blurred; I confused their names. If a man desired me, that was enough. But my primary focus was always on those canvases: canvases which gradually became larger, filled with colours that grew more lush, figures that became less and less recognizable until there were no figures at all, just thrusts and eddies of palpable colour.

The heat and frost that flowed from my brush seemed linked to my love life—or its lack. I made poor choices, doomed myself to failure. I opened my arms and my legs to the cruel, the vapid, the inept; I expected the worst and always found it. The more empty a liaison, the more violent and sensual my work became, and I theorized that perhaps a void of one kind might actually be a fullness of another sort.

I supposed it was very Zen.

By the time I settled in Minneapolis and my paintings became popular with those who set such trends, I had given up men entirely. My work was displayed at the Ardith Crawford Gallery, the best in town, the best in the region. Ardith became my agent as well, and began to find a national audience for my paintings.

I bought a house in the city, a century-old Queen Anne with stained-glass windows and a turret and parquet floors and six fireplaces (and a long list of needed—and expensive—repairs), and happily set to work steaming wallpaper and stripping varnish. And painting more paintings so that I could write out cheque after cheque to the endless army of pants-at-half-mast plumbers, electricians, carpenters, roofers, and repairmen who tracked mud over my threshold for the next year.

I spent most of my time in the studio, a gutted and airy remake of the old servant's quarters. I went out little and entertained less. Years passed, their seasons marked only by how many layers of clothing it took to make it to the market or Shepherd's Art Supply without freezing or sweltering; and whether, on my pilgrimages downstairs, I lit a fire or threw open the windows.

I clung to my brushes and colours more fiercely than I had ever clung to any man of muscle and blood. A clean, blank surface was to me a virgin, faceless lover, ready to be granted intelligence, persona, desire; ready to be schooled and imbued with the languorous sensuality or savage passion of the moment.

I was true to my canvases, and they to me. They pleased me perfectly, exited with grace when the time came, and never made me sleep on the wet spot.

For some reason it was Brigston, the old days,

and especially those lean young small town boys, Bobby Daws in particular, that I thought about while I waited for Chips to pick me up for the exhibition. I stuck my boots up on the coffee table and sipped at a Scotch—purely medicinal, since I was fairly certain that an opening at the Ardith Crawford Gallery was not the best place for a panic attack—and remembered how cocksure Bobby'd been, all those years ago, and how cocksure I'd tried to give the appearance of being.

The truth was, I'd never been sure of anything, except in front of my easel. Not that what I do is easy: it is, in many ways, the hardest thing I've ever done, or can imagine doing. But there's a surety in it, a sense of command.

The rest of the time? Just pretending.

I wondered if Bobby had ever made it to San Francisco. He'd wanted to grow his hair long and be a rock-and-roll star. This had always struck me as hilarious, since he could barely carry a tune and knew only three chords on his guitar, but at the time I'd usually just take another hit, nod, and mumble, 'Far out.' I supposed he'd at least succeeded in growing his hair.

I wondered what Bobby looked like now, or if he or Jimmy Lightfoot or any of those hometown boys were still alive. Strange to be thinking about them at all, considering that any minute Chips would be cheerfully driving me to what I was sure was certain doom; but Bobby had been my first, if you didn't count Norman. Perhaps, in times of quiet terror, a person needs something sentimental to cling to, no matter how trivial.

The realization that it *was* so trivial made me want to cry. I was relieved when the doorbell rang.

Chips was out there, thumbing the button over and over, gleefully shouting, 'C'mon, damn it! We're burnin' moonlight!'

4

Alex

By a quarter to seven I'd talked my gonads into taking a temporary vacation where the French paintings were concerned, and I was up on the rear balcony, arguing with the bartender. We'd ordered three cases of champagne; he showed up with one. I heard Darryl unlocking the front door too early and turned around to yell at him, too.

Then I saw who he was letting in.

There's no mistaking Chips Quincannon any day, and that night she was all beads and feathers, very hot in a Vegas ballbreaker kind of way. She had a friend with her, a really pretty girl I'd never seen before.

She was tallish, but shorter than Chips (who's practically an Amazon), and her hair was a sort of palomino blond, cut in a blunt bob that swung past her shoulders. She wasn't thin or fat, but she had the kind of hips you'd want to hang onto when you danced close. She was leggy and wore scuffed-up knee-high boots—brown ones with high heels—and these really tight, really beat-up jeans. You could see little patches of pale skin through the holes on her thighs, and when she turned around I saw a bright yellow handprint on her backside.

I found myself wishing I'd put it there.

Darryl was standing out on the main floor with them, talking Chips's ear off and looking lovesick, and the blonde kept looking down, looking away, like she was either really embarrassed about something, or really shy, or really didn't want to be there. In this weird sort of way, she was one of the sexiest women I'd ever seen.

A couple of minutes later, she and Chips pried Darryl loose and disappeared down the hall. I heard the door to Ardith's office close behind them. I waved Darryl upstairs to the bar.

'Guess what,' I said. 'We're short of champagne. You're elected to make a run to the liquor store.'

He straightened the knot in his tie, flicked some invisible speck off his lapel. Perfect Darryl. All teeth and tan and forty-dollar haircut. 'I'm not going now, Alex. It's almost time to unlock.'

'Yes, you are, Darryl. I can't leave, Ardith *won't* leave, Roxanne's underage, and Betty's husband dropped her off. She doesn't have a car.'

Darryl was staring toward Ardith's office. He

was so goofy for Chips it was pathetic, but anybody could tell Chips wasn't interested, if she ever had been. Darryl hadn't figured it out yet. He lived to trip over his own dick.

'Betty can take my car,' he said. 'I'm staying.'

'Betty's busy. Don't give me any shit about this, okay?'

He looked like he wanted to punch me. I just stood there and stared down at him. Darryl may have me in years, but I've got a job title and four or five inches on him.

Finally he dropped his eyes. He started digging in his pocket for car keys and mumbled, 'Gimme some money then, damn it.'

'I'll call ahead and have them charge it,' I said, then added, 'Who's the blonde with Chips? You think Ardith's gonna let her stay on the gallery floor dressed like that?' We all knew how Ardith felt about anything less than haute couture.

Darryl found his keys. 'You nuts?' he grumbled. 'Ardith'd let her walk in here naked if she wanted to.'

We all knew how Ardith felt about pretty blond girls, too.

I guess nobody in their right mind ever said life was fair, but I still felt like somebody'd just punched me in the gut. 'She's one of Ardith's...? I mean...shit. What happened to Gloria?'

Darryl shook his head. 'No, no. Jeez, Alex, what planet do you live on? Don't you know who that is?'

I shrugged. 'Some friend of Chips', I thought.'

'Maybe,' he grinned a little nastily. It must

have shown on my face that I was hurting a little, and the son of a bitch was loving it.

I snorted at him and slouched back on the bar. 'OK, fine. Don't tell me.' I checked my watch. 'It's five till. You'd better get going.'

He cocked his head and pursed his lips like he was about to make a great deal on a used car. 'OK. I'll tell you. *If* you'll have them load it for me.'

I was going to do that anyway just to save time, but I said, 'You win.' I wanted a smile on his face for the opening. And I wanted to know who the blonde was. 'All you'll have to do is honk and pop your lousy trunk, okay? So who is she?'

He tossed his keys into the air and caught them with a pass of his hand. 'That, my dear asshole, is Little Miss Cum-on-a-canvas herself—Sally French.'

At 7:30 Sally French still hadn't shown her face, and by then the place was packed and noisy. We'd already 'red dotted' a couple of big pieces, and Ardith was in top form: all kiss, hug, gush, and sell. The main room had begun to reek of liquor and too much expensive perfume and some sort of weird cheese the caterers used in the canapés, and there was the beginning of a yellow cigarette-smoke cloud forming near the ceiling.

I'd gone back to the storeroom to cut in the main gallery's exhaust fans, and to dig out a fresh halogen bulb for the number three spot. I was sorting through cartons and mentally cursing Darryl for not checking *all* the lights, when I heard Ardith's voice in the office, next door.

'You can't hide in here all night,' she said. 'You made it this far, Sally. Nobody's going to *bite* you, for Christ's sake...' She didn't sound like she was smiling.

I heard her heels click down the hall before her footsteps got muffled in the carpet, and then I heard her say, all sweetness, 'Dr and Mrs Fitzpatrick! I'm delighted you could be with us this evening! Have you seen...' She faded out.

I found the right carton and was trying to ease out a bulb without breaking it when I heard the office door open again.

'You'll be fine.' It was Chips.

There was this little squeak, and then, 'Oh, Chips, I don't think I can do this...'

That flutey little voice was Sally French?

'You want a tranq? I think I've got—'

'No. No, I don't think so.'

'If you're sure,' Chips said, then, 'You'll be fine. It's just an hour and a half. Two hours, tops. And then we can blow this pop stand and get bombed and listen to Beatles records and try to remember what we were doing in 1970. You'll like *that* part, I promise.'

I thought I heard a half-laugh, kind of thin and wispy and maybe not quite so scared anymore. Then, 'What makes you think I'll live that long?'

'Me knowum everything.' Chips in Tonto mode. I could practically see her forcing her features stony.

Sally French laughed. It was great, like music. 'Stupid Indian,' she said.

'Dumb blonde.'

It sounded like they'd gone through that little routine a couple hundred times. I heard them walk away toward the main gallery, then realized I was standing in the middle of the storeroom with an eight-dollar light bulb in my hand, and that I was grinning like an idiot.

Chips had shed a trail of little black and red feathers down the hall, and I followed it out onto the main floor.

She and Sally French were across the room in front of this really huge piece titled *Nearctic Number Three*. It was at least eight feet long and maybe six feet high, and had a focus—a core, really—off to the right side; all this tiny, tight detail like beads and pearls made out of melting ice. All that tight stuff swirled out like oil on water until it practically exploded over the canvas.

It broke all the rules. The colours were cold, almost icy, but they couldn't have come across any hotter. She worked the paint to make it seem you were looking at her paintings through a different kind of air: there was a thickness in the atmosphere around them that reached out and enveloped you.

The closest I can get to describing it is the feel you get from some Vermeers: dense and sparkly and misty and incredibly clear all at once. And something about the way she glazed and layered the colour made it almost throb, like a heartbeat.

Christ, I wish I could paint like that.

It was really weird, seeing her stand there in front of that gigantic canvas. She was so scared she was almost transparent, or at least looked like she wanted to be. This frightened little blonde in a baggy sweater and torn jeans had created all that power? It was like one of those puzzles you'd find in magazines when you were a kid: What's Wrong with This Picture?

Darryl's radar had already bleeped on Chips, and he was zeroing in. I beat him there.

'Here,' I said, and shoved the light bulb at him before he could start to drool. I jabbed my thumb toward the dead spotlight across the way.

'Alex, gimme a break, willya?' he hissed, then turned to smile over his shoulder at Chips. Chips gave him a 'go screw yourself' look. He didn't get it, the stupid bastard.

I said, *'Now,* Darryl.'

'Alex, couldn't Roxanne—'

'Is there a problem?' It was Ardith. She was decked in bright red from lips to spikes.

Darryl grabbed the bulb out of my hand. 'Not at all, Ardith,' he said, and shot me a dirty look before he went for the ladder.

Ardith shook her head and muttered, 'You're going to have to talk to him,' before she sank her nails into my elbow and pulled me over to Chips and Sally French. 'Alex, dear, you know Chips, of course.'

I nodded and stuck my hand out, reflex action.

All that beaded fringe on her arms rattled

51

when she took it, and she lost a half-dozen feathers before she finished saying, 'Hiya, Alex.'

'And this,' Ardith said, 'is—'

'*Ar*dith! *Dar*ling!' Baldwin Baylor's hand was on Ardith's shoulder. He planted a kiss on her neck.

'Peaches!' she squealed—well, it was as close to a squeal as Ardith gets. 'You came!'

He pursed his lips, rolled his eyes. 'Not yet, my tawny beast. But judging from the look of things, I may before the evening's over.'

Ardith kissed his cheek, then rubbed away the lipstick with her thumb. 'You're evil.'

'My job, darling.' He held out both arms and swept them toward the walls. 'An absolutely astounding show, Ardith. Even better than last year's! My review will be scintillating.'

Baldwin Baylor (Peaches, to his friends) was the most powerful critic in town, and he and Ardith go back forever, I guess. He scared the bejesus out of Darryl, who was convinced Peaches sat up nights thinking up ways to slip him the salami.

When Peaches had a crowd to work, like that night, he was full steam ahead: Baldwin Baylor, Nellie Art Critic at Large. But when there's no crowd and you both stick your feet up on the table and knock back a few beers, he's a pretty down-to-earth guy.

I liked Peaches a lot. Sure, he played all those old stereotypes to the hilt when he was in the mood—and he wasn't above being purely ornery, just for effect—but he was also one of the most genuinely kind people I'd ever known. He nursed me through my breakup with Suzanne, and he was always talking me up to Ardith. I always thought he was at least partly responsible for my promotion to manager. I mean, I deserved it and everything, but sometimes things like workplace performance sort of slip past Ardith. Peaches always managed to point it out when I did something he considered particularly brilliant.

He's a pretty smart guy, too. He knew more about postmodern art than anybody I've ever met. He even wrote a book about it that's required reading at a lot of colleges, and his articles turned up in the national art rags with regularity. He also had a vintage Bentley that he's taken apart and put back together more times than he could tell you. Of course, he didn't always put it back together so great because it broke down about every three months, but he loved that damn car. He let me help him work on it a few times. Amazing piece of machinery, if you're into that sort of thing.

And Darryl didn't need to worry about Peaches bending him over the balcony rail; Peaches had been living with the same guy, a history prof from the university, for almost twenty years.

Of course, that didn't stop Peaches from driving old Darryl nuts. Peaches knew exactly which buttons to punch. Sometimes he practically tap-danced on them.

Anyway, he'd been scanning the room the whole time he was talking to Ardith. You could practically see him running through his mental

Rolodex, making notes on who was there and how much they were worth and what kind of collections they had. If he was in the mood and he liked what he saw (which it looked like he did), he'd move more paintings than all of us put together. The Baldwin Baylor seal of approval goes a long way. And in the middle of all that mental file flipping, he spotted Darryl, who was up on the ladder changing that stupid light bulb, and he got this big nasty grin on his face.

'Yoohoo, Darryl!' he called over the crowd, 'We missed you at the baths last night!'

About a dozen people snickered, and Darryl went bright red.

'Poor dear,' Peaches said to Ardith. 'You can almost hear his sphincter snap shut from here, can't you?'

Darryl wobbled on the ladder and Roxanne ran to steady it.

Chips cracked up, and Peaches zeroed in on her. 'Chippewa! My favourite savage!' He gave her a hug and came away brushing feathers off his coat and grumbling. 'I wondered who was moulting.' He tilted his head to look her up and down. He clicked his tongue and folded his hands. 'Ah, my poor, brave Chips. Another tragic explosion at Bob Mackie's?'

Sally French was actually laughing by then, and while she was paying attention to Peaches, I had a chance to study her.

At first I thought her eyes were blue, but then decided they were grey: really light grey with blue-green flecks. She had these long lashes

54

that you could tell were hers, not phonies, and a cute little nose dusted with freckles, tiny, light ones. There were little crinkles at the corners of her eyes when she laughed, which she was doing just then. She was also shaking hands with Peaches.

'Hi,' she said. A single, clear note.

'My dear Miss French.' He lifted her hand to his lips. 'May I call you Sally?'

'Please.' She pulled her hand away, although she kept smiling.

'And you'll call me Peaches, won't you?'

She smile went to a grin. 'Okay, Peaches.' I wanted her to grin at me, too, but not quite like that. She looked like she'd just found her long-lost favourite aunt.

Ardith forgot to introduce me. She had already excused herself and sidled up to what is known as a prominent old-money congressman. He'd been standing in front of *Bartok and Blasphemy* for the past three minutes, trying to act like he didn't have a boner. I should have been working the crowd, too, but I couldn't make my feet move.

'Well then, Sally,' Peaches was saying, 'you and I must have a nice long chat about these fabulous paintings of yours.' He put about three extra A's in 'fabulous.' Good old Peaches. He was on a roll. 'You'll have to think up some nice, pretentious quotes for my column.'

'But—'

He cut her off. 'Oh, don't worry, dear. I'll make it up for you if you want. Actually, I'll

55

probably do that anyway, so let's just not worry about it, shall we?'

She laughed.

'You know,' he said as he led her away. 'I've been coming to your exhibits since practically the Ice Age, and I have to utterly *drench* my system in saltpeter before I leave the house.'

He grabbed a couple glasses of champagne off a waiter's tray, pushed one into her hand, and kept walking. That pretty little ass with the big yellow handprint was getting farther and farther away. The only reason I could still hear them was that Peaches was talking about two hundred decibels louder than everybody else.

'Terribly heady stuff, your work,' he said. 'Practically obscene. By which I mean absolutely delightful. It's a miracle Tipper Gore hasn't lobbied for stickers. Although perhaps she should. It'd make exquisite press. Do you think I should FAX her?'

He flagged down another waiter and grabbed a handful of hors d'oeuvres. 'Fabulous trousers, my dear,' I heard him say as he stuffed one of those smelly cheese things in his mouth. 'You *must* tell me who does your laundry.'

They disappeared into the crowd.

'You're gonna need a shitload, kid.' Chips wove her arm through mine, and I jumped a little. I'd forgotten she was there.

'Huh? Of what?'

'Luck, angel, luck.' She stared at me for a second, then threw back her head and laughed. 'Jeez, you're blushing!'

It was turning into a great show. By 8:30, a half-hour to closing, those little red dots that signify "Sold" were on better than three-quarters of the title cards. I hadn't had a chance to go over and introduce myself to Sally French, but it looked like she was in good hands with Peaches. He was sticking close, introducing her to everybody who mattered.

Chips was off in the corner with some Nordic ski instructor type. By the looks of it, he didn't plan on going home alone. I hoped he'd talk Chips into it, because that'd mean our guest of honour might need a ride home.

I just happened to be available for chauffeur duty.

Each opening night was unique. Of course, there's always the clique who showed up mainly to be seen and drink a lot of free liquor and have their pictures taken for the columns. They'd cluster in the middle of the main floor and drink and smoke and hug each other and wave at their friends and try to pretend they had a clue as to what was going on with the art.

But outside of them, the general feel you got from the crowd depended on what you had on the walls or on the floor. At a Chippewa Quincannon show, people got really touchy-feely. Not only with those bronzes of hers, but with each other. They talked about Our Magnificent Heritage and dredged up their own (mostly apocryphal) Native American blood ties. They drank too much champagne and made too many bad jokes about 'firewater.'

57

When we had a Bartlett show, people spent the evening clustered in small, quiet groups, talking about neo-Impressionism and the effect of light on water. And, of course, asking if the bar on the balcony was still open.

At Sally French shows, you always saw these solitary people standing in front of this canvas or that as if they were mesmerized. Sometimes they'd sway a little, sometimes they'd stand stock-still. Sometimes a friend would come up and tap them on the shoulder and they'd turn around laughing and all embarrassed. If it was a guy, you could usually see the reason why. The women just blushed. Women have it easier that way.

I was trying my best to avoid that situation. Whenever I had to look at a French, I tried to focus on just a little piece of it, never the whole canvas. I couldn't afford to let myself get sucked into one tonight.

The last thing you need when you're trying to sell somebody a thirty-thousand dollar painting is a big fat woody.

I kept myself busy shaking hands and making small talk. And answering questions. So far, I'd explained the difference between oil and acrylic three times, the difference between cotton and linen supports twice, defined abstract expressionism (okay, *tried* to) a half dozen times, directed four people to the restroom, and called a cab for a lady who was too full of bourbon and branch to find her car, let alone drive it.

Some guy in a Brooks Brothers suit and a turban, who said he wasn't liquid just at the moment, showed me a palmful of what he claimed were emeralds and asked if we'd trade. I referred him to Ardith.

I spent ten long minutes with a guy who kept saying, 'But what *is* it? I mean, is it supposed to be flowers or a landscape or what?'

But things got better. Rob Winston, one of our best clients, was there. He and I had a great time with our noses about an inch away from a big piece titled *Nasty Habits,* trying to figure out how the hell Sally French did her glazes. And we both had a kind of nervous laugh about not being able to stand back and *really* look at it in mixed company.

Oh, and I sold him the painting. He and his lady friend left right after that. They looked like they were headed for the nearest motel.

Ardith sold *Nearctic Number Three* (or, as she called it, 'The Big Kind of White and Silver One') out from under me, but I sold my client on a smaller piece, which she ended up liking better, anyway.

Everybody was happy.

While all this was going on, I tried to keep an eye on Sally French. It was hard to find her in the crowd, which was just as well; that yellow handprint on her backside was beginning to have the same affect on me as the paintings I was trying so hard not to look at.

59

When I did catch a glimpse, it looked like Peaches was doing most of the glad-handing for her. He must have noticed—I had, anyway—that she balked at touching people. Every time she had to shake hands with somebody, she acted like she was hooked into some sort of really unpleasant, low-voltage current. But she must have warmed to Peaches, because within fifteen minutes of the time he squired her off, he had an arm around her and she didn't seem to mind at all.

Maybe she figured it was an insulation against all those other people.

And it looked like Peaches was doing a good job of fending them off. At least, I hoped he was, because it didn't seem to me that Sally French was up to too much hand-shaking or small talk.

But then, at about a quarter to nine, Anthony showed up. He's the history prof Peaches lives with, and he doesn't have much use for art unless it's at least a couple thousand years old. Peaches must have already got plenty for his column, because he waved goodbye to me and kissed Sally French's hand, and he and Anthony were out the door.

She was just standing there in this sea of people (pretty drunk people, by then), looking very pale. Some guy was shoving a drink at her and she was doing this little skittery movement with her head, like she was trying to find Chips or Ardith or the nearest exit.

She looked like Bambi in the middle of that forest fire.

5

Sally

'How long does it take you to do one of these things anyway?' 'Do you give lessons?' 'Would you sign my brochure?' 'We're having a little cocktail party next week, and we wondered...'

After a while, the faces blurred together. I never said what I was thinking. And I filtered out most of what was said to me. The voices turned into a brown, muddy background buzz.

'We'd buy that one, but...do you think you could do one just like it, only smaller and in mauve?' 'So, baby, are you as hot as your paintings?' 'I used to paint a little, too, dear. Isn't it fun?'

The half-finished canvas waiting in my studio nagged at me: I felt like I'd cheated on it by coming here tonight. I kept working on it in my head, laying down glazes three, five, then ten days ahead of myself. I'd be lost in mentally swirling paint into medium, getting the right translucence, the perfect refractions of light through tint, when Peaches would nudge me. I'd look up, remember where I was, nod, and smile at another featureless face. I said as little as possible. Peaches did most of the talking: not only for me, but for everybody. He was a wizard.

But just when I had begun to think I'd live

through it after all, he said, 'Sally, my love, this is Anthony Sutton. My better half.'

Tall, tweedy, and decidedly handsome, Anthony put me a bit in mind of a middle-aged Cary Grant in horn-rimmed glasses. He took my hand and shook it firmly, without smiling. 'My pleasure, Miss French,' he said, before he turned to Peaches. He even had a faint English accent. 'Are you ready, Baldwin?'

Peaches was. He kissed my hand, waved at a few people, and suddenly I was stranded in the centre of a milling mob. I remember wondering if this was the same crowd that always gathers at street accidents, like in that Ray Bradbury story. The only difference tonight, outside of the spangles and flitter, was that the victim was still on her feet.

I was looking for Chips or Ardith when another drunk on the make moved in. This one had oiled, slicked-back hair and a bored, indifferent look, and he wore an Armani suit; he also appeared to be one of those people in whom inherited wealth fosters a geometrically increasing stupidity. He'd spoken to me earlier, and Peaches had neatly dispatched him. But Peaches was gone and he was back.

He touched my hair, and my skin prickled unpleasantly. 'So, Miss Painter Lady,' he said. 'You ever ridden in a Lamborghini?'

Just over his shoulder, I caught a glimpse of Chips. She was across the floor, talking to some guy. 'Excuse me,' I said, 'I really have to—'

'Wassa matter, honey? You're a star. You got your picture taken for the paper. What's say you let Vic put a cap on the evening for you?'

His hand went from my hair to my arm. I jerked away, but he held on.

Remember to breathe, Sally, remember to breathe, you can't have a panic attack here, not now; God, I wish I had a Scotch; God, I wish I was home.

Chips would've known how to handle this. She'd have got rid of this idiot, probably with a neat one-liner that'd shrivel his balls for life, but I couldn't think of a thing. I was too out of practice. Of course, ten years ago, I'd have gone with him and done it on the hood of his fucking Lamborghini and never asked his name.

Oh, please, mister, if I do what you want, will you make me give a damn about you, about anything?

So much for the good old days.

He shoved his drink at me. 'Here, babe. Have a shot of this.' He leaned down and winked. 'Got a little nose candy in the car.'

I hadn't heard that one for over a decade, and I was surprised when it almost shocked me. 'Listen, I really don't—'

A hand loomed in from the crush of bodies behind me and took hold of Mr Nose Candy's wrist. 'Excuse me,' said a pleasant but persuasive baritone. 'Miss French is needed on the balcony.'

Mr Nose Candy let go and stared up and past my shoulder. 'Oh,' he said, with a spoiled sneer. He took back his drink. 'Your loss, honey,' he said to me. 'Maybe I'll see you later.'

'Don't count on it, asshole.' The baritone again. He'd said it under his breath, as if he

63

thought no one would hear. I turned around.

'Sorry, Miss French. When I saw Peaches leave, I got over to you as soon as I could.'

He was very tall, probably six-three or so, and was standing so close I had to crane my head up. He had a young, strong-jawed face that framed startlingly sagacious eyes. A sense of recognition flickered, then passed.

He bent down a little and whispered, 'C'mon, I'll get you clear of this.' When I balked, he said, 'It's all right I work for Ardith.'

I'd been drowning in all those people, but he parted them like Moses commanding the Red Sea.

The balcony was deserted save for a frazzled bartender who nodded dully as we passed. A sleek grouping of furniture, upholstered in Ardith's trademark lilac, huddled against the balcony's rear wall. My rescuer led me to it.

'It's almost closing,' he said. 'You've done your duty.'

I dropped into a chair and stared at the patch of dove-grey carpet between my boots. I hadn't realized how exhausted I was. 'Thank you,' I said. 'Thank you very much.'

I expected him to join me, but he just stood there for a moment, rocking from foot to foot.

'The bartender's going to start packing up in a couple minutes,' he said at last. 'Would you like something?'

'Christ, yes.' So much for polite conversation. I'd been nursing the same glass of flat champagne for over an hour. 'Scotch, please. Rocks.'

And put a Seconal in it, would you? Just for colour, you understand.

He moved away, and I let myself lean back just a little, let my eyelids drift closed. The crowd seemed far off, like a distant, chattering flock of geese. I started to think about the painting on my easel. Tonight it would be ready for the next major glaze. Alizarin with just a touch of—

'Chivas okay?'

I opened my eyes. 'What? Yes, thanks.' It was one of those plastic airline glasses, cupped in a damp cocktail napkin. He'd got himself something, too, and he sat down on the couch.

He poked at his ice cubes with a fingertip. 'I need one. Been bedlam around here. But I guess you know that.' He grinned, and little wings fanned at the corners of his eyes. How could a face that young hold such confidence, hold eyes so ancient? A person could get lost in there.

'Blue,' I said. The colour of his eyes.

'Beg pardon?'

I felt my face go hot. 'Nothing. Sorry.' I fumbled for the pack of Salems I'd tucked inside my sweater, and dropped my lighter in the process.

He picked it up. It was one of those disposables; when he clicked it to light my cigarette, it looked lost in his hand. I'd forgotten how big and beautifully made a man's hands can be. Why had I picked this boy's to remind me?

He reached over and pulled a cigarette out

65

of my pack. It was a casual move, as if he'd known me for years. 'Mind?'

I shook my head. How old was he, anyway? Twenty, twenty-two? He was quite handsome, actually: strong-featured, wide-browed; a trace of a smile tugged at one corner of his mouth. He was probably one of those people who was completely relaxed in any circumstance, always making everyone else feel at ease without knowing or trying. And where did he get those eyes? I remembered what Chips had told me, and said, 'You must be Alex.'

'Guilty.' He was leaning forward, elbows on knees, suitcoat open, his tie belling out from his shirt. A shock of hair, slightly wavy and the colour of wheat, tipped over his forehead. I almost reached to brush it back, then caught myself. This wasn't me. I shouldn't be here, drinking Scotch with him, wanting to touch his face. I should be home, alone, making love to a canvas.

I took a too-big gulp of Scotch and nearly choked.

His hand cupped my shoulder. Long fingers tapped my back. 'You okay?'

'Yes, I—'

'Well, *here* you are!' Ardith swooped down like a scarlet vulture on uppers. She perched on the sofa next to Alex and gave him a hug before she reached across his knees to squeeze my hand. As I had all evening, I made a conscious—if not too successful—effort not to pull away. I'd had enough hand-squeezing to last the rest of my life.

66

'Wasn't it wonderful? An absolute success, Sally, practically a sellout! And Alex, you were marvellous! Isn't he marvellous, Sally? He sold that big orange thing to the Findales. *Twice* as much as they've ever dropped in here before. And what else, Alex? The dark blue one to Rob Winston, and the little one with the cranberry stuff in the middle to—' Her head snapped toward the bar. 'Don't you dare pack that away until you bring me a rye and soda, young man.'

The bartender slouched dejectedly, then began looking through the case of half-empty bottles he'd just set aside. He was muttering under his breath.

Ardith got her drink just as Chips came up the steps. She was joined at the hip to a windburnt blond who looked like he ought to be skiing Norway instead of gallery-hopping.

'Hiya,' she said, and flopped down in a chair. The Viking stood behind her, one hand possessively curled around the side of her neck. She leaned her head back into his groin and popped a stick of gum in her mouth. ' 'Bout everybody's gone. Betty's pushin' the last of 'em out the door. Great show, you guys. Paintings weren't bad, either. This is Eric.'

Eric nodded without looking up at any of us. He just kept staring down at the top of Chips' head, probably wishing she'd turn it around and open wide. His forehead was all but flashing *Valhalla or Bust*. It didn't look like there'd be any Beatles-fest tonight.

She wadded her gum wrapper into a tiny ball

67

and pitched it toward an ashtray. It landed dead centre. 'Two points,' she said. 'So, you ready to go, Sal? I thought maybe the three of us could grab a bite somewhere.'

'That's okay, Chips. You can just drop me off. I'm not hungry.'

'Well, all right, but are you sure—'

Alex leaned forward to squash out his cigarette. 'Why don't you and Eric go on, Chips? I'll give Miss French a lift. She's on my way.'

Chips tried not to look hopeful. I knew she'd take me without complaint, and that she and Eric, would probably come in for a drink just to be sociable. But I also knew I didn't want to be stuck for a half-hour making small talk with Eric, and that Chips was in a hurry to get him into something more comfortable: that big waterbed of hers, for starters.

'Sally?' She tilted her head and the Viking stifled a groan. 'Hey, it's no trouble. I *planned* on it.'

I looked over at Alex. He looked calm and steady and unsettling all at once, but I decided he was safe so long as I didn't look at those eyes of his any more than I had to. Besides, he was practically young enough to be my son. He'd probably drop me neatly at my door, tell me what a pleasure it had all been, then speed home to his girl. I'd be alone again that much sooner.

I took a breath. 'If Alex doesn't mind driving me... It's okay, Chips, really. You two go on.'

Chips looked puzzled, but relieved. 'You sure about this, Sal?'

Alex smiled at me. His eyes were like clear summer sky. A good colour for a painting.

I said, 'Yes, I'm sure.'

His car surprised me. I figured that if he was managing the gallery for Ardith, she'd be paying him an override and he'd be making good money. I imagined he'd drive some hot little flash of a sportscar, or maybe a yuppie special.

But when we went to the parking lot, the door he unlocked and held open for me was attached to a vintage Cadillac: the chunky, sturdy kind they made before the stretched-out models with the overdone tail fins. It had rained, and beneath the parking lot lights the Caddy's two-tone paint, white and Copenhagen blue, sparkled. The chrome glistened with beads of water. It had wide bench seats—real leather—and the interior looked showroom-new.

'This is something,' I said, when he slid behind the wheel.

'My fifty-six,' he said with a grin. 'You like her?'

I nodded. 'It's not what I expected.'

He turned the key, and we pulled out into traffic. I'd forgotten how steady and solid a car could feel. It was like riding in an upholstered steel womb.

A skin of rainwater had turned the streets wet-black, a mirror alive with blurred reflections: tail lights, street lights, neon signs. The effect was almost virulent, like those black velvet paintings. Day-Glo matadors. Huge-breasted women. Jesus hauling Elvis into heaven by his microphone cord.

'How long are you going to make me call you, "Miss French"?'

'What?' My face went hot again. For no particular reason, that simple question seemed fraught with overtones. 'I...Sally. I mean, call me Sally. Please.'

'Sally,' he said.

I hugged my door. It had been a long time since I'd heard a male voice speak my name in the dark, even longer since I'd liked the sound of it. This was ridiculous.

He pulled onto the freeway. He drove casually, with one hand lopped over the top of the wheel and the other riding the bottom curve. A tape deck, snuggled inconspicuously beneath the dash, played Mahler. Another surprise.

'You cold?' he asked. 'I can turn on the heat.'

'I'm fine.' I nodded toward the road ahead. 'You'll need to take the ramp at—'

'I know.'

'You know where I live?'

'You forget, Sally. I'm on intimate terms with your file.'

'Oh. Of course.'

Neither of us said another word for the ten minutes it took to get to the house. He pulled into the narrow, rock-walled drive as if he'd done it hundreds of times and drove forward to the sideyard steps.

'Here we are,' I said. Stupid thing to say.

He opened his door and swung his long legs to the pavement. 'I'll see you up.'

'Really, you don't need—'

He was already out and rounding the Caddy's nose.

We climbed the steps, then followed the stone path that curved to the front walk, and I realized I felt more nervous on my own territory than I'd been at Ardith's.

Well, I wasn't going to invite him in. Not into my house, not into my life. Life? Where had that come from? All he'd done was drive me home and walk me to my door. He was just a polite young man being nice to a business associate. Well, I still wasn't going to invite him into the house. Surely he wouldn't ask...

'Maybe you should open the door.'

'What? Oh.' I dug into my purse and fumbled with the keys.

He took them. 'Here, let me do that.' He held the ring to the light and started sorting. 'This one?'

'Yes. The deadbolt.' All evening I'd been escaping into the painting upstairs, couldn't wait to get back to it. Suddenly I couldn't remember what it looked like.

Something brushed my leg. I jumped.

'It's all right,' Alex said. 'Take it easy.' He sank down on his heels and reached into the murk beyond the porch light's range. Something stirred beneath his hand and he grinned up at me. 'Your kitty?'

The damned thing. 'He's a stray. Just hangs

around the neighbourhood.'

A raspy purr rose as the cat, a lean-flanked orange tabby, moved into the light. Alex scratched its neck and ears.

'You ought to feed him. He's awful skinny.'

'I would, but I'm afraid he'd move in.'

He stood up and put the key in the lock. 'Would that be such a bad thing?' The bolt retracted, the door swung open. 'There.'

'Well, thanks for—'

He was already past me. 'Where's your kitchen?' he said from the front hall, then, 'My God, what a great house! Is that a real Tiffany window?'

6

Alex

Thank God for the cat. I wanted to get to know Sally French more than I could ever remember wanting anything (except maybe my first horse, when I was ten), and that fleabitten tom gave me my excuse. It was a flimsy one—and Sally looked at me like I was out of my mind—but it got me in the door.

I wasn't anywhere near prepared for what I found inside. There are a lot of rambling old Queen Annes and Gothic and Colonial Revivals in her part of the city. Most of them have been converted to apartments or rooming-houses. If they're still single-family houses, they're either run down and ready for the wrecker's ball, or they've been irretrievably bastardized over the decades by those well-intentioned (but tasteless) folks the restoration people call 'remuddlers.'

I just assumed hers was probably one of the latter. My dad's an architect—and fervently wishes I'd go back to school and become one, too—and he specializes in restoring places like this one back home in Denver. Summers, I used to help out at his office and in the field, and I figured I could walk into Sally's house and impress the hell out of her: tell her how to bring it up to nineteenth-century snuff. Big expert.

Well, she didn't need any help from me. I didn't know how much of it was original, but it all looked like it could have been, right down to the parquet pentacle in the foyer floor and the grandfather clock and the brass gaslight sconces along the walls.

To my left, above the staircase's first landing, was what looked like an honest-to-God Tiffany window. It was mostly blues and lavenders and greens: a field of irises surrounding a blue-cloaked Art Nouveau goddess. Her head was tilted back and her lips were parted, as if in some quiet, secret ecstasy. The wind lifted her cloak. She cradled more of those lavender irises in her arms. The only yellows were in the iris beards and the wisps of hair that escaped the goddess's hood. Even with just the feeble light from the side yard lamp coming through, it completely blew me away.

'Jesus,' was the most intelligent comment I could come up with.

The cat tried to sneak in, and Sally shooed it back outside before she closed the door. 'Exactly what I said when I saw her the first time,' she said. She came to stand beside me at the foot of the stairs. 'She's real, all right. I guess you wouldn't consider her original, though. To the house, I mean. It was built in 1882. The guy who restored her thought she was added around the turn of the century.'

I took the two treads to the landing in one step, then reached up and ran my fingers over the goddess's skirts. Most stained glass has thick lead caming to hold the pieces of glass; not this one. Lead was too clumsy for the guys who made this. All those intricate slivers of iridescent glass were held together with barely visible soldered seams. Copper foil underneath, probably.

'My God,' I said, 'this thing's a miracle.'

She came to the bottom of the steps. 'Neat, huh? When I moved in, there was just a pane of clear glass, like a picture window. We found the Iris Lady by accident when the guys came to replace the furnace. She was behind it, under a bunch of junk. This place has gone through fourteen owners since it was built, twelve just since the Eisenhower administration. That's when it started being a rental. I guess somewhere along the line somebody stuck her down there for safekeeping. The next guys either forgot about her or didn't figure she was worth anything, and after that...'

74

I looked at Sally over my shoulder. Her voice had gone kind of hushed and breathy, and that last speech was probably more than she'd said all evening at Ardith's. She was smiling at the Iris Lady, looking past me as if I didn't exist.

She'd crossed her arms over that baggy sweater, and I got a hint of how lush her breasts might be beneath it, enough of a hint that I wanted to see her out of the thing in the worst way. There was a little flush of colour in her cheeks, and all of a sudden she looked kind of dewy to me, like an English schoolgirl: an English schoolgirl past the age of consent, with round breasts and round hips and...

I started to get hard, and reminded myself that the Iris Lady had put that look on her face, not me, and I was pretty sure that a great big erection wasn't going to endear me to her at the moment. I shifted my weight and thought about lima beans. I went soft again. Works every time.

When I thought it was safe, I said, 'I'd love to see her in the sunlight.'

She focused on me again. Her smile sagged. 'Out front, you said something about the kitchen?'

Oh yeah. The kitchen. My excuse.

I turned my back on the Iris Lady. 'Where is it?'

She pointed to the second set of double pocket doors off the entry hall. 'Through the dining room. But—'

I slid them open. 'Dinner is served, Madam. Sorry. I've always wanted to say...'I took a step

75

inside. 'Wow. This place is a barn! Where's the light?'

I heard her high-heeled boots clicking along behind me, then the snap of a switch. The chandeliers blazed.

It really *was* a barn of a dining room. In the centre, under twin chandeliers, was a claw-footed table for ten, and there was enough floor room left on all four sides to hold a shuffleboard tournament. There was a tiled fireplace in one corner, a bronze bust and several Boston ferns in another. To the left were two sets of French doors that led to a small conservatory. Through the glass, I could see the silhouettes of potted plants and queen palms. There was probably a small fountain, too: I could hear a faint splash and trickle.

Opposite the conservatory was a set of pocket doors that had to lead to the front parlour. On a hunch, I looked under the table. Sure enough, there it was: a brass push button in the floor, the latest in modern technology for the newly electrified family. I wondered if it was still hooked up to ring a buzzer in the kitchen. Dad would've loved this place.

I don't know how long I stood there gaping before she cleared her throat and said, 'Alex? It's straight ahead.'

The kitchen. Almost forgot about that again.

The door swung with a soft *swoosh* when I touched the brass push plate. Sally stepped in after me and flicked the light switch.

'Here it is,' she said. 'Did you want a glass of water or something?' She started for the sink.

That yellow handprint curved over her fanny like an engraved invitation.

Put your hand here, Alex. Can you say 'cop a feel'?

'No,' I said. 'I don't want anything. For me, I mean.'

'You just collect kitchens?'

God, she was making me nervous. 'No, I only thought...' I went to the refrigerator. It was one of those side-by-side jobs with the ice dispenser in the door. In that old-fashioned, high-ceilinged kitchen, it looked like a UFO.

There wasn't much to choose from: a half bottle of screw-cap Chablis, a couple of six-packs of Diet Coke, an open pack of smoked turkey lunchmeat, three oranges, a plastic-wrapped chunk of cheddar. I grabbed the turkey and the cheese.

'You got a knife and a little bowl or something?'

She was staring at me like she was trying to decide whether to dial 911 or just hightail it. I smiled at her. I'd got myself in with this ruse, and I was stuck with it.

She handed me a paring knife and a soup bowl, then stepped back, presumably out of range.

'Thanks,' I said, and cut a thick slice of cheddar into little cubes. I did the same with a couple slices of turkey, then went to the back door. 'Does he come when you call?'

'Who? What in God's name—'

'Your friend the cat.'

'Oh.' She relaxed a little, and one corner of

her mouth turned up in an actual partial smile. Progress. Our most important product. 'I don't know,' she said with a shrug. 'I never tried.'

He didn't just answer to 'kitty-kitty'—he came skidding in at twenty miles an hour, purring and meowing all at once and generally making an idiot out of himself. I can't say I blamed him. Cold cuts probably beat the hell out of roadkill sparrow any day.

We both stood out on the porch while he inhaled his dinner. She hadn't turned on the light, and I was glad. I stood a little to the side so I could watch her in the moonlight. She was staring off into some secret place she had, someplace where I wasn't. She looked incredibly vulnerable: soft profile, half-lidded eyes, lips just parted. A few strands of her hair played in the breeze, like the Iris Lady's on the landing.

Earlier, I'd read the bio on her brochure, and it said she was thirty-nine. I made a mental note to have them knock something off our printing bill for that little typo. Twenty-nine, maybe, but not thirty-nine. Hell, my mother was just three years past that, forty-two. And Sally French was definitely not my mother.

The cat finished his dinner, flopped out on the porch, and began licking his shoulder between yawns. I filled the bowl with water and left it out for him.

Sally came back from whatever mental plane she'd drifted to, and by the time I finished water detail, she'd cleaned up after me. The cheese and turkey were gone, the counter was clean, and she was wiping her hands on a dishcloth.

She gave me another half-smile. I appreciated the effort, but I was going to get better than that before I left. I took the towel and looped it through the pull on the refrigerator door.

'Thanks,' she said. 'It was sweet of you to drive me home, Alex. But now that you've done your Dr Doolittle number, I really have to get to work. I've got a long night ahead.'

She wasn't getting rid of me that easy. 'Great,' I said. 'I'd love to see your studio.'

The first floor of the house had been tidy to the point of anal-retentive. The studio was a disaster area.

Paint-splashed throw rugs were scattered around the easel, one of those custom hydraulic jobs for oversize canvases. Clamped to it was a painting in progress: deep, cranberried purples and reds. It wasn't pure sex yet, but it looked like she had it at least to second base.

Next to the easel was a galvanized steel garbage can. Crumpled cigarette packs, paper towels, and pop cans overflowed the plastic liner to spill out over the rugs. Little mismatched, paint-streaked tables and stands fanned a crooked semicircle around the work area. Each brimmed with an unsteady jumble of twisted Windsor-Newton tubes, chunks and splinters of graphite sticks, and capped baby-food jars half-filled with paint. Bottles of alkyd or copal medium, turpentine, and linseed oil filled in the holes, along with more wadded paper towels and ashtrays crowded with Salem butts.

Brushes—brand new and battered and everywhere in between—splayed from coffee cans, pickle jars, cracked vases, and chipped pitchers. A long counter, shelves above and below, ran the length of the front wall. A mayo jar crammed with brushes stuck up from one of the twin steel sinks, and the countertop was jammed with bottles and jugs of everything from liquid latex to Liquid Plumber.

Except for a few painty fingerprints, the white walls were bare: no pictures, no clocks, no calendars. Toward the rear of the room sat a beat-up recliner and a wheeled cart that held a small portable television. Orange extension cords and a white TV cable snaked across the polished plank floor in untidy loops.

Several stretched and primed canvases leaned against the back wall. No finished paintings, though. Ardith must have cleaned her out for the show. Pencils, markers, and grey wads of kneaded eraser cluttered a monster of a drafting table that hulked beside the door. Next to that was a banged-up wall unit that held a stereo and about nine million CDs. A big Bose speaker sat in each corner of the room. The air was heady with the mingled smells of turpentine and oil paint and varnish.

'My kind of place,' I said. It was, too.

The narrow stairs we'd taken from the kitchen came up just about dead centre of the studio, and she was waiting there, leaning against the guard rail, watching me like she couldn't wait for me to go away or possibly die.

I sat down on the high stool by the drafting

table and leaned back. All right, I'd practically shoved my way into her house, but all I wanted was for her to like me and let me get to know her. Well, okay, maybe a little more than that. Instead, she looked like she was a phone call away from hiring somebody to break my legs.

I was beginning to understand how the Jehovah's Witnesses must feel. I figured it couldn't get much worse.

'So, Sally,' I said. 'Could I interest you in a copy of *The Watchtower?*'

I thought she'd say *I beg your pardon* or at least look at me like I was nuts; instead, she started laughing like crazy. Boy, did I want to kiss her.

'Am I really that awful?' she finally managed.

Her face was all rosy from laughing, her eyes sparkled, and she was combing that long golden hair with her fingers, pushing it away from her face. I wanted to do more than kiss her—a lot more—but instead I said, 'Does this mean I'm off your hit list?'

She smiled. 'You want a Coke or something?'

She loosened up after that. I told her about growing up in Colorado, about my dad and mom, and how I used to spend summers, until I was twelve or thirteen, on my uncle's ranch outside Pueblo. I told her about my short stay at the institute and how I'd come to work for Ardith, and how I had my Aunt Barbara's recipe for the best beer-basted barbecued spareribs west of the Mississippi. I left out the part about my so-called love life, and especially the part about

81

Suzanne; but basically, I talked my ass off. It was like I couldn't shut up.

I didn't touch her, though. I stuck to that drafting stool like my backside was coated with Duco. She sat down in front of the easel and propped her elbows on her knees and her chin in her hands and listened, I mean listened hard, like she was really interested.

She looked straight at me. She didn't squirm in her chair or glance around the room or fiddle with her hair or her nails. A lot of women do that, like they're just waiting for you to clam up so they can tell you something *really* interesting... About the only thing Sally did, other than listen, was laugh or smile or ask a question. Or lick her lips. She was doing that a lot. Sometimes she'd catch the edge of her lower lip between her teeth and kind of roll it back and forth.

Can you say blue balls, *Alex? I knew that you could.*

After a while my motor ran down, and we just sat there for a couple minutes, looking at each other.

'You know,' she said finally, 'besides Chips —and the movers who helped get *Nearctic Number Three* out the door—you're the only person who's ever seen my studio.'

My cock buzzed again. 'I am?'

'Ardith says I'm a hermit. Since the renovation, nobody's been in the house at all except Ardith and Chips and a couple of Chips', uh, friends. And the cleaning lady. A couple workmen. Oh. And my Aunt Mariah. She

82

visited once.' She got a strange look on her face for that last bit. It lasted less than a second. Almost a tic.

'When was that? I mean, when they finished the house?'

'Let's see...' She twisted her mouth. Beautiful mouth. 'Seven years. Seven years last April.'

That floored me. 'You mean nobody's...I mean, well, you go out, right?'

She smiled at me and stood up. I'd never seen anybody make getting out of a chair seem so completely and unconsciously sinuous. 'I paint. It's what I do. It's *all* I do. Would you like to see more of the house? I never had anyone who—I mean, well, Chips is into contemporary stuff, and Ardith never pays attention. I've never had a chance to show it of to anybody who'd really appreciate it.'

'You kidding?' I was on my feet. 'Sure!'

She started for the door. There went that yellow handprint again.

'How about your aunt? What'd she think?'

That funny expression again, the half-tic. 'She didn't like it,' she said. She opened the door and slid her hand around the corner to flick on the lights in the next room. 'She said that if I was making so much money, a person would think I could afford a *nice* house.'

'A nice—*what?*' I couldn't have heard her right.

She didn't answer me. She just walked through to the next room. 'This was the nursery, originally,' she said. 'It's my library now.'

I forgot all about Aunt Mariah.

It was a great little room. Three walls were wrapped by floor-to-ceiling bookshelves she said she'd salvaged from another house. There was another of those delft-tile fireplaces, this one crowned by a gilt-framed Townsend: a pawing Arabian horse tethered beside a stone water tank. In the centre of the room was a Hepplewhite desk—Federal rather than Victorian, but it worked great.

On the desk, a Bogucki bronze horse reared next to a MacIntosh computer, and the glass-fronted shelves were crammed with all kinds of books: shelf after shelf of those big coffee tables things on practically every painter you've ever heard of; rows of beat-up paperbacks; shiny-jacketed bestsellers; worn reference books; gold-stamped, leather-bound antiquarian volumes you wanted to open just to smell the years on their pages.

The rest of the upstairs was just as terrific. Charming, my mom would have called it. Dad would have said it had architectural integrity.

She showed me two medium-sized bedrooms, the first a guest room, rigged out in exact high-Victorian detail. 'My mother did these,' she said softly, and pointed to a wall done entirely in framed book jackets. They were all children's books: *The Blue Elf, A Rose for Baby Sarah, Billy Joe and the Big People,* a bunch of others.

I touched one of the frames. *The Spotted Pony.* I said, 'I know this one. Mom used to read it to me when I was little. Your mother did these?'

'Just the illustrations for that one,' she said,

blushing, and ushered me out.

The next bedroom she showed me was used primarily for storage, so there wasn't much to see, but the next room, the bathroom, was great. It had been converted from a small bedroom, and it had its own marble-mantelled fireplace. An oversized, brass-fitted clawfoot tub sat smack in the centre of floor, and even the john was a turn-of-the-century repro: wooden seat, and an overhead tank with a pull chain.

It was the fireplace and the tub that got me, though. I thought about how nice it'd be to soak in that tub with her, with the fireplace crackling close by, and her breasts, her body, all soapy and warm and wet.

'That's about it,' she said. We were back out in the hall. Well, gallery, really. It was one of those big wide ones that was really a long room in itself. Doors opened off one long side and the back, and the other long side overlooked the open stairwell.

Sally was leaning against the balustrade, absently trailing her fingers over the woodwork. Ever since we'd started the tour, she'd been doing that: sliding her hands over the panelling, pressing her cheeks to velvet drapes and lace curtains, curling her palms over doorknobs, bedposts, her own elbows; stroking marble and wood and fabric as if they were lovers. And she seemed completely unconscious she was doing any of it.

I didn't get it. How could she be so sensual with all these *things* when she acted as if human touch repulsed her? Well, *I* hadn't touched her.

Not yet. It was hell, but I kept my hands off.

She started toward the head of the staircase. 'C'mon, I'll show you the downstairs.'

'What's in here?' It was the first door at the top of the stairs. I put my hand on the knob.

She shook her head. 'That's my room.' She looked a little nervous. 'I don't think I know you well enough.'

'But—'

She went down two steps to the first landing and smiled up at me. 'Come *on*, Alex...'

When she smiled at you that way, you couldn't help but follow.

We went down past the Iris Lady to the foyer. 'Parlour's in here,' she said, and started to open the double pocket doors.

'Oh, no. Is this thing right? I didn't hear it chime from upstairs.' I was looking at the grandfather clock. I checked my watch. Yes, it was right—2:20. I'd been here almost five hours? No wonder my nuts were in a knot and I was so tired I could barely see straight.

She turned around, leaving the parlour doors a quarter open. 'I don't wind the chimes. Oh. This is probably pretty late for you, isn't it? I mean, you're one of those people with a *real* job...'

I grinned at her and her cheeks coloured a little.

'Maybe you'd better skip the downstairs,' she said. 'I'm sorry I was so inhospitable before. It's just that I don't, I mean, I...' She opened the front door for me.

Less than six inches stood between us. Jesus,

it was like she had this 220-volt aura. I could actually feel the current, feel my hair standing on end, my skin crisping. I reached through the current, put my hand on her shoulder. She looked down, but she didn't flinch.

'I, uh...' She was blushing like crazy now. 'I...well, I'm glad you came in. Really. Maybe some other time we—'

I bent down, tipped up her chin, and kissed her.

She was all stiff at first, with her arms clamped at her sides and her lips pressed tight together. There was no give in her, no flex, but I just kept kissing her and thinking, *Come on, Sally, come on, girl, relax...*

I felt her lips soften about the same time her fingertips touched my waist. The current surged, washed over me. I pulled her closer, and her hands slid up my chest, then around my neck.

I was straight up, and I knew she could feel me pressing into her belly. I sure could. But there wasn't a damn thing I could do, or wanted to do, about it.

I just kept on kissing her, and she kept on kissing me back. My tongue slipped past her teeth, my hands were on her hips. I felt like I was burning that yellow handprint right off. There was more pure sensuality, more heat in that kiss than in a lot of three-day weekends I've had.

She made a soft sound in the back of her throat and squirmed against me a little. I was afraid I'd go off in my shorts. It killed me to do it, but I broke off the kiss.

Her eyes were barely open, her lips parted and a little swollen. Her hands slid back down my chest, then dropped to her sides. I wondered if there'd be scorch marks on my shirt.

I whispered, 'I'll be back to see the parlour, Sally.'

I had a hell of a time walking to the car, and I almost scraped a fender against the rock wall when I backed out. When I pulled onto the street and crawled past the house, the front door was closed, but I could see Sally's silhouette through the etched glass. She was still standing exactly where I'd left her.

I thought she was swaying a little.

7

Sally

The phone wouldn't shut up, no matter how many pillows I piled over my head. On the tenth or twelfth ring, I pulled myself up on one elbow and, cursing, slapped my hand along the top of the nightstand until I found the receiver.

'It's barely noon,' I growled.

'Touchy this morning, aren't we?'

'Serve you right if I bought one of those machines, Chips.' I pulled myself up to half-sit against the brass headrails and groped for a cigarette. The pack was empty, but there was

a half-smoked Salem in the ashtray. I lit it.
'How'd the Viking work out?'

She laughed. 'Not bad, kiddo, not bad at all.
He just left. We've got a date tonight, if I can
walk again by then. He's takin' me to a revival
of *Downhill Racer*. Figures, huh?'

The cigarette was stale and hot, and I stubbed
it out. 'You taking up winter sports?'

'Just winter sportsmen. Jeez, you sound wrung
out. You stay up all night painting again?'

'No, Alex came in. I showed him the house.'

'*What?*' I heard a crash on her end, a muffled,
'Aw, crap,' then, 'You telling me you actually
let somebody in your house?'

'Well, I didn't exactly let him in. He just sort
of...got in.'

'Well, what happened? How come you're so
tired? How long did he stay? Don't tell me
you—don't tell me you actually did it with that
child!'

I laughed. 'You break something a second
ago?'

'No, I sat up so fast I dumped the ashtray,
and—'

'Chips! Did you start smoking again?'

'Sue me. And quit trying to change the subject.
You sleep with the Boy Wonder or not?'

'Of course I didn't. We just, um, talked.'

'Sure you did. You don't *sound* like you "just
talked". You sound like—oh, hell. I realize this
is unprecedented, since the requisite decade
between visits has not yet fucking expired, but
I'm coming over.'

She hung up.

I took a quick shower and threw on some clothes, then wandered down to the kitchen and put on the coffee. The coffee was for Chips. I grabbed a Diet Coke. I don't like coffee, but I need that morning jolt. I remembered there were bagels in the freezer, and by the time I'd zapped one in the microwave and wolfed it down, Chips was leaning on the bell.

She grabbed me by the shoulders and studied my face until I laughed. 'What are you *doing?*'

She stepped back and nodded her head. Wise Old Indian mode. 'Don't tell *me* nothing happened last night. It's all over your face.'

'Honest, Chips, nothing—'

'Uh-huh. Sure.' She dug into her purse, an oversized, fringed leather bag big enough to carry a couple of human heads, and pulled out a metal tin. 'Brought you a present.' She shoved it at me, then rummaged in her purse again.

I turned the box over ion my hands. It rattled dully. 'What is it?'

She found her cigarettes, jammed a Winston in her mouth, and lit it before she took back the tin and twisted off the lid. 'For the girl who has everything—including a twelve-year-old lover—a super-deluxe condom sampler. Twenty-five in all.' She riffled the packets with her fingertip. 'Super thin, textured, coloured, ribbed... Hell, there's prob'ly one that glows in the dark.' She shoved the tin into my hands and took a drag on her cigarette. 'Welcome to the Age of AIDS, baby.'

90

I stared at it. 'Jesus, Chips. I told you, nothing happened. And he's not twelve.'

'Okay, thirteen.'

'Chips!'

She took back the tin, clamped the lid on and started upstairs. 'I'm gonna put this in your room. Do I smell coffee?'

Chips poured her third cup and slid back into her chair. The kitchen table was littered with her accoutrements: half-spilled purse, a Sunday paper, crumbs from the bagel she'd gobbled with her first coffee, a chunk of cheese she was slowly mutilating into bite-sized pieces. 'So that's the story on Eric,' she said. 'And now we get back to you and child.'

I shrugged. 'Nothing to tell.'

'Oh, sure.' She lit another Winston before she remembered to put the last one out. 'Try that one on somebody else, Sal. You can't fool your Auntie Chips.'

The doorbell rang.

'Ha!' she shrieked. 'I knew it! It's him, isn't it? I can leave by the back door if—'

'Oh, shut up.' I was certain it wasn't Alex, didn't want it to be Alex. All the same, I'd felt a little charge of shivers zipper along my backbone. I stood, a little shakily, and started through the dining room, toward the front door.

Chips was on my heels. 'Well, who'd have the nerve to drop by here—on a Sunday, no less? Besides me, I mean.'

I hadn't the slightest idea. But what if it *was*

him? I took a deep breath before I opened the door.

It was a uniformed deliveryman. He looked incredibly bored, and he was holding a long white box tied with an enormous pink bow. I wasn't sure whether I was relieved or disappointed.

'Miz French?' he drawled around a wad of gum.

When I nodded, he shoved a clip board at me. 'Sign at number eight.' When I handed it back, he muttered, 'Have a nice day,' and gave over the box.

Chips had it away from me before I could get the door closed. 'Hmm,' she purred. Both her eyebrows were working. She carried the box into the dining room and put in on the table. Her fingers rubbed at the embossed logo at the box's upper corner. 'Flowers by Felix. Very expensive. Very trendy. The kid's got class, I'll give him that.'

'Oh, Chips! Why would Alex send me flowers? And stop calling him "the kid." '

'Jesus, you should see your face!'

I didn't need a mirror. I knew I was bright red.

'Well, don't just stand there, Sal, open it!'

Flowers. Alex had sent me flowers. My fingers were trembling as I pulled off the bow, lifted the top off that long white box.

'Hurry up, willya?' Chips grabbed the lid and pushed aside the top veil of tissue.

I gasped as an unmistakable scent filled my nostrils.

92

'Whoa,' Chips breathed. 'Yellow roses. Must be two dozen. If I'd known he...hell, I would'a screwed him *years* ago!'

I was too floored to tell her to shut up. They were beautiful: long-stemmed, perfect, soft yellow blossoms. I picked out one and trailed the moist, silky petals over my cheek. It had been a long time since anyone sent me flowers, and I couldn't remember ever being quite so touched by the gesture. I closed my eyes, inhaled the perfume...

'Earth to Sally.'

I looked up. 'Oh. Sorry.'

'In case you're interested, Cradle Robber, there's a card.'

'I... You open it, Chips.'

'Chicken.' She slit the envelope with her nail, pulled out a sheet of paper and unfolded it. 'Damn.'

'What?'

'Well, there's no God, kiddo.'

'What are you talking about?'

She held up the note again, and read, 'Thank you for a delightful evening, Sally dear. Having a little soirée at my house Monday evening at 8 which you absolutely must attend. No excuses. If you are not here by 8:30, I will send Anthony for you. I warn you that Anthony has no sense of humour. Hugs, Peaches. P.S: The Chippewa Person will be here, too. P.P.S: I trust you read my review this morning? I'm sure we agree it was brilliant.'

I slumped into a chair and dropped the rose back in the box. It had been terribly sweet of

Peaches to send me flowers. And after all, I'd spent the better part of the night telling myself that no matter how attracted to Alex Langley I might *think* I was, the whole idea was ludicrous. So why was I disappointed he hadn't sent me flowers when I never expected—or wanted—him to in the first place?

'Chips, go home. I need to paint.'

She sat down next to me and elbowed the box out of her way. 'Hey, you really like this kid, don't you?'

I plucked at the tablecloth.

'Come on, Sally, it's Chips. You okay?'

I shrugged. 'Yeah, I'm fine. I just feel stupid, that's all.'

She cocked her head to one side. 'Might one ask just exactly how stupid you feel?'

I smiled at her. 'Not as stupid as you'd like to think. He kissed me, that's all.'

'You kiss him back?'

'I...yes.'

'Are we talking a "gee-it's-been-swell-but-I-gotta go" kiss, or a "practically-sex-standing-up-with-all-your clothes-on" kiss, or something in between?'

I didn't say anything, but I felt myself go red again. It's hard to be a private person when your hormones are all over your face.

'And then he left?'

I nodded.

'He didn't try t'get you in the sack?'

'No.'

'Shit.' She looked away and twisted her mouth. 'Y'know, this could be serious.'

94

We both sat there for a couple of minutes, staring at the flowers, before I pushed back my chair. 'I'd better get these in water, huh?'

Chips looked relieved. 'Good idea. You White Eyes always know what to do in a crisis. I hear that's what happened to Custer at Little Big Horn. He would'a won but he just couldn't get his boutonniere straight.'

While I dug a vase out of the pantry, Chips rifled through the paper until she dug out the magazine section. By the time I'd run the water and started snipping the tips of the rose stems, she'd found Peaches' column.

'Ready?'

'Shoot.'

She leaned back in her chair, propped one foot on the table, and began.

The ART SCENE
by
Baldwin Baylor

Last night I had the privilege of attending another gala opening at the Ardith Crawford Gallery, and the rarer privilege of meeting one of the gallery's most renowned (and reclusive) talents, Sally French.

Ms French, whose large, erotically charged canvases are in great demand both here and abroad—

'Hold it! What's he mean, "here and abroad?" '

Chips pursed her lips. 'Don't you have a couple of paintings in England?'

95

'Well, yeah, but only because the people bought them before they moved there.'

She shrugged. 'That counts.'

'Oh, brother.'

'Shut up. Where was I? Oh. Okay...

...here and abroad, has mounted a show of exceptional strength and maturity. Some of the large pieces, including the impressive 'Nearctic Number Three' and 'Gods of the Heather,' are—

'I'm gonna skip this part. It's just titles and stuff, okay?'

I dropped another rose into the vase. 'Okay.'

'Lessee...blah, blah, blah...biography stuff.' She was scanning fast '...*Native of Kansas, moved to the Twin Cities in 1981...*' She looked up. 'I didn't know you moved here in '81. I thought you—'

'Get on with it, Chips!'

'Touchy, touchy! All right. Here we go. Oh, you're gonna *love* this part!'

'Just read it, will you?'

She snickered, then began again.

'I paint pure, raw emotion,' said Ms French. 'Emotion from the soul rather than from the heart.'

'What? I never said—'

'Wait,' she grinned. 'It gets better.'

'...from the soul rather than the heart.'
Very true. There is nothing even faintly maudlin

about these canvases. They are imbued with a raw, yet sophisticated, sensuality—and sexuality. French's flawless use of colour and design couple with her masterful use of old-world glazing techniques to create works unlike those of any other contemporary artist.

When asked about the painstaking work involved in creating those multiple glazes, a technique foreign (or at least intimidating) to most contemporary painters, Ms French said, 'The necessities of the soul are complex matters. I could not express them—'

'Chips, I swear to God, I never—'

'Shut up, willya? You get real poetic here in a second. Um, where was I? Oh, yeah...'

'...could not express them by simple direct or wet-in-wet painting: my subject is too complex to be handled in a cavalier manner. Like human emotion and human need, the paintings develop, evolve. The root of any emotion, like the first tint in a series of thirty glazes, may not be easily seen, but it makes its presence known, even if only subliminally.'

Among those attending last night's opening were Dr and Mrs Jeffrey Porter, Mr and Mrs Howard Locke—'

She tossed the paper to the table. 'Rest of it's a list of who's who. Pictures of you and a few locals.'

I was still reeling from the quotes. 'Pictures? They were taking pictures?'

'Christ, you *were* dizzed out. Take a look.'

The biggest one was of Peaches and me. He

97

looked like he owned the place. I looked like a ragamuffin.

'Ick. Why did Peaches make up all that stuff? This is all Ardith's fault. I never would have gone if she hadn't—'

'Oh, don't worry about the quotes,' Chips said around a fresh cigarette. 'Peaches does that to everybody. Except the people he hates. He makes up really dumb stuff for them to say.'

'And mine wasn't dumb?'

'Bitch, bitch, bitch. God, the flowers look great.'

They did.

'You okay with this Alex thing?'

I ignored the question. 'Do I really have to go to Peaches' party?'

'Command performance. Don't worry. Peaches' dinners are usually small. Maybe a dozen people.' When I grimaced, she said, 'Face it, kid. Like it or not, you've got a social life.'

I flicked one of those yellow roses with my index finger. 'I'm gonna kill Ardith.'

8

Sally

Chips finally gave up pumping me for information and went home. I put Peaches' flowers in the centre of the dining room table, checked the plants in the conservatory, and then climbed

98

the back stairs to the studio. I wanted to kick myself. Maybe I was getting senile, but I really had wanted those flowers to be from Alex. That child.

I sat down in front of the easel and stared at the canvas. The night before, at Ardith's, I had known exactly what the next step would be; but for the life of me, I couldn't bring it to mind, couldn't get started.

When the phone rang, I nearly fell out of my chair. I practically galloped over to it, but once my hand was on the receiver, I couldn't bring myself to lift it. *Please, let it be a phone survey, no, please let it be Alex, no...*

On the fifth ring, I picked it up.

'Uh...hello?'

'It's about time you answered. I was about to hang up.' Aunt Mariah.

She asked what was new. I told her I'd had another show. She said that was nice, dear, and then spent fifteen minutes telling me about Millie's new convection oven which did such a wonderful job on roasts, and Little Meg's bunion, and Mavis's arthritis and how it was so difficult for her to do her quilting and it would be so nice if I would send her a card.

'There was an article in the paper, Aunt Mariah.'

'About what?'

'My show. Would you like me to send you a clipping?'

She wasn't listening. 'Norman has an appointment in Minneapolis next week,' she said, and I felt the bottom drop out of my stomach.

'Appointment?' Why in the world would Norman need to come to the Twin Cities? He hadn't been out of Aunt Mariah's cellar in twenty years. Thank God. 'Is he sick or something?'

'Certainly not!'

I'd forgotten that Mariah considered illness a sign of moral compromise. 'Then—'

'It's his Magic Cuber-Viewer,' she said, with about as much pride in her voice as I'd ever heard there.

'His what?'

'His latest invention. Mister Chippy's wants it.'

Mister Chippy's? It sounded like a cute name for a pimp, as in *Mister Chippy's House of Tarts*. Certainly nothing the Aunts would be happy about. 'You lost me, Aunt Mariah.'

'Pay attention, for heaven's sake! He's selling it to Mr Chippy's Breakfast Bars. They're going to put one in every box, and Norman's going to buy me a real mink coat.'

Aunt Mariah is one of the few people left in the Western Hemisphere who still think the ultimate celebration of good fortune is being heaped with animal skins.

I said, 'How nice.'

'Don't take that tone with me, Missy. We'll be there on Wednesday, and I certainly hope you'll be able to muster a little more enthusiasm by then. After all, we finally have a genuine success in the family. We always knew Norman was a genius, and the world has finally caught

100

up with us. I should think you'd be proud of your cousin.'

I sat down at the drafting table and found a pencil. 'Where's the Mr Chippy's office? I'll try to get you a hotel close to—'

'Hotel!' She let out a long-suffering sigh. 'Why on earth would we stay at some dirty hotel where God-only-knows who's used the potty? Besides, you and Norman haven't seen each other for over twenty years, and if that isn't a disgrace, I don't know what is! A normal person, Sally, would have come home to visit every now and then, but you left here like you were shot out of a gun. I suppose we weren't good enough for you.'

'Aunt Mariah, I—'

'Well, what's done is done, young lady. You always thought you were so smart, so superior. God is always watching you know. I'd think you'd welcome us into your home. Unless, of course, you've got some reason you'd rather we didn't stay with you...'

'Of course not, Aunt Mariah. You're always welcome here.' Even as I said it, I could not believe the words were coming out of my mouth.

'Fine, then.' She gave me the flight number and time of arrival. I wrote them down, all the while picturing the airport, the crowds, the blaring lights, the noise. Where did a person park at the airport? It'd been years since I'd been there.

And then Mariah was off and running about the new minister who was just too darned *young*

101

and who had these three little children that she was certain were just going to make a mess of the manse, '...and of course you know who'll have to clean that up, once he gets transferred, which he certainly will if he doesn't start paying more attention to our rummage sale and less to his hobbies. He's practically a hippie. Well, we church women will be the ones saddled with it.'

'Saddled with what?' I was still thinking about the airport. I'd probably have to walk through millions of people to find the gate. Would I have to hug Mariah and Norman when they got off the plane? People always did in movies. An unexpected spasm of revulsion twisted through me. I jerked, almost dropped the phone. I think I made a choking sound.

'Sally, pay attention! With cleaning up after those children of his after they leave, that's what. Honestly, Sally, you never change. You never listen to anything I...'

As Chips would say, *blah, blah, blah.*

After she got off the phone, I went downstairs and poured myself a glass of wine. I drained it before I got all the way back to the studio, and went back for a second.

Nothing was happening on the canvas, even after a third glass. I put on ZZ Top—they usually pump me up into painting gear—but even that driving bass didn't help. It was as if the contents of my cerebellum had been jigsawed, then dumped (in a mess I imagined to be the colour and texture of tapioca and strawberry preserves) on my brain pan. I couldn't hold any

102

train of thought for more than a few seconds. Irritation with Aunt Mariah; mooning—stupid, ridiculous—over Alex; worrying over Peaches' dinner party and dreading the advent of Norman; wondering if Chips thought I was a total jackass; hoping I'd never see Alex again; trying to figure out my share of last night's proceeds; wondering if Alex would call: I was overwhelmed by everything except painting.

I kept thinking about that kiss, too, just like I'd thought about it practically all night after Alex left. I didn't believe I'd ever been kissed quite like that in my life. It hadn't had anything to do with technique or timing. It was more that, for a few seconds, corny or not, I felt as if he was part of me, or that maybe I was part of him, and that the two of us, together, had been for a moment transmuted into one bright tongue of light: orange that glowed pure and bright, and gave way to a hot, butane blue.

I'd felt stronger, stronger than I could ever remember feeling, as if he had all this power, and he'd just made it a part of me without my even having to ask.

And I'd never been so aroused by just a kiss. I couldn't begin to explain it, but as good as it made me feel, as strong and as desirable, that kiss carried with it an enormous dose of guilt. Part of the jumble in my head was a series of quick cuts, like newsreel footage, of myself as the subject of a two-part 'Geraldo': *'Middle Aged Women Who Love Boys—Or Focus for Today: Fetal Attraction.'*

The phone rang again. This time I dropped

103

my wine glass. Fortunately, it landed on a pile of wadded paper towels and didn't break.

'Hello?' *Please be Alex, please don't be Alex, oh God, it's Geraldo, he knows already...*

'Sally?'

I sagged against the drafting table. 'Hello, Ardith.'

'Are you all right. You sound funny.'

'I'm fine. I was just, uh, preoccupied.'

'Well, I had to tell you, Sally dear, how delighted I am that you came for the opening last night. I know it was difficult for you, but it paid off. It is now, officially, a complete sellout! I got a call at home from the Brick Lowell this morning, and he bought the last piece! I hope you're busy doing me some more...'

I let her rattle on. Yes, I'd do her some more work with all possible speed. Yes, I'd read Peaches' review. No, I wouldn't 'do something' about my clothes.

After she hung up, I went back to staring at the canvas. I considered pitching it and starting over.

It was almost dark, and I had to grope for the light switch. If you're not going to accomplish anything, I always say, you should at least be able to see what it is you're not doing. Very Zen.

The phone rang again just as the lights blazed on. I stared at it. It couldn't be Ardith, couldn't be Aunt Mariah. Wouldn't be Chips: she was probably with Ever-Ready Eric, the Viking stud, by now. Maybe, just maybe...

'Hello?'

'Hi there!' A male voice, too chipper. 'This is Steve from Snow King Carpet Cleaning, and—'

I slammed down the phone, and I was only a tiny bit sorry for being rude. I took it off the hook again, laid it on the table, and went down to the kitchen. By the time I came back up (this time with the wine bottle instead of a glass), it had finished making that horrible *hey-stupid-your-phone-is-off-the-hook* whine. It was dead. I drank a toast to it, then stared at the colour of my wine.

By seven o'clock, Mariah and Norman and their impending arrival had disappeared from my thoughts entirely. There wasn't any space for them, what with trying not to think of Alex taking up so much room.

I was still pretending to work, though. I'd taken the painting off the easel, leaned it in the corner, stared at the empty easel, and brought the painting back. Twice. I'd switched from ZZ Top to Paul Simon to Carly Simon to Wynton Marsalis to Beethoven. Nothing worked. Mainly because I kept staring at that phone, wondering if I should drop the receiver back into its cradle.

After all, I reasoned, there could be an emergency. The Viking might've turned out to be a creep, and Chips could be making a distress call from some deserted gas station. I might have won the Publishers' Clearing House Sweepstakes, and they could be dialling me that very second. Maybe there was a gas leak in the neighbourhood, and the police were trying to break through to warn me.

Alex might call.

I walked over to the drafting table, then gingerly picked up the handset. I slid it into the cradle. I rested my palm on it, stared at it. I was too old for this horseshit.

It rang.

I jumped, knocked it to the floor, then dived for it.

'Hello?' I gasped from beneath the drafting table.

'Sally?'

I stood up, brought the phone with me. 'Yes?'

'Hi. It's Alex.'

I thought my heart would pound through my rib cage. What was wrong with me, anyway? I could never have an affair with this kid—I'd have a coronary before we ever got to bed.

'Hello? Sally?'

'Uh, yes. I'm here. Hi, Alex. Sorry. I dropped the phone.'

'I know it's late and it's really nervy of me to call on such short notice, but, um, I was wondering if maybe you'd like to have dinner. If you haven't eaten yet, I mean. And see a movie?'

My internal alarms went off. My chest went tight. Restaurants, theatres, too many people, too many lights.

'I...I don't know, Alex. I mean, it's nice of you to ask, but, uh, I'm not very good with crowds, and...'

'Oh. Of course. I knew that. That was pretty

106

dumb, wasn't it?' There was a short pause, then. 'Did you have dinner yet?'

He had the most beautiful voice, even over the phone. I wondered what it would be like to be twenty again, to have a twenty-year-old body and the energy that went with it; to be naked with him in the dark, to hear that voice in the dark. *If you'd been twenty when I was twenty, would you have, could you have...?*

'Hello? Sally? Are you there?'

'Oh. Excuse me. No, I haven't eaten, but—'

'Okay. Well, if you won't go out to dinner with me, I guess I'll have to think of something else.'

'Pardon?'

'Don't go anywhere, okay?'

'Alex, what on earth—'

'Bye, Sally.'

I had another glass of wine and three aspirin.

When the doorbell rang a little after 8:30, Alex was standing on my porch, a big cardboard carton in his arms. He brushed past me into the house, deposited it in the kitchen and said, 'Hang on, there's more. And no peeking!'

I watched him walk down to the drive and pull another carton from the Caddy's back seat. He really was a beautiful young man, and not just his face; he *moved* beautifully. When he came back in, I followed him through the darkened dining room. There was so much adrenaline flowing through my system, I was afraid I'd glow in the dark.

'All right,' he said, once both boxes were

on the kitchen table and he'd taken off his jacket. He was grinning. 'If Miss French will have a seat?'

I sat down.

He waved his hands in a magician's hocus-pocus flourish over the first box, and opened it. Suddenly, my kitchen smelled like a short order diner.

'Now, I know you're in a hurry to get back to your easel, so you'll want something fast, and I also wasn't sure what kind of food you liked, and I didn't want to take any chances, so...'

He reached in. 'Kentucky Fried. Extra Crispy and Original.' A box of each slid onto the table. Both hands went in the box again. 'Slaw. Mashed. Gravy. Corn.' He started a new row. 'Pizza Hut!' Three of those flat cardboard boxes. 'Pepperoni. Sausage. Vegetarian with pineapple.'

'Subs,' he said with a grin, and produced three long white sacks. 'Turkey and swiss, roast beef and onion, meatball and sauce.' The first big box emptied, he dropped it to the floor before he opened the second.

'Chinese! Let's see...' Out came carton after little white carton. 'Moo goo gai pan, barbecued spare ribs, sweet and sour pork, chicken fried rice, egg rolls, crab puffs.' He lined them up neatly next to the KFC red and white containers.

I couldn't stop laughing. 'Alex!' I finally managed, 'what are you *doing!*'

'Feeding you, m'dear.' Then, in a surprisingly excellent imitation of Dan Ackroyd doing a

Bass-o-Matic commercial, he said, 'But wait! There's more! Candles, to ensure a romantic ambience. Paper plates and napkins, to keep the grease off the table and madam's dainty fingers. Plastic silverware, to spare milady those nasty dishpan hands.'

He piled the utensils on the plates and with a flourish, produced a pink and white paper bag. 'For dessert, Mrs Field's finest chocolate chippers. Semisweet, milk chocolate, and semisweet macadamia.'

A corkscrew came next, then two wine bottles. 'Red for the pizza. White for the Colonel. Michelob for the subs,' he added, lifting a six-pack. 'Tea—well, okay, tea bags—for the Chinese. Also Pepsi, Coke, Diet Coke, Seven Up. A & W, and Vernor's.'

He sat down propped that beautiful sagacious, boyish face in his hands and arched a brow. 'And where,' he said, 'did the yellow roses come from?'

I could hear Geraldo—Oprah and Phil and Sally Jessy, too—in my head. A talk show chorus. *And so, Ms French, are we correct that this innocent young boy merely brought you a little fast food, and on the strength of that, you raped him?*

'I, uh, P—Peaches sent them.' I could barely look at him. I had never wanted any man so badly in my life.

Alex smiled. He opened the extra Crispy and held it toward me. 'Breast?'

I couldn't tell you what was said or who stood

up first, or even whose hand was the first to reach for and touch needy flesh. I do remember, however, that there was no coercion in it, and not one protest. I was beyond that, beyond rational thought.

I only knew I wanted him.

Wanted him? I needed to devour him, needed him to devour me.

We made it only halfway up the studio stairs before we were down, twisting on the risers, Alex pulling me atop him as he kissed me and slid his hands under my sweater, then inside my jeans.

Elbows thumped walls, feet kicked railings, buttons popped, hips and knees found pockets of space, gained purchase. I tore at his clothes and kissed him back in a greedy, bright orange fever.

His hands, his fingers seemed to be everywhere at once: on me, in me, splaying over my breasts, lifting my fanny, snaking my pants down my legs while I kicked to be rid of them the faster. I hugged him tight, then scratched him, bit at his shoulders, inhaled the scents of clean male skin and aftershave and need. In a blur, I felt his teeth scrape my throat, his lips tug at my nipples, his hands twisting me, turning me, opening me.

He came into me in a rush, and it could not have been more perfect—or more necessary. We were like two animals, caged for years, who had just been set free at the height of rut. I moved beneath him, then atop him, in a frenzy that only just missed being violence, and came quickly to a climax so intense that my bones nearly rattled.

Panting and slick, we lay contorted on the stairs. My bluejeans and panties were a tangled heap at the foot of the stairs, overlapped by his Levis and capped by his shorts. One of his shoes rested precariously on the third step. The other was in the centre of the kitchen floor, right next to that chicken breast he'd offered me just before my hormones bludgeoned my brain into submission. His shirt was under us. One sleeve trailed out from beneath my backside.

Only then did I realize I still had my sweater on, although it, along with my bra, was tugged up over my breasts. It struck me that I must look reasonably idiotic, and then it struck me that I had just done a very foolish thing.

Even as Alex's hand slid lazily from my belly to cradle my hip, I cursed myself for a fool. I'd given in. I'd been so weak. Had anyone ever been weaker? And he was only...what? Twenty? They'd probably bypass Geraldo and Phil and put me directly in prison.

Well, all right, I thought, *not prison. He's legal. But they'll do something. Maybe make me wear a big letter 'A' on my blouse. No, a 'C,' for Cradle Robber.*

I won't look at him, I told myself. I'd make myself ignore his scent, warm in my nostrils and incredibly heady; his body, so close that our breathing had nearly synchronized. I'd make myself believe that his shoulders weren't broad, that his skin wasn't sleek and taut and velvety as only a man's skin can be. I'd convince myself

111

that this encounter was nothing, meant nothing. An accident.

I told myself that his smile was common, that he had no sense of humour, that his eyes held no secrets, that his voice wasn't music, that he moved with no grace, that we had nothing in common except for this horrendous sexual *faux pas*.

And I thought I might just be able to manage it, if only I didn't look into those eyes.

I moved to pull my sweater down, hoping to regain at least some of my dignity, but Alex stopped me.

'No.' His whisper vibrated through me. 'Not down,' he said. 'Off.'

He eased it over my head, along with the tangled bra, then tossed them down the steps before he brought his hand back up to trace a slow circle around my nipple with his fingertips. He never looked away from my eyes, and by then I was lost in his. So blue, so clear, they were; painting after painting, canvas after canvas could be done in nothing but the subtle tones and variations that went into the blue of those eyes.

And by then I didn't care about Geraldo or Oprah or Phil or jail or scarlet letters. I didn't care, I didn't think. I just wanted more of this, of him.

'C'mon,' he said, half-carrying, half-guiding me up the steps to the studio, then through it and the library to the bedroom. We fell upon the perpetually unmade bed, and his arms enveloped me.

'Sally,' he said, in a whisper hoarse but Puckish. 'My brilliant, gorgeous, sexy Sally. We're in deep trouble. I only had one condom on me.' He flicked his hand toward the wastebasket, and I heard the tiny rustle of impact.

At least one of us had retained some presence of mind, then. I didn't remember his producing one, let alone putting it on or taking it off.

The smile must have blossomed over my face, because he gave me a quizzical look, kissed my nose, and said, 'What're you grinning about? This is a major dilemma!'

I shook my head. 'Chips.'

'What?' He was grinning, too. 'If you're planning to call Quincannon for a mercy run to the drugstore—'

'No needs. She's psychic.' I wriggled one arm free and reached toward the nightstand. Chips's box of goodies. I handed it to him.

He propped himself on an elbow and twisted off the tin's lid. He smiled a little too wickedly.

It set my heart racing.

He reached into the tin and began sorting through the contents. 'Couple dozen. Going to be Monday before we use these up, Sally French.'

'Braggart.'

He pulled out a packet and wagged it at me. 'How do you feel about orange with ripples?'

I took it from him and tore it open. 'Right at the moment,' I said, reaching for him, 'it's my favourite.'

9

Alex

I was deep beneath the ocean's surface, miles from land, swimming naked. Whales sang. Light filtered softly through the warm murk in waving bands that shifted from blue-grey to pale gold to milky green, and I was slipping through the water effortlessly, feeling spent and exhilarated all at once. Bubbles rose around me, sparkling and refracting the light, shifting the colours.

But then the whales stopped singing and I began to rise, and just as the clear bright surface came into focus, I realized I'd been dreaming. And in the dream I hadn't really been underwater so much as I'd been swimming through one of Sally French's paintings.

Sally. I reached for her, but the other side of the bed was vacant. The only light in the room was the luminous dial of her bedside clock, which read 4:07. The only sound that seeped into the room was soft music: Ray Lynch, 'Deep Breakfast.' No wonder I had dreamt about whalesong and weightlessness.

I stood up, wrapped a sheet around my middle, and followed the music.

She was in her studio, dressed in nothing but an old flannel shirt that hung halfway to her knees, and she was painting. She hadn't heard me come in, and I stood there, watching her work.

It was a new painting, huge, and she was moving along it, sweeping wide, translucent washes of deep Indian yellow across its surface. She worked quickly but with an incredible intensity, as if she were aware of the most minute nuance of the linen's weave, the colour, and nothing else. By the time she left one area of canvas and moved to the next, the application was so flawless that it seemed the pigment had simply materialized there and had never known a brush.

She switched to cadmium yellow without cleaning her brush, and then I noticed that she'd been busy mixing paint: one of the small tables at her right hand been cleared of the previous clutter and now held several sizes of glass jars, each half-filled with paint in varying colours and consistencies.

How long had she been awake and working? I wondered if she'd slept at all.

The cadmium yellow began to mate with the first colour, and bright swirls began to emerge as the focus of the thing came clearer. She walked the canvas slowly, then rapidly: adjusting a tone here, a nuance there. She was swaying with the music, almost conducting it on canvas. The synthesizer swirled, and so did her hips. An electric crescendo coincided with an upsweep of her arm, a sweep of bright, clear yellow that semed to melt away, at the edges, to nothing. Her bare feet made a slow, silent dance on the piled rugs, a soft, patting rhythm on the bare wood when she moved to the painting's far end.

The Ray Lynch disk ended and a new one started: some sort of Gaelic music, lush, haunting, almost pagan. Sally switched to a soft lemon, this time an opaque, and without breaking rhythm, she began to weave it into the previous colours. She slid thin ribbons of bright colour into the pattern so delicately that if I hadn't seen them applied, I suppose I'd have picked them up only subliminally.

And then, in a tiny slice of silence between songs on the stereo, my stomach growled.

She spun round, her freshly dipped brush spattering pale sunshine across the rugs. Her mouth opened, soundlessly for a second, and then she said, 'Oh.'

I think I blushed. My face went awfully hot, anyway. I felt like I'd just been caught peeking in someone's bedroom window.

She ducked her head, as if she were the one who should be embarrassed, and carried her brushes to the sink.

'Don't stop,' I said, and almost tripped over my sheet when I stepped forward. Ever graceful—that's me.

She dropped the brushes into a jar of turpentine, then turned on the tap. 'I can't do any more tonight anyway,' she said. She began gently working the first brush through the yellowing turp. 'This layer has to set up.' She didn't look at me.

I cinched the sheet a little tighter around my waist and braved another two steps into the studio.

She said, 'I brought some chicken up from the kitchen,' and pointed down the counter to a paper plate. A breast, a leg, and some bones. 'I packed all the rest in the fridge so it wouldn't spoil.'

I inhaled the chicken before she had the last of the turp squeezed out of her brushes, then shoved the plate away and picked up a glass half-full of brown liquid. I sniffed at it. You have to be careful what you drink in a painter's studio.

'It's Coke,' she said, and looked away quickly. She squeezed liquid soap into the hollow of her palm and began to gently work the brush bristle through it. 'Probably warm.'

I'd already gulped it down. 'S'all right.' I watched the bristles glide across her lathered palm, and decided it probably hadn't been such a swift idea to sneak into her studio. She was either really angry or embarrassed, because she sure wasn't making any conversation, let alone eye contact.

I gathered up my sheet again and went to stand behind her. I reached around her and cupped my hands over hers, the brush in the centre. 'Mind if I borrow a little of your soap?' I said, and wiggled my fingers. 'Chicken grease.'

Now, there's a romantic phrase for you: chicken grease.

I started soaping my hands with hers. Her fingers were so tiny, so slim. I said, 'Sorry I snuck up on you. I won't do it again.'

She didn't say anything for what seemed like an awfully long time.

'Sally?'

I still couldn't see her face, but she stood up a little straighter, as if she had just remembered I was there. She gripped my soapy index fingers. The way my body reacted, she might as well have gripped something else. She said, 'I don't suppose I can skip Peaches' party?'

I dipped my head down a little. I could smell the sweet, clean tang of her hair. I cleared my throat. 'Command performance.'

'What...what does a person wear?' She let go of my finger and began to rinse her brushes.

I stuck my hands under the tap. 'Anything. Everything.' My sheet fell off. I felt it slide down my legs and come to rest around my ankles. 'Nothing.'

She laughed, a breathy *hmm* sound deep in her throat. 'Nothing?'

I said, 'It's an eccentric crowd,' and kissed the top her head.

She swayed a little, her hips brushing back against me. I wished I could see her face. With wet hands, I lifted the golden silk of her hair and kissed the nape of her neck.

'I...I guess it must be,' she breathed.

I kissed the side of her neck, the top rim of her ear. 'Must be what?'

She let out a tiny, fluttery breath before she said, 'Eccentric.'

'Um-hm.' I had her earlobe between my teeth, worrying it gently. I loved the taste of her.

Her head tilted back a bit father. 'I, uh...' She dropped the brushes. They clattered into the stream of running water as her hands gripped the edge of the sink. 'I can't get out of going, then?" Her voice was throaty, broken. I could barely hear her.

I slid my hands apart, across her shoulders, then down her sides to lift the hem of her baggy shirt. She wore nothing beneath it but a pair of panties, and I slipped one hand inside to stroke her belly while I tickled the underside of her breast with the other. She had wonderful breasts. If I could paint like she did, I'd have done a whole series of paintings in the pale salmon pink of her nipples. I said, 'Peaches' party isn't the only thing you can't get out of, Sally.'

She leaned her head back against my shoulder and uncurled one of those tiny hands from the sink's edge to push at the elastic of her panties and slide her fingers atop my hand. She guided it downward, between her legs. 'Do it here, Alex,' she whispered. 'Do it now. Like this.'

Nothing—and I mean nothing—would have pleased me more, but the damn rubbers were in the other room. I swallowed hard, kissed her ear and whispered, 'Honey, we need Chips's goody box.'

'No.' It came out as a long sigh. Her right hand was still on top of mine, riding it. 'You trailed some in.' She let go of the sink just long enough to point to the floor at my side. I guess we'd dumped the box, and a few had got caught in my sheet. She grabbed for the sink again, then nudged backward, into me, with her hips. 'Now, Alex. Please.'

I bent quickly and picked up the nearest

119

packet. Just before I ripped it open with my teeth, I noticed that it was yellow. The same yellow as those last little lemon ripples she'd painted.

It was a good thing Ardith closed the gallery on Mondays, because it was nearly three on Monday afternoon before I managed to pry myself away from Sally French. And when I kissed her goodbye at the door, I very nearly didn't leave at all.

What was it about her? On the drive home, I tried picking her apart, piece by piece. Not that I was trying to talk myself out of her, mind you; it's just that I'd never been quite this, well, *drunk* on any woman before. I figured I'd better take what chance I had to try and figure it out, since when I was with her I was so besotted I couldn't think at all.

It was crazy. I'd always gone out with very stylish girls. You know, the tall, willowy, glamour types with just the right clothes and makeup. That probably doesn't say much for me, but it's the truth. Even back home, when I was in high school, I went steady with Georgia Baer, and she ended up going off to New York and signing with the Ford Agency. She was in *Vogue* again last month, draped in white vinyl.

After Georgia there was Colette, then Nancy, then Suzanne. I thought I loved each and every one of them, once upon a time.

But along, as they say, came Sally. She wasn't any six feet tall, she was sure no slave to fashion, she didn't wear makeup or do anything special

120

with her hair, but she left all the others in the dust. I guess there's no fighting chemistry.

When I got home, I almost phoned my folks. I generally call them every two weeks or so just to see how they're doing and let them know what's new with me (and give my dad another opportunity to remind me that it's never too late to go back to school, and didn't *Langley & Son* have a nice ring to it?), and I was due to phone them. But I didn't. My parents—my mom especially—are practically psychic, and I didn't want them noticing anything unusual in my voice and asking uncomfortable questions. How could I explain to them the way I felt about Sally when I didn't understand it myself?

So I wandered around my condo, absently picking up dirty laundry from one corner and dropping it in another, and feeling alien in my own home. At about five o'clock I finally sat down on the sofa and looked around me. It was a nice condo, and I made nice fat mortgage payments. Downstairs was a trendy address, valet parking, and a doorman who called me Mister Langley, even though he was old enough to be my grandfather. I was on the tenth floor, in what the real estate lady had called the Junior Executive Floorplan: 1350 square feet featuring a vaulted living room with a fireplace, two big bedrooms, formal dining, a great view of the city, even a Jacuzzi in the master bath.

It had been pretty stark when I'd moved in—what they call 'lite and brite'—and I hadn't really done too much to alleviate it. Oh, I'd hung some paintings and prints. There were a few things from home scattered on the shelves, a couple of nice pieces of furniture mixed in with the bargain stuff, a rowing machine in the middle of the living room floor. But it was hardly what you'd call 'homey.' I guess I'd never paid much attention before. After all, I never spent much time there.

Before, there'd been work and Suzanne to take up all my time. Lately, there'd been work and...and what? I had to think about that. It didn't seem to me that I'd been home that much more since Suzanne and I had broken it off—well, all right, since I'd broke it off and Suzanne had mailed me that dead fish—but what had I been doing? Movies alone, meeting some client or other for a drink, a few ballgames, nothing spectacular.

It struck me that I'd been doing a whole lot of nothing, just to keep from coming back to this house that wasn't a home. It also struck me that I'd felt completely at peace in Sally's house. I could have closed the door behind me and never come out again.

Of course, I reasoned, Sally French had an awful lot to do with that. That was how deep and how fast she'd got to me: less than forty-eight hours together, and already I didn't feel whole without her.

Something within me had been looking for her forever, and the way I felt about her made my so-called passions for her predecessors seem trivial. I wondered who Sally was looking for, and prayed she'd discover it was me. Maybe she'd been searching for me all this time. Maybe those glorious, brilliant paintings had been her way of calling out.

Messages in bottles.

I began to think that all those metaphysical yo-yos might have something after all. Maybe there was such a thing as a soulmate.

Maybe I'd just found mine.

10

Sally

When I called Chips to tell her she didn't need to pick me up for Peaches' party—and why—she nearly jumped through the phone at me.

'Calm down,' I said, once she gave me a chance to get a word in. 'I don't...I don't want to talk about it yet. I don't think I *can* talk about it.'

There was a long pause before she said, 'Okay, kiddo. Think you might be a little more glib at the shindig tonight?'

'Chips...'

'Okay, okay. I won't bug you about it. But Sal? If you wanna talk, I'm here.'

'Thanks. I know.'

After I hung up the phone, I wandered into the studio. I couldn't paint, of course. There wasn't enough time to get much of a start before I'd have to change for the party. I stood before the canvas, staring at it, trying to plan the next

123

series of glazes. But as much as I wanted to get back to work, my mind wandered.

The studio had the alien air of tainted sanctity. *Do it here, Alex, do it now.* Good God. I'd spent years attempting to gain a tenuous control over my life, over my heart, and in one weekend I'd managed to set myself back a decade. No, it was worse than that—it had been more than sex, more than a little cat-in-heat rumpy-pumpy.

And the new painting was yellow. Had I ever done one entirely in yellow? I didn't think so. Of course, they always changed. They never ended up as what they'd started out to be. But even now, in this early stage, it was beginning to pulse.

Suddenly, I couldn't bear to look at it. I turned away, toward the long counter. A bad choice.

Do it here, Alex, do it now.

Dear Lord in heaven.

My brushes still lay where I'd dropped them. One had landed on an angle with half its badger hair bristles bent, and it had dried that way.

'Ruined,' I muttered, and flipped on the tap. 'A forty-dollar brush.' I straightened the soft calico hairs under the water's stream, reshaped them, blotted them between paper towels, then carefully lifted the top layer of towelling.

In slow motion, half the bristles lifted and twisted back into that sick, spoiled angle.

'Damn it,' I whispered through clenched teeth. Then, 'Damn it, damn it, damn it!'

I hurled the thing. It made a loud *pop* when

it bounced off the far wall. I later discovered it had put a nice ding in the wall as well, but at that moment I was too busy crying to notice.

What was wrong with me? What had I done? My self-control wasn't just slipping away, it had fled on the first fast-moving train. I wanted Alex—to touch him, to see him smile, to hear his voice—more than anything; and at the same time I wanted never to see him again. I doubted Dr Ruth could sort this one out. Maybe not even Oprah.

I ripped a paper towel off the nearest wall and scrubbed at my tears, then blew my nose.

'Get a grip, Sally,' I muttered as I pitched it, in a wad, toward the wastebasket. I straightened my shoulders. I took a deep breath.

'You're making too big a deal out of this,' I told myself as I made my way into the bathroom and ran a rub. 'So what if he's younger than you? Okay, a *lot* younger. He's legal. He's a grown up. It probably didn't mean a thing to him except that he got lucky and got laid. It's not like he's in love with you or anything. It's not like you're in love with him.'

That stopped me. I couldn't lie to myself—I did feel something for him, something inexplicably deep. But love? I barely knew him, other than in the biblical sense. Besides, I wasn't certain I knew what love was. I wasn't sure that it existed outside of romance novels and old movies.

By the time I finished my bath, I'd decided to call up Alex—and Peaches—and beg off. I hadn't wanted to go to the stupid party in the

125

first place, and going with Alex would just get me into deeper trouble.

'I'm sorry, Alex, I'm not feeling well,' I practised over the gurgle of the drain as I towelled off. No, that sounded dopey. Besides, he'd probably come racing over with two aspirin and a hot water bottle. It had to be something long-term, something really discouraging.

Alex, my application with Dr Leakey was approved, and I'm leaving for the Kalahari at noon.

Of course, Sally, I understand. What are the lives of two little people compared to the science of anthropology?

Yeah, sure.

I couldn't tell him the truth: he'd awakened in me something I'd thought either nonexistent or long dead. If I let it come fully awake it would trample me into the ground, then eat me, whole and alive. It was too fast, too intense, this thing we'd started. It would never work. Romance was for teenaged girls, love was an illusion, hope was for the simple-minded.

The years had convinced me that lust and art were the only two pure—if sometimes ugly—human truths. I had harnessed them, controlled them in my solitude.

It was a fine balance I'd struck. My art, the colours and layers of my soul and heart, trembled precariously upon the narrow tightrope to which I'd narrowed my world. The longer I allowed this relationship with Alex to continue, the more entangled I let myself become, the more devastating the consequences of the inevitable breakup, the most disastrous the plummet.

It wasn't his fault, of course, unless you could say he was to blame for being caring or witty or handsome or smart, or for being the most attuned lover I had ever known. It wasn't his fault that the sound of his voice or the brush of his hand touched a shrouded place deep within my psyche, not his fault that I hadn't known that that place existed, that I had no control over it and was therefore terrified of it.

Wrapped in a towel, I went back to my bedroom, lay down on rumpled sheets, and without thinking, reached for his pillow. The faint scent of aftershave mixed with the barest trace of musk clung to the slip. I buried my face in it, crushed the fine texture of linen against my skin, breathed deeply of those last lingering evidences of Alex.

And with that one small action, that one whiff of complicated scent and the memories it triggered, my resolve melted like blued ice under a yellow August sun. Alex meant certain disaster, but I couldn't stay away from him.

Just one more night, I told myself, and hugged the pillow closer. *Just one more night can't hurt, can it?*

Alex had said he'd call for me at seven, and he was five minutes early.

I'd decided on my green silk blouse: one of those big, full-sleeved poets' shirts with a wide collar and deep V neckline. Aunt Mariah always said I shouldn't wear green, but I loved that blouse. I'd bought it back in '85 and had

127

based at least four paintings on its bottomless emerald.

'You look great!' he enthused, after a long kiss that nearly dissolved me into the foyer floor. 'I like your hair that way.'

I'd done a French braid, which is about as fancy as I get. It had been so long since I'd done one that it had taken me almost an hour to get it straight. And even. But I said, 'Thanks,' rather dismissively, as if I'd just whipped it off in a few seconds, and pointed to my jeans. This pair, in honour of the occasion, bore no paint spatters or holes. 'You're sure this is all right? What I'm wearing, I mean?'

'Terrific.'

His smile made me shiver inside.

'And we sorta match,' he added. He had on jeans, too, with a pullover cableknit. It was the colour of mid-summer sky over ocean, and made his eyes look that much clearer, that much more like windows into forever.

'Cowboy boots?' They made him another two inches taller, so that I barely came up to his shoulder.

He opened the front door and ushered me out onto the porch as he drawled, 'Yes, ma'am. The footwear of choice for us Colorado cowboy types.'

I laughed. 'Cowboy?' We started down the walk toward his car. The sun had nearly gone, and the western sky held the last tinges of orange and pink. There was a wonderful damp pine scent in the chilled air, along with a barely

128

perceptible undercurrent of electricity. Rain was on the way.

'See how you are?' he said, feigning indignation. 'You city women think that just because a fella knows a Manet from a Monet he's never landed face-first in a fresh pile of steer manure. I'll have you know that back home, my mother is standing guard over a whole closet full of my old stock horse trophies.' He opened the Caddy's door for me, I slid in and was immediately enveloped by the rich scent of leather.

I arched a brow teasingly. 'I'm supposed to be impressed? What's a "stock horse," anyway? Sounds like something wooden, like a first cousin to a stick horse.'

He shook his head, long and sad. 'Woman, I can see you have a lot to learn about the fine art of reining.'

He walked around the car, slid in, and turned the key. I fought back the urge to scoot closer to him.

'Raining? This has something to do with riding a horse in the rain?'

He backed down the long driveway and into the street, and with his hand on the gearshift, he turned toward me. One corner of his mouth slowly curved into a purely ornery smile.

'Nope,' he said. 'Reining, as in reins. You know, long strips of leather that hook onto the bit and you hold them in your hands and—'

I laughed. 'Smartass.'

He nodded. 'Yes, ma'am, guilty.' He put the car into drive and we started down the street.

'No, really, you do things like figure eights and fast lead changes and three-hundred-and sixty-degree spins. Sliding stops, stuff like that. I was Junior State Champion two years running. Not that I mean to brag or anything.'

I punched him in the arm and he broke out laughing. So did I. 'I know what a stock horse is.'

It had started to mist a little, and he switched on the windshield wipers. To their steady *whisk whisk whisk* he said, 'Mine was Mountain Annie. Slick little mare. My folks've still got her.' Without looking at me, he smiled. Just the corner of his mouth. 'You know about that stuff?'

'I'm from Kansas, remember? 4-H country.'

'You ever—'

I shook my head. 'I sat on a horse once, but it was standing nice and still.'

He signalled and turned onto the freeway entrance ramp. 'You'll have to come out to my folks' place. Meet Annie. I'll teach you to ride.' He must have seen the terror on my face, because he quickly added, 'Or not.'

It wasn't the thought of horses that had scared me, though. It was the not-any-too-veiled *Come and meet my parents* part. I stared at my lap.

We rode in silence for a few minutes before he said, 'You know, nothing much really happens at Peaches' parties until at least nine or so. Want to take a ride? Go the scenic route?'

It was really raining by then—and good and dark as well—but I said, 'Sure, I'd like that. Around the lakes or something?'

He smiled. Intermittent passing headlights turned his eyes from ice to sapphire to turquoise. 'Or something.' He stretched his arm along the back of the seat and stroked my temple with two fingers. 'Don't stay way over there.'

He drove slowly through the city, around Lake of the Isles, then along quiet back streets that grew less and less recognizable until I was lost. I didn't care. I could have ridden like that with him for the rest of my life. He kept one hand on the wheel. The other casually cupped my shoulder, rubbed my neck or arm, traced my ear.

We didn't talk. Mozart played softly on the stereo, an accompaniment to the rain that pelted the old Cadillac's roof and streamed down her fogging windows.

I closed my eyes and nestled into the curve of Alex's shoulder. His sweater was as soft under my cheek as his chest was solid, his understated aftershave a lazing aphrodisiac. All the doubts that had tortured me that afternoon were forgotten. When I was with him each moment seemed to ring clear, unsullied and untroubled by reality.

With my eyes still closed, I felt the car make a slow but sharp turn to the right. The smooth asphalt under the tyres gave way to the crunch of wet gravel. Against Alex's chest, I murmured, 'Are we there yet?'

His breath washed warm across my scalp as he kissed the crown of my head. His hand slid to my side, and he squeezed me gently. 'Not yet.'

131

We began to climb, and when my lids fluttered open, I saw we had left the tidy houses and neat yards of suburbia behind. Wild, towering trees, black-green and dancing in the rain, lined the narrow gravel lane. The leaves of their lower limbs made wet scuttling sounds on the Caddie's roof.

'How did we get to a forest?'

He chuckled. The sound rumbled through his chest and my cheek. 'I want to show you the view. We're on Rob Winston's estate.'

'Who?'

'Client.'

A few minutes later the gravel road wound up out of the trees and onto a grassy bluff. Alex eased the Caddie up to a low stone wall, then cut the motor. He kissed the top of my head again, then gave me a little nudge. 'Look.'

It was a Maxfield Parrish sky if ever there was one, crowded with thunderheads and lit by a full moon that slipped in and out of hiding to lend the clouds silvery edges and deep, nearly ochre bodies. Far below, the swelling river ran dark and wide, the colour of pewter. Beyond its fat, rushing ribbon, the city sparkled like a million fairy lights.

About us, rain made music on glass and metal and filled the car with the scent of wet earth and fresh-scrubbed trees. I thought how wonderful it would be to sprawl naked in the grass, beneath the storm.

I had leaned forward and propped my forearms on the dashboard, and Alex was rubbing my back in slow, light circles, bathing

132

me in warm gooseflesh.

'Sally, I was thinking.'

Was there any headier draught for the senses than his voice in the rain? I bit my lip and looked down at the river.

'Thinking?'

'About tonight. About the ways I'd like to make love to you after we do our duty at the party. And I've come to a decision.'

His hand slipped round my side, his index finger tracing my breast's underside. A short gasp of anticipation escaped through my teeth. 'Decision?'

Gently, he eased me back against the seat and leaned over me. His eyes purpled by the shadows, his lips a scant inch above mine, he whispered. 'I can't wait that long.'

I found I couldn't, either.

There is little to be said for the comfort level of the average teenager's obligatory backseat lovemaking. However, when the car in question is a '56 Caddy with a rear seat the size of a camp cot, and when the participants are past the clumsy adolescent stage and are as inventive—and game—as Alex and I were, the possibilities are endless.

My braid was the sole casualty. All the way back into town I tried to replait it with no success, and finally just brushed it out. 'Are you sure it looks all right?' I asked Alex for the third time as he parked in front of Peaches' house.

'Beautiful,' he soothed. 'And you don't need

133

to be nervous. Peaches is practically family.'

Peaches and Anthony had a Tudor house in Kenwood, part of the old mansion district not far from the Guthrie Theatre. I've always loved the houses up there. They're beautiful old things, some of them absolutely huge. If a neighbourhood can be quaint and spectacular all at once, this one was.

It had stopped raining, and Alex and I walked down the wet brick drive arm in arm. Light poured from the wide, mullioned windows, and I could see people inside. They were holding drinks, giving each other a peck on the cheek or a pat on the shoulder or backside as they passed. I heard laughter and music. I thought I caught a glimpse of Ardith, her arm around the shoulders of a blond girl.

Alex rang the bell.

'It's about time!' Peaches said less than five seconds later as he hauled us through the door and into foyer. 'Everybody! Attention!' he called. He held me captive on his right, Alex on his left. 'These naughty and completely *un*punctual people have arrived at last. Dinner will be served in five minutes. If my ducks haven't turned to cinders.'

Everybody laughed and went back to their private conversations. My first impression was that there were at least a million people crowded into the living room. Some were dressed in evening wear, but most people seemed to have worn casual clothes. Some wore what looked like either jogging or gym gear.

Anthony, tweedy and decidedly unruffled,

tended bar across the room. His lifted his hand and sent us a rather bored wave. Chips in a denim miniskirt and fringed leather jacket, wove through the crowd toward us, dragging Eric behind her. Across the room, a tall, extraordinary pretty girl in a short black dress seemed to be staring at me, but looked away when I turned toward her.

Too many people, too much noise. A surge of panic pushed at the top of my skull.

Above the din, Peaches said, 'Sally, I adore that blouse!' You'd make a fabulous pirate.' He cocked his head at Alex and clicked his tongue. 'And just what have you been up to, you wicked thing? Our little Sally appears just a little too freshly fondled to me. Anything your mother should know?'

My cheeks went hot. I thought my heart might pound through my rib cage. Before Alex could reply, Peaches added, 'After the festivities, you've got to come out and have a look at the Bentley. It's my carburettor again, I think. Or maybe the plugs. Or the wires. Thunk, thunk, thunk.'

'What *kind* of thunk, Peaches?' Alex asked. He looked relieved at the change in subject. 'Is it a sort of—'

But Peaches was already scurrying off toward what I supposed was the kitchen. I grabbed Alex's arm, and he smiled. The panic washed out of me and was gone. Magic. I smiled back. 'Freshly fondled? Be honest, Alex, do I look like I, I mean we...and do I really look like a pirate?'

135

'There you are!' Chips joined us. 'You don't look like a pirate. You look like Lord Byron's mistress. Or maybe Percy Shelley in drag.' She grabbed the sides of my blouse and held them wide. 'Christ, I love these poets' shirts! And don't believe him about burning dinner on your account. He never serves much before nine-thirty, anyhow, and you beat that by ten minutes. Where'd you find this in green silk? Snazzy.'

'Had it for years, I just—'

Somewhere, someone struck a gong. Peaches materialized between Chips and Alex. To a hushed and smiling crowd, he announced, 'Ladies and gentlemen, the culinary experience of a lifetime, or at least this week, awaits.'

My dining room could have fit into a corner of this one and gone unnoticed.

All thirty of us—I counted—sat at the same long table, and no one suffered for lack of elbow room. The ceiling was beamed in dark wood that punctuated long stretches of stamped antique tin. The walls were darkly panelled, but not much of the panelling had a chance to show through the artwork hung over it.

They were good paintings, too. I didn't recognize the authorship of all of them, but I saw two Frankenthalers and a Rothko, a Mark Tobey and a Franz Kline; a de Kooning; three Motherwells. Directly across from me, partially obscured by Eric, was a Larry Rivers.

It was an amazing, if eccentric, collection, one that any museum would have been proud

136

to show if it had been regrouped a little bit. And while most of the pieces were quite large, the room was proportioned so beautifully that they didn't seem crowded.

Anthony reigned over one end of the linen-draped table, which was fairly staggered with crystal and flowers and mismatched but gorgeous antique china. Peaches held court at the other end. They apparently didn't believe in place cards, but Alex guided me toward a seat roughly a third of the way toward Peaches' realm and sat on my left. Chips grabbed the chair to my right. Ever-Ready Eric, who so far hadn't said a word, slipped into a vacant seat exactly opposite Chips, probably with hopes of playing footsie.

Peaches tapped a knife against the side of his wine glass and waited for the room to quiet. 'Ladies, gentlemen, and otherwise—and you know who you are—dinner.' He raised a small silver bell and gave it one tinkling shake. 'Richard? Helen? You may serve.'

Beside me, Alex pressed his palms to his forehead. He was grinning. Chips leaned across me. 'Gets better all the time, doesn't it?'

I poked her. 'What?'

'The show,' she said. 'And just you watch. Nothing's gonna match.'

I heard Alex chuckle, but I didn't look at him. 'What do you mean?'

'Peaches is into eclectic this year,' Alex said. I felt his arm slip round the back of my chair to press against my shoulders. I leaned into the safety of it.

Chips shook out her napkin and draped it

over her lap. 'Last time he served enchiladas and quiche and some weird melon shit with coconut.'

A slender, fine-featured young man and an equally slender fair-haired girl, both dressed entirely in white and pushing serving carts, emerged from the kitchen and made their way down the length of the table. 'It was avocado mousse *en* cantaloupe,' Alex said, as the waiter slid a shallow soup bowl in front of him. 'Coconut on top. The time before that was the chicken with Mexican chocolate sauce and french fries.' He looked down at his soup just as the waiter served mine. 'Borscht?'

Chips took hers out of the waiter's hands and sniffed at it before she lowered it to the table. 'Wouldn't be surprised,' she said.

After the borscht came the duck—a quarter of a roasted bird per person, served on a bed of wild rice and mushrooms, with a gardenia on the side.

'A flower on the plate?' I flicked away a few grains of rice, then twirled the short stem in my fingers.

Chips nodded. 'You're supposed to eat it.' When I made a face she added, 'No, really,' and tipped her head toward the lady across from me, beside Eric. She was munching away at hers, in between telling anyone who would listen how 'tasty' everything was. She looked as though she might munch away at the tablecloth if given half a chance. Poor Eric looked as if he were afraid she might try him with a little hollandaise, and looked pleadingly at Chips.

138

So did I. 'You going to eat yours?'

She picked it up. 'Not enough money in the world.' She flicked it into my fingerbowl.

'Gee, thanks.'

'Anytime.' She was already busy with her duck. 'Looks like a decent bird, doesn't it?'

The lady across the table pointed at my fingerbowl. 'If you're not going to eat that...?'

I nudged Alex with my elbow and tipped my head toward the paintings on the opposite wall. 'Art critiquing must pay pretty well.'

Alex slid a forkful of rice into his mouth, then shook his head. 'Nope,' he said, once he'd swallowed. 'It's Anthony's money. Family's rolling in it. Peaches does the buying, though. The rest of the collection is just as pushy. Did you try your rice yet?'

'No. Alex, this stuff is worth a couple million!'

He scooped another pile of rice on his fork and paused. 'Oh, way more than that. Wasn't when he bought it, though.' He pointed, with his fork, to one of the paintings across the way. 'He told me he picked that one up for twelve hundred dollars back in the mid sixties. Now it's worth about three hundred and fifty grand, give or take.'

Rather facetiously, I muttered. 'I'd be more impressed if there was one of mine in here,' and when Alex laughed, I added, 'What?'

He wiped at his mouth with a napkin. 'You're sitting in front of it.'

I twisted around so quickly I nearly tipped my chair. There it was: *Moonlight and Madness,* one of my favourites from roughly five years before.

139

I was suddenly a little impressed with myself, or at least the company I was keeping. I think I gasped.

Alex grinned and gave me a wink before he turned back to his dinner. I wondered if he'd noticed that I'd stopped breathing for a half-second.

Odd, how the close proximity of friends can buffer fear. Sitting safely between Chips and Alex, I began to feel almost cocky, as if I might be able to talk to an actual stranger should the need arise. After all, I was hung on the same wall with Georgia O'Keefe.

While everyone was occupied with the main course, I studied the company. There were a few people I assumed were Anthony's university friends, since they had gravitated towards his end of the table and seemed almost normal. Ardith was across from us, about halfway down towards Peaches. Ardith had power, that was for certain. Peaches seemed to be the only one present who didn't kowtow to her. She waved at me and gave me a *see-I-was-right-you-should-get-out-more-often-and-don't-you-look-lovely* look but most of her attention was lavished upon a blond girl, the same one I'd seen her with earlier.

'That's Gloria,' Alex said, when he caught me watching. 'How you doing?' His hand slipped beneath the table to rub my knee, and he smiled. The rest of the room faded away for the second it took me to fall into his eyes and imagine we were still back on the bluff, in the rain.

'Sally?'

140

A frisson passed through me—warm and totally inappropriate—and the room came back into focus. 'Fine,' I said, over the clatter of silver and chatter. I cleared my throat. 'Who, uh...do you know that girl down there?' Anything to distract my thoughts.

'Where?'

'The pretty one with the black hair. Between Ardith and the man with the green bow tie.'

He glanced toward her, then quickly looked down at his plate. 'Why?' Fork in hand, he pushed at his duck.

'She keeps staring at me,' I said. 'Or I think she does. Every time I catch her eye out of the corner of my eye and turn, she looks away.'

Alex sat back a little in his chair and smiled at me softly. 'Nobody important. I mean, nobody for you to—'

'Suzanne Moore,' Chips interrupted. She leaned close, so that our shoulders bumped. 'Works for Bing Taylor, over at Cross Street Galleria. Bing's never invited here, but she always is. A real go-getter, that girl. A real barracuda.'

'Huh?'

'She wants to be Ardith when she grows up.' Chips sat up straight and took a long drink of water. 'In the business sense only, of course. She likes boys. Or so I hear.' She studied her glass. 'What do you hear, Alex?'

A tick of irritation seemed to tug at one corner of Alex's lip, but it was gone so quickly I decided I'd imagined it. He had his mouth

141

half-open to reply when Peaches rang the little silver bell again.

'If all you handsome, adorable, marvellous people would kindly shut the hell up, we have an event planned before the next course. Maestro?'

Alex nodded. 'Be right back,' he whispered against my ear, before he pushed his chair out and left the room.

I looked at Chips.

'Must be music involved,' she said, and dropped her wadded napkin on her plate. 'Peaches can't work the stereo and Anthony won't leave the room when they've got guests. Don't ask me why.'

Two men, both from Anthony's end of the table and both in rather conservative suits, rose, made their way toward the middle of the one side of the hall, and began to take off their clothes beneath a Jasper Johns flag.

'Misters Johnson and Rojack have ever-so-graciously consented to entertain us,' Peaches went on, 'with a sample of their current revue, which may be seen at the Arlington Club through Friday next.'

None too softly, Chips said, 'Dontcha love it when he's pompous?'

'I heard that?' Peaches snapped happily. 'And I'm not pompous, I'm affected. Are we ready, Mr Johnson?'

'A moment, please,' said the one I assumed was Mr Johnson.

Both men, far from slim had stripped down to their shorts and turned their white, fatty backs.

I caught a glimpse of Mr Rojack's hand as it darted into a black case and brought out something red. Mr Johnson reached in and brought out something white. After a moment, they traded, and after another moment, they both reached into the case again.

A few seconds later, Mr Rojack produced what looked like a large canvas laundry bag with a frill at the opening, and proceeded to pull it over his head and most of his torso.

'Chips?' I whispered. 'I, uh...how old do you think Alex is?'

She cocked a brow. 'Why don't you just ask him?'

She leaned away to make room for the waiter's arm. He whisked away our plates, dropped them atop the growing stack on his service cart, and moved on without a word. Across the room, Mr Johnson wriggled headfirst into a laundry bag similar to Mr Rojack's.

'I can't,' I said. 'He might—'

She nodded, cutting me off. 'He might ask you the same question. Okay, kiddo. I'll find out. You okay? Really, I mean.'

That was probably the most complicated question I was likely to hear all week. I said, 'I don't know.'

When I looked back toward Mr Johnson and Mr Rojack, any individual distinction had vanished. They were simply two fat men, dressed in nothing but bikini shorts and upside-down-laundry bags that covered their heads and shoulders and ended, in a ruffle, just above their elbows. Both stood with their backs to us, and both had folded their arms behind them.

Chips began, 'Sal, I think you and I oughta have a little talk about—'

One of the men, perhaps Mr Johnson, loosed a muffled cry of, 'Music, please!'

The beat and the chant—*oooma-chucka, oooma-chucka, oooma-oooma-oooma-chucka*—thundered through the room at the instant Johnson and Rojack leapt round to face us. The laundry bags had become outrageous hats over the huge, outlandish faces painted on their undulating bellies. The lines where stomach fat rolled over belly fat were transformed into wide, red-lipped mouths that opened and closed, smiled and frowned. Greasepaint eyes, bright blue and huge and staring, narrowed and widened beneath the flopping flounces of their canvas hat brims.

Chips was laughing. She lifted a glass and held it towards Peaches. 'Too much,' she called over the din once she caught his eye. 'Too much!'

The man with the green bow tie gripped my hand. 'Such an honour, Miss French. I deeply admire your work.'

'And I suppose that's why you don't own one,' Ardith said as she joined us. 'Don't believe a word Osgood says, my dear.'

He clamped a hand to his chest. 'Ardith, why must you always cast aspersions on my character? You know I'd *adore* to own one of this young lady's pieces. I simply can't afford—'

'Oh, Osgood,' Ardith sniffed. She was holding

a rye and soda, and looked as if she might have already had one too many. 'Everybody in this room knows you've got more money than the Vatican.'

'Liquidity, Ardith,' he said, and managed to look hurt. 'Liquidity is the key.'

They began to bicker, and I sidled up to Chips. 'Where's Alex?' I whispered, nervous again.

'Right here.' His breath warmed my ear at the same time his hands slid up my arms to my shoulders. He pulled me, rather subtly, back against his chest.

'Can we leave yet? I've been introduced to so many people my fingers are practically bleeding, and dinner's been over for an hour.'

He chuckled. 'Try fifteen minutes.'

Chips, sipping on something green in a tall glass, elbowed a sequin-dripping fat woman out of her way and moved in a little closer. 'Sal's never had the slightest sense of time,' she muttered. 'Never knows what the hell day it is. It's a miracle she remembers my name or yours. And by the way, has anybody seen my Viking?'

Alex's hand left my shoulder long enough to gesture across the room toward an open door bracketed by two huge Warhol silkscreens. 'He's hiding in the library. I overheard Mark Gerling ask him if he'd ever posed nude, and I think it scared him.'

Chips lit a cigarette. 'Poor baby's out of his element. Well, better go save him. Back in a sec, Sal.'

As she turned away, Alex lifted my hair and kissed the back of my neck. Warm tingles diffused through my scalp and down my spine as I heard myself whisper, 'Someone will see!'

He kissed my ear. 'So? Let 'em. Besides, nobody's paying attention.'

He was right. The bodies were as thick in that room as the cigarette smoke, with people clustered into little conversational knots, each trying to hear and be heard over the other.

A fiftyish woman in one of those shiny stretch gym outfits, a little scarf-skirt tied round her waist and martini in her hand, wiggled through a cluster of bodies and stopped in front of us. 'I heard someone say you're Sally French. Is that true?'

I nodded.

'My husband and I have two of your paintings—one here, and one in Scottsdale. We winter in Arizona, you know.'

I nodded again, and wondered what she was doing there. Everyone else I'd met was either an artist, in the art business, or had something to do with the university.

'In fact, we planned the entire motif of our Scottsdale house—well, not the *entire* house, you understand...' She paused long enough to emit a rather artificial laugh that exposed probably ten thousand dollars worth of caps, each as white and perfect as a Chicklet.

'*Sun Wraith,*' she said, still smiling. 'I did all the main rooms to match the colours. Well, the decorator did. It's such a pretty painting. Such pretty colours. My husband will just sit

146

and stare at it for hours.'

Behind me, Alex said, 'I remember that painting.'

I was glad he did, because I certainly didn't.

'Marvellous piece,' he added. 'From the show two years ago, if I remember correctly. You must be Mrs Edlin.'

She aimed a blank look up past my shoulder, toward him, and said, 'Why, yes, I'm sorry, but I don't recognize you. Should I? I mean, are you anybody?'

'No.' There was a smile in his voice. 'Not anybody at all.'

'This is Alex Langley, Mrs Edlin.' I said it rather more indignantly than I'd planned. With Alex so near, I was braver than usual. 'He's with the Ardith Crawford Gallery.'

'You work there, do you?' She cocked her head rather condescendingly. 'But you seem so—'

'Alex! There you are!' Peaches skidded in between me and Mrs Edlin, who spilled most of her martini. Peaches stepped on the olive, but didn't notice. 'Dear heart, you *must* come and have a peek at the Bentley. And no, don't look at me like that. It can't wait. The poor thing's ill and I need it tomorrow.'

'Peaches...'

'My boy, I insist.'

Alex still had his hands on my shoulders, and he turned me to face him. 'You be all right for a few minutes?'

I made myself smile. I supposed I could always join Eric in the library, and we could cower there together. 'Go on ahead. I'll scream if I get into trouble.'

I watched Peaches and Alex weave away through the crowd, and with every step Alex took I felt myself grow smaller and smaller.

'How rude.'

'Oh. Mrs Edlin.' I'd forgotten her.

'Call me Marci, dear. That's Marci with an "i".'

I'd have wagered good money that she dotted it with a little heart. She added, 'He's a mechanic? I thought you said he worked at the Crawford Gallery. I haven't been in there for an *age*. Lou—that's my husband—he does the buying.' She was watching Alex and Peaches make their way toward the door. 'Dear Lord, the child can't be more than twenty. Do you suppose Professor Sutton is serving him liquor?'

She was really beginning to irritate me, which was fine. I figured I could use the distraction. I said, 'He's not a mechanic, Marci. Professionally, I mean. And he doesn't just work for Ardith. He manages the gallery.'

She wasn't listening. She was up on her toes and waving at a tall man in a grey V-necked sweater. 'Lou! Lou! Over here! I've got Sally French! You know, the girl who did our paintings?'

'So that's who you are.' A woman's voice, husky and purring. I turned toward it. It was the girl who'd stared at me during dinner, Suzanne Moore, if Chips was correct. With one finger, she casually pulled back a few strands of glossy

148

blue-black hair from her brow. 'Been seeing Alex long?'

'Beg pardon?' I stammered.

'Oh, he's sweet, isn't he?' she said, so softly that I could barely hear over the party noise. 'Terribly sweet, even if he is fickle. But then, I take it you're not in for the long haul. I suppose you just like the young, pretty ones. Sascha O'Brien's like that, too. She looks about your age. Do you know Sascha? We carry her over at Cross Street. A new boy on her arm every few months. All pretty. All at least fifteen or twenty years younger than she.'

She stood up a bit straighter. She was at least five-foot-ten, quite slender, and looked as though she might have just stepped out of *Harper's Bazaar*. Cheekbones you'd pray for, huge green eyes, lush lips; not a hair out of place, not a pore on her face.

I hated her.

'I suppose Alex really is perfect for you, then.' Her voice had risen to a normal volume, which was still difficult to hear over the party noise. 'He never seems to last long with his girls,' she continued. Although she couldn't have been over twenty-five she had a look of bored sophistication, as if she'd just come back from Cannes for the fifth time and had nothing more important to relate than that the shopping wasn't quite up to snuff.

'Oh, hello, there!' said Marci, who had just rejoined us, along with the man in the grey sweater. Marci had a fresh martini, too. 'Should I know you?'

149

Suzanne ignored her. 'And really, Sally, he *does* seem awfully friendly with Peaches. A little too friendly, if you get my drift. I mean they do spend an inordinate amount of time together.'

Marci patted my arm. 'This is my husband, Lou. Lou, this is Sally French. See, I *told* you we'd meet somebody famous tonight!' Loud grabbed my hand and shook it too enthusiastically.

'One might wonder,' Suzanne continued, 'if Alex isn't a closet case. Some of those are the biggest studs around until they decide to come leaping out of—'

'Excuse me,' I said. *Don't panic, don't panic, don't panic...* I yanked my hand away from Lou without looking toward him. 'I don't know why you're—'

'You surprise me, though,' she said, her perfectly plucked brows furrowing delicately. 'I mean, that he'd pick you. I've never known him to—'

'Miss French?' Lou's voice, dripping with endorphins, in the background. 'I love your paintings. I mean, I really *love* your paintings.'

Suzanne pursed her lips in a finely tuned pout. 'If I may be frank, I'm surprised to see him with a woman so much more...mature.'

'Well, if it isn't Subtle Suzanne.' Chips to the rescue. I wished she'd throw a blanket around me and carry me outside. Eric, looking harried in a Norse sort of way, was with her as she slipped through the crowd to stand beside me, facing Suzanne. 'Slaughtered any good mice, lately, dearie?'

150

Suzane's nose tilted into the air. 'Only rats, Quincannon.' Her gaze swept quickly up and down Eric before she added, 'I see you brought something to play with, too.'

Lou took my hand again. 'May I call you by your first name, Miss French? I feel as if I know you. From your paintings, of course. I can't begin to tell you what an effect they have on me. Well, I suppose you know that. I suppose you plan it that way.'

He rubbed the back of my hand with his thumb and I flashed on Norman: *Gonna pinch your nips, Sal, let's play doctor.*

I pulled my hand away again and muttered, 'Sure,' my voice quavering. The top of my head felt light, as if it were about to lift off, and I thought, *Please, God, don't let me freak out now.*

Where was Alex? I didn't see him anywhere. He was probably up to his elbows in engine gunk and grease, and I was a little angry with him for not being there to protect me. But then, that wasn't really his job, was it? Nor was it Chips', although she seemed to making a valiant effort.

I took two deep breaths, concentrated on slowing my heartbeat, pushed the panic aside. For the moment, at least.

'Suzanne?' I said, as sweetly as I could. She broke off her verbal skirmish with Chips and stared down at me with poorly disguised disdain. 'Suzanne, I'm sorry, but I'm not interested in anything you have to say.'

She didn't say anything for a moment, and

151

then she smiled. 'But it's too late, isn't it, dear? You've already heard it.'

Chips stepped forward. 'Listen, bitch—'

I grabbed Chips' arm. 'Never mind.' Suzanne smiled again, then lost herself in the crowd.

'What a lovely young woman!' said Marci, all white, wraparound smile. 'Is she a model? An actress, maybe? She looks like an actress.' She leaned forward a bit and whispered, 'I was hoping Prince might be here. Do you think he's coming?'

'No, this is his night for cribbage at the governor's,' Chips said dryly before she whispered, 'He's twenty-two,' in my ear.

'A little too pushy, if you ask me,' said Lou, looking after Suzanne. 'Say, this is some party! Did Marci tell you we live next door? Never been to one of these shindigs, but tonight when we saw the cars pulling up we said, "What the heck," and came on over to say hi, and Professor Sutton invited us to stay. You know—'

Somebody banged on the dinner gong again. The room immediately quieted, and all heads turned toward the foyer. It was, I realized, a well-trained crowd. Peaches appeared in the wide foyer doorway, where he'd trapped Alex and me when we'd first come in. 'Misters Johnson and Rojack have to be leaving us,' he announced with a small flourish. 'Let's all give them another resounding *merci* for that captivating performance!'

Everyone applauded as Johnson and Rojack, dressed again in sober suits, gave a stoic tandem bow and exited. I wondered if they'd wiped all

152

that greasepaint off their bellies before they got dressed, and suddenly Norman was before me again: Norman at fourteen, with the laundry marker in his hand, and I was terrified and trapped, my panties yanked down around my ankles and my dress hiked up: Norman's knee held down my legs, his hand pinned my heaving chest as the marker, indelible, travelled cold slow letters over my battered, prepubescent groin.

I'm gonna write it here so you won't forget where it is, Orphan Annie.

Norman, don't, please, please let me up!

I'm gonna write it so you won't forget what you are. That's capital C, Capital U, capital N—

'Do you do it on purpose?' Lou asked, and I jumped.

Breathe, Sally, breathe...

I focused on the tiny pair of crossed golf clubs embroidered on the breast of his sweater. Red stitch, red stitch, red stitch, gold stitch...

'Do...do what on purpose?' I said, once I'd shoved Norman out of my brain.

Lou gave me a wink and a thinly disguised leer. 'I think you know what I mean, don't you, Sally?'

'No,' I said, 'I don't.' I wanted to leave. I wanted to go home, where it was quiet and safe and I didn't have to pretend to be clever or sociable or even nice. Home, where I could battle my ghosts in private. I was fairly certain that if I didn't get out of there soon, I'd either explode into a full-blown panic attack or take all my frustrations out on Lou.

Noted artist K.O's upper-middle-class golfer at swank dinner party! Details at six, film at eleven.

To Chips, I said, 'Peaches and Alex are supposed to be out fixing the car, and I need to—'

'We were.' Alex materialized beside me and planted a kiss on my nose. 'It was the plug wires.'

Relief washed over me, through me. I said, 'You've got grease on your forehead,' and wiped it away with a cocktail napkin. That face: that beautiful chiselled, taut-skinned face, the face that chases away my spectres.

Dear God. Twenty-two.

And I was falling, falling into him, falling in love. The sort of love I'd been so sure was myth. I knew it at the exact moment I wiped the smudge from his face. And I also knew that I couldn't afford the pain if it went wrong; and it could go wrong so easily. I had to make him understand it was impossible. I had to make him realize what we were up against. But I was so close to being overtaken, swept away.

I had only the strength for one protest. I had better make it a good one.

Alex grinned. 'Miss me?'

'She pined,' Chips said drily. 'Anybody got a smoke? I'm out.'

Marci latched onto Chip's elbow. 'You look like...' Her brows furrowed. 'Should I know you?'

'Absolutely,' Chips replied, as Eric lit a cigarette and handed it to her. 'I'm fuckin' legendary.'

154

11

Alex

She was so quiet on the way home.

Staring out her window, she hugged her car door so tightly that she might as well have been welded to it. When I asked her if she was cold, she just smiled—that little Iris Lady half-smile of hers—and said no. She barely looked at me.

I asked if she'd enjoyed the party.

'It was interesting,' she said. The half-smile again, no eye contact.

Maybe I'd left her alone too much after dinner, maybe she was ticked at me. I volunteered this suggestion, but she just gave me the Iris Lady look again.

'No, Alex, it was fine.'

By the time we got back to her place, she had me nervous enough to ask a stupid question. 'Sally, what is it? What's wrong?'

She closed the front door behind us and leaned against the foyer's wainscotting. She stared at the floor.

'Sally, if I said or did—'

'No.' She shook her head. When she finally looked up at me, those big grey eyes of hers looked forlorn. 'It's just...I mean, I...'

She took a deep breath, as if she were about to dive headfirst into cold water.

She said, 'I don't think we should see each other anymore.'

She might just as easily have hit me between the eyes with a hammer. 'But—'

'No, stay where you are. If you touch me, I'll...' She crossed her arms tightly, hugging herself, shielding herself. 'I need to say this. I...Alex, this is doomed. You and me, I mean.'

Something black and unexpected swirled, just for a moment, at the back of my skull. Anger? Indignation? I tried to ignore it. 'Doomed? What are you talking about?'

She backed up to stand just beneath one of the wall sconces. The light washed over her face. 'Look at me, Alex. I mean, really look at me. I'm not...I'm not a girl.'

As sombre as she was—and as frustrated as I felt—I couldn't help but smile. 'I've got you there, Sal. I have first-hand evidence that you're no boy.'

'That's not what I mean.' She almost barked the words, and I think I flinched. 'I mean, I'm not a girl anymore. I'm not young. I'm not...I'm not what you seem to think I am.'

I took a deep breath. Whatever interior monster was eating at her was sure taking big bites. As calmly as I could, I said, 'Sally, how can you know what I think?'

She bit her lip. 'You don't see me, Alex. You see what you want. How old do you think I am?'

I was so flummoxed by the question that I couldn't remember the stuff from her bio sheet, except some vague recollection that it needed correction. I very wittily replied, 'What?'

'I said, how old do you think I am?'

I didn't understand where this attitude came from, and I didn't appreciate being held as some sort of psychic hostage in her front hall when all in the world I'd wanted was to bring her home and make love to her.

That thing in the back of my head swirled up into a little black, buzzing cloud. 'What the hell does it matter?'

She winced as if I'd physically slapped her, and I immediately wanted to snatch the words back, or at least their tone. *Too late, Alex. Can you say 'big mistake'? Can you say 'fix it quick'?*

'Oh, it matters,' she said, too calmly, too softly. 'I'm thirty-nine. I'll be forty next month. Do you know what that means?'

'Dear Lord. Don't tell me you voted for Nixon!'

'Stop it. It's not funny. I'm old enough to be your mother. I've got seventeen, almost eighteen more years of road under me than you do. My God, Alex, you weren't even born in time for Woodstock! You never saw the first space launches or listened to Walter Cronkite explain two hundred times what a "cherry picker" was. You missed John-John saluting his father's coffin. You missed hula hoops and Roy Rogers and the *White Album* and—God. I should know better than this. I should have known better from the start. But you, you...' She paused, almost panting.

She suddenly looked so small, so lost. I took

157

a step toward her. 'Sally, I—'

She pulled back, flattening herself against the wall like a spent rabbit trying to make itself invisible to the coyote. 'No. We have to stop this...this *thing*. We have to stop it now, while we still can. It's not fair to you. I'm not some sweet little virgin you can take home to meet the folks. I've been around, Alex. I mean, *really* around.'

I held out my hand. 'Sally,' I said softly, 'it doesn't matter.'

She ignored my hand. 'It does. It matters a great deal, Alex, I've lost count of the men. I can't remember their faces, most of them. I didn't know half their names. But I changed everything, you see? I made it all right. I live alone, completely alone; not just in this house, but here.' She pressed a clenched fist to her breast. 'I can't let you in. You're too damn scary. You need someone your own age, someone who isn't terrified to talk to a stranger, somebody who hasn't been backed into a corner. You need somebody less...used up.'

She stopped, biting at her lips. I was afraid to move, to say anything. She looked as if she might bolt and run out into the street.

At last she seemed to collect herself and added, more softly, 'You see? We have to stop this now. It'd be far too easy to love you, Alex. It'd be too easy for both of us to be disappointed. To be hurt. I can't take that chance. I just can't. So goodbye, Alex.'

This time, when I stepped forward, she didn't leap away. She lifted one arm, like she expected

158

me to shake her hand—all very civilized—then leave. I took her hand all right, but I didn't shake it. I pulled her toward me and held her. She was limp, as if she'd used up every ounce of energy in her body.

'It's all right,' I whispered. I rubbed her back. 'I don't care. I don't care what you did or who you did it with. I won't hurt you, I couldn't—you ought to know that by now. And if it'll make you feel any better, we'll try to find a hula hoop and you can teach me how to use it.'

Within my arms, she quaked slightly as she began to cry, soft little sobs that brought tears to my eyes, too. I blinked them back. Big boys, especially ex-kiddie-cowboys, don't cry.

'No, Alex, please go away. Don't hold me. I can't think...' A muffled murmur against my shoulder.

'I want to be with *you*, Sally, whether you're eighteen or forty or sixty. I think I love you. I think you just might love me. Shouldn't we give ourselves a chance to find out for sure?'

She really began to cry then, and all I could do was hold her and rock her, there in the hall, and whisper, 'Shhh, shhh, shhh.'

The phone woke us both. I opened one eye just far enough to see that it was a hair past 7:30, and that Sally was about to wiggle across me toward the nightstand.

'Hello?' Her voice, deep with sleep, gave me ideas a man shouldn't have when he knows he's already going to be late for work. She was half

159

across me, her belly covering mine at a right angle. I pushed away the sheet so I could rub her pretty bare bottom.

'Chips? What is it?' She motioned at me to stop. 'Are you at the hospital now?'

I stopped. 'Chips is in the hospital?'

Sally shook her head. 'Of course I can,' she said into the phone. She sounded fully alert. 'Right away.' There was a pause, and then she asked, 'Are you okay?' A longer pause. 'Hang on, I'll be there. What floor?'

A few seconds later she slid the phone back into its cradle, then sat up, hugging the sheets.

'What is it?' I'd grabbed her cigarettes off the night table, lit two, and handed her one. 'Something wrong with Chips?'

Sally took a long, ragged draw on the Salem, then shook her head. 'It's Pops. Her father. He had another episode in the middle of the night. There's a clot or an aneurism or something.' She looked away and took another drag. 'He's in surgery right now. I have to go.'

We both dressed hurriedly; but downstairs, before she opened the front door, I took her arm. 'This isn't the way I had this morning planned, Sally. I want you to know I meant what I said last night. You're not getting rid of me.'

She reached up and touched my face with her fingertips. I went straight up and hard, just like that. She said, 'I think...I think I just might believe you.'

160

I kissed her on the forehead. 'Call me at work, let me know how Chips' dad is. And I'm taking you to dinner tonight, if you're willing. Someplace quiet and casual, don't worry. If Chips is up to it, she's invited, too. Okay, honey?'

She smiled. 'Okay. Thank you.'

On the porch, she fumbled in her purse for her car keys. We'd had the first frost of the season during the night. The last traces of sparkle were melting off the grass, and the walk was damp. There was a wonderful nip in the air, even if the skies were on the grey side. I was down to the second step when she said, 'Alex?'

I turned. She was still on the top step, and her face was even with mine. She threw her arms around me and hugged me tight, which did nothing at all to alleviate my woody. 'Thank you again,' she whispered. Sparrows argued in the trees. A block over, somebody leaned on a car horn.

My Caddy was parked behind her old Impala, and as I unlocked my door and swung it open, I heard her call my name.

'Yes?'

She was already in her car. She stuck her head out the window and grinned. 'How do you walk with a hard-on that big?' And then she rolled up her window, turned her key, and honked for me to get going.

Women.

Like my dad once said, you gotta love 'em, otherwise you'd have to kill 'em. He was patting

161

my mom's fanny at the time.

'You're late.'

My desk was on the main gallery floor, toward the back. I slid into my chair and shoved a couple of folders out of my way. 'Thanks, Darryl, I knew that.'

He had the coffeepot in his hand, but I didn't notice him offering. 'Ardith's pissed.'

'There's a shock.'

'Is that Alex, *finally?*' Ardith's voice, from down the hall.

I leaned back in my chair, ignored Darryl's snotty grin, and hollered. 'Yo.' I laced my fingers behind my neck.

Ardith appeared at the mouth of the hallway and stepped into the main gallery. She was having a fuchsia day. Everything matched. 'You're late,' she said. She didn't sound too upset.

'Sorry.'

She sat down opposite me in the client chair, lit a cigarette, then gestured toward the coffeepot in Darryl's hand. 'Get us some cups to go with that, would you, Darryl?'

He gave her a big, toothy smile. 'Of course, Ardith.' When she looked away, he mouthed *Fuck you* at me and stalked off.

I said, 'Chips Quincannon's father is in the hospital again.'

Ardith frowned, then blew thin twin jets of smoke out her nostrils. 'Same thing?'

I nodded. 'He's in surgery now.'

'Poor Chips.'

162

'What *about* Chips?' It was Darryl, back with two coffees in pale lilac cups.

'Her father's sick again,' Ardith said. She picked up her cup and scowled at it.

Darryl took it back. 'Not enough cream?'

'Too much.' He slumped off again and Ardith turned to me. 'Find out what hospital he's in and send flowers. Don't go over forty dollars. Usual sentiments on the card.' She took another drag and leaned back in her chair as she exhaled the smoke. 'You brought Sally French to Peaches' last night?'

Here it comes, Alex. Act nonchalant.

I nodded. I took a sip of my coffee.

'That was nice of you. She needs to get out.'

Darryl brought her a new coffee. I was waiting for the other shoe to drop. The coffee met with her approval this time, and after she took a sip, she reached for one of the folders on my desk. 'Let's go over the figures from the French show,' she began, and put on her glasses.

I allowed myself a small sigh of relief. She hadn't noticed the way I'd been fawning over Sally. Not that I minded anybody noticing, really, but I didn't think I was ready for the sort of discussion Ardith might want to have about artist-agent relationships and all that crap. Besides, I wasn't sure I wanted to talk to anybody about what I felt for Sally, mainly because I wasn't yet certain how the hell I really *did* feel.

I knew I was besotted by her body, her

163

face, her talent, her voice, and the way we fit together in bed. I knew that I missed her every minute we were apart. I knew I had to see her again, and keep on seeing her for a long time.

But what did any of that mean, really? Was it love, or just hormones in high gear? I knew about the latter, and I'd confused it with love before. I wanted to make sure this time. It was too important.

Ardith shoved a few more inventory sheets at me. I scribbled notes on them, but I was still thinking about Sally. What was it she'd said in the hall last night. Seventeen years between us? It didn't seem possible. I'd told her it didn't matter, that I didn't care, and at the time I truly hadn't. But today I wasn't sure. And what about a year from now, or ten?'

Around a fresh cigarette, Ardith mumbled something about New York. I nodded and took the next sheaf of consignment sheets. I hated all that busywork, but Ardith was bound and determined to be the last business on the face of the earth to computerize.

Alex, you are a total jerk, I told myself, as I copied information from one set of papers to the other. *Sally's wonderful. She's the most incredible woman you've ever had the impossibly good fortune to meet. Stop thinking of reasons to screw it up.*

I decided that when I called the florist to order flowers for Pops Quincannon, I'd have them send some to Sally, too. Peaches had sent her a couple dozen yellow roses, but I could outdo that. None of that gauche long-stemmed red stuff, either. Pink ones. Pink Sonia roses. And not two dozen, but three.

I guess I was grinning, because Ardith said, rather incredulously, 'You like the idea?'

I looked up. 'What idea?'

She pursed her lips. 'Alex, are you listening to me?'

I set aside my pen. 'Sorry. Not really.'

'Good God.' She squashed her cigarette in the ashtray and lit another, grumbling, 'I might as well be talking to Sally French. I'm surrounded by daydreamers.' She looked me in the eye. 'Have I got your attention now?'

I grinned at her and nodded.

'It's the Lowells.'

'What about them?' I shrugged. 'They flew in from New York for the French show, stayed ten minutes, and left.'

'Without buying anything. Well, Brick Lowell called me at home Sunday morning to see if the green and blue swirly one—'

'Ebbtide?'

'—Might possibly be available. Well, you know it was. It was the only thing that didn't sell, and that was only because that nouveau riche idiot Terry Woodard reserved it right after we opened the doors, then changed his mind two minutes before closing. That's the second time he's pulled that shit on me.'

She lifted her coffee cup halfway to her lips before she realized it was empty. She twisted her head up toward the balcony. 'Darryl!' He leaned over the railing. 'Could we get a refill, please?' she looked back at me. 'I would have told you at Peaches' party, but you fled the scene so early...'

'So the show's a sellout,' I said.

'Mm.' She took off her glasses and slid them back into their case. 'Brick wants it installed, so you're going to New York.'

I nearly spilled coffee down my front. 'Ardith, there's no reason that *I* need to—'

She waved her hands. 'I know. I told him we could ship to Fenner & Gross and they'd hang it as well as anybody, but he insisted on you.' One of her brows arched disapprovingly. 'You know why.'

I did. Brick-the-Prick Lowell was filthy rich and about as obnoxious a man as you'd want to meet. His was second-generation money, and he'd never done a day's work in his life. He and his wife had a daughter about my age, Stephanie.

Stephanie was as pretty as orthodontia and plastic surgery and enforced spa retreats could make her, but she was as vapid and spoiled as her father was mean. For some bizarre reason Brick had decided I was the perfect man for Stephanie, and he'd been trying, none too subtly, to fix us up for two years. Needless to say, I was somewhat resistant.

'I'm sorry, Alex,' Ardith said as I rubbed my temples. Excedrin headache number forty-three. 'I know he's a pain in the ass, but he's a good client. I've made your plane reservations and booked you into the Plaza.'

166

'The Plaza?' Usually she picked something about two steps down from the Motel 6.

She shrugged. 'I'm feeling generous. Don't push your luck. You're leaving Thursday and coming back Saturday.'

'Why so soon? The show's supposed to hang here for another week and a half.'

She pressed her lips together and raised a brow. 'Because he's a good client, and he wants it now. Besides, it's not exactly the crown jewel of the show, is it? Now, while you're in New York, I'd like you to make a few courtesy calls...'

I didn't pay much attention to the rest of it. Of all the lousy timing! I considered suggesting she send Darryl or Betty in my place, but didn't. Ardith was right—Brick Lowell spent a lot of money with us, and if it was me he wanted, it was me he'd have to get.

I entertained a brief fantasy in which Sally went with me, and we initiated each other into the Mile High Club. It also crossed my mind that, considering what she'd told me last night, she'd probably gained entry years ago. And then I was pissed at myself for thinking it.

After Ardith disappeared into her office and left me to my paper-shuffling, I called our usual florist and sent a big arrangement to Pops Quincannon and three dozen Sonia roses to Sally.

Five minutes later I called back and changed it to four dozen.

167

12

Sally

I'd been so distracted with worrying about Chips and Pops—and, I admit, Alex—that I was in the hospital and had followed the coloured lines in the corridor floor most of the way to the recovery room before I panicked.

There is something about hospitals that floods me with terror.

Part of it's simply that hospitals are big, public places, and I don't like big, public places, not one bit. Part of it is the too-clean stench of them, and the horrible little squeaks that nurses' shoes make on the high-gloss floors. I have never been a patient in a hospital, and I've never had anyone near and dear to me die in one, but still they fill me with horror.

Maybe it's precognition. Maybe one day I'll find myself trapped in one, the victim of some horrible accident or lingering disease, tethered to machines by invasive yards of plastic tubing and wires, at the mercy of strangers with cold hands and colder impersonal stares.

All I can think about, when I'm in a hospital, is the Nazis and Dr Mengele. And, well, Norman.

By the time I'd followed the yellow line

around the last corner and found myself in Recovery's stark, airless waiting room, I had broken out in a light sweat and my heart was hammering toward the doubled rate that always accompanied a full-blown anxiety attack.

And it was too late to head this one off.

'Jesus, sit down.' Chips touched my shoulder and I nearly screamed. She shoved me into a chair and knelt beside me. 'Breathe,' she said, and rubbed my arm. 'No, slow down. Breathe slowly.'

I did, and relaxed into the attack, letting it run its course. After what felt like an hour (but was never really more than a few minutes, at least for me) my heart began to slow, the chest pains ebbed along with the fear, the heat began to drain from my face. I made myself focus on my surroundings, tried to lose myself in their details.

The little waiting room seemed a white cell, despite the things intended to make it seem less institutional and more comfortable. A Coke machine with a *Quarters Only!* note taped beside the coin slot hummed against the far wall. A vase of cheap plastic flowers and a ragged fan of tattered, outdated magazines sat untidily on the scarred coffee table that separated Chips' and my chairs from a matching sofa. They were barely cushioned, and unholstered in cracked cobalt blue vinyl that smelled faintly of vomit.

I hoped I never got sick. I hoped that if I did, they'd let me die at home.

Again, Chips wiped at my forehead with a tissue. It came away soaked. 'Better. A little slower. You're okay, Sal. Just relax. Shit, I didn't think about this until after I'd called you, and when I tried to phone you back you were already gone. Better now?'

I nodded. I was still a hair's breadth away from screaming, but the chest pains and shaking had stopped.

'I'm sorry,' I said, my voice catching. I was still a little breathless. 'How's Pops?'

She bit at her lips. She looked awful, I realized. Even when Chips dressed casually, she was always perfectly pulled together. Unlike me, she has a real knack for clothes. But this morning she had on green leather pants with a lavender print blouse. Her hair, a stray section of which she kept nervously pushing off her face, was hap-hazardly tied back with a metallic gold ribbon. Dark crescents made half-moon pools beneath her eyes.

'They don't know yet.' She began rummaging through her purse. 'The surgery went fine. That's what they said. But I didn't like the way they said it.'

She produced a brown plastic prescription bottle and tipped out a white tablet, which she shoved at me. 'Take this,' she ordered, and handed me a half-drained soda to wash it down with. 'Valium,' she said, when I hesitated. 'It's only five mils, Sally.'

I swallowed it.

She squinted at the bottle. 'Oops. Ten mils. Oh, well.'

'When'll you know more? About Pops, I mean.' I was wondering just how blasted I'd

170

get on ten milligrams of Valium. Probably not very. Just enough, I told myself, to stop me shaking on the inside.

Chips tipped one out of the bottle for herself and gulped it down. 'They won't let you smoke in here,' she grumbled, and shot a dirty look toward the nurses' desk. 'Remember that time you and me and Pops went up to the lake and he rented the helicopter and I threw up on the pilot?'

I put my hand on her arm.

She made a face. 'I don't know why I was thinking about that. Jeez, I'd give anything for a good lethal blast of tar and nicotine.'

'Go on downstairs. Have one outside.' I tried to ignore the stink of alcohol and disinfectant and God knew what else. 'I'll stay here in case there's any word.'

She managed a lopsided grin, her first since I'd arrived. 'And have your coronary on my conscience? I don't think so. I'll wait till your medication kicks in, thanks.'

'Well, at least brush your hair. You look like hell.'

She dug into her purse again, muttering. 'Gee, thanks for comin' down to cheer me up.'

'Your shirt's buttoned crooked, too.'

She paused, brush in hand, to look down at her front. 'Shit,' she whispered. She closed her eyes so tightly that her forehead, normally so high and clean, creased with the effort.

'Oh God, Sal, what'll I do if he...what'll I do if he dies?'

171

Ten milligrams of Valium, when one isn't used to it, can have a very calming effect. I braided Chips' hair for her and she got her blouse fixed, and then she went outside to chain-smoke a few to tide her over. When she came back, we played gin rummy with a deck she got from the nurse whose name tag read *Molly Tiggs, R.N,* but to whom Chips referred, behind her back, as Lieutenant Shit Head.

At about eleven, Pops Quincannon's doctor made an appearance. Pops had been moved out of Recovery, but to Intensive Care rather than a private room. I listened as he spoke to Chips in soothing, practised tones intended to make the actual message seem less harsh.

Chips went up to Intensive Care, and since vigils there could only be held by family members, she sent me home. 'I'll call if there's any change, Sal. And...and thanks. You know.'

The Valium, still in effect, seemed to have no effect on my driving ability, but it did take its toll on my sense of direction, or, more precisely, my sense of purpose. I didn't go straight home. Instead, I drove out through the city, making great loops that once or twice took me over into St Paul and back again, and what I did was think.

I am ashamed to admit that very little of this rumination was directed toward Chips and Pops. Mostly I thought about Alex, what he'd said last night and this morning. I wanted to believe him. I can't remember ever wanting anything more.

But he's so young, I reminded myself, as I

crossed the interstate for the fifth or sixth time. *Even if he says a thing, even if he truly believes it when he says it, that doesn't mean it'll be true for him tomorrow or a week from now.*

I had once been twenty-two.

I remembered how it had been.

Something else bothered me, too. It was one of those feelings where you know there's something important you should be doing or taking care of, but you have not a clue as to what it is. Of course, these feelings were nothing new to me. Sometimes things had a way of slipping out of my head until it was too late, like the time I forgot to pay the yard man for two months straight, and didn't realize it until I walked out one day and noticed that the lawn was halfway up to my knees.

But the only thing I connected with the current niggling sense of foreboding was my studio. And it had nothing to do with the painting on the easel. This was something to do with the drafting table. Something *on* the drafting table. But what, I had no idea.

'Maybe I wrote a note,' I muttered, as I started toward home down a quiet, tree-lined boulevard. I was always writing myself notes and leaving them on the drafting table. *Order canvas.* Or, *Leave cheque for cleaning lady tomorrow.* Or, *Find new gardener, pay in advance.*

It was a good thing I had my seatbelt on. I jammed the brake to the floor as, nonplussed, a grey squirrel scampered across the road as if screeching tyres and smoking skid marks were nothing out of the ordinary, and rodents had a

173

God-given right-of-way.

I put the car, still sprawled on an angle across the centre line, into park and sat a moment, panting and grateful there'd been no one behind me. The squirrel spiralled up a tall maple and disappeared into its yellowing leaves.

The little son of a bitch.

I was relieved when I pulled into my own drive. The postman had come. After I unlocked the front door, I paused to sort through the mail. Power bill, water bill, an advertisement addressed to 'Sally Fronck,' the *New Yorker*, a Dick Blick catalogue, and three blind ads addressed to 'Current Resident.'

I crumpled the ads in one hand, intending to drop them into the hall trashbasket. 'Waste of trees,' I muttered, and stepped into the house. But before I had a chance to close the door behind me, I felt a brush against my ankle. A streak of orange flashed down the foyer, then disappeared around the corner, into the dining room.

That cat! This was Alex's fault. I never should have let him feed the thing. I followed it into the dining room and found it butting its head against the kitchen's swinging door. How do cats always know where the kitchen is in a strange house? Must be radar or something. The poor thing was trying so hard to open the door—and with such little success—that I went over and opened it for him. He shot into the kitchen and leapt up on the table, purring.

'Well, you've got balls, Kitty,' I said.

He mewed and turned in a prancing circle,

174

tail up, as if to show me I was indeed correct. He mewed again, this time more insistently.

'Okay, okay.' I filled a bowl with leftover chicken and some lunchmeat and cheese, then carried it out onto the back porch.

He really was a pretty cat, I decided, as I watched him devour his meal. Bony, but a pretty colour. His orange stripes weren't really stripes at all, but rather thumbprint-sized spots that covered his creamy flanks and faded into faint bracelets on his lower legs and darker ones on his tail. Smaller broken stripes formed a fuzzy M on his forehead. Such big green eyes.

It wasn't until the doorbell sounded that I realized I'd crouched down and was actually petting him.

I stood abruptly and wiped my hands on my jeans. 'Going soft, are we, Sally?' I muttered, then stepped quickly into the house and headed for the front door.

It was a deliveryman who, once I'd signed my name, presented me with two huge florists' boxes and a card. *Peaches again*, I thought happily, and carried them to the dining room, where his previous delivery, the long-stemmed yellow roses, already crowned the table.

I pulled free the ribbons and opened the boxes, both at once. Then I sat down, hard. They were the most gorgeous pink roses I'd ever seen. Or smelled. Four dozen of them, two dozen in each box, glowed an impossibly rich shade of rose madder against the white of the tissue.

'Oh!' was all I could say. 'Oh!'

Still staring at the roses, I fumbled the card open and thought that Peaches would have to stop this. If he sent this many flowers—this often—to all his pet artists, it must be costing him a fortune.

The card read, *See you tonight. Alex.*

He picked me up at about six.

I phoned the hospital and tracked down Chips, and she agreed to take a dinner break. She met us out front—just as well, for the Valium's soothing effect had long since faded, and I wasn't up to another trip inside. Alex took us to a small (and, mercifully, dimly lit) seafood restaurant a few blocks off Hennepin.

Chips looked worse than she had that morning. She barely touched her scampi. Pops had yet not risen from his anaesthesia, and she said she'd spent the afternoon alternately pacing the waiting room and sitting beside his bed, holding his hand.

Alex was so kind to her. Without ever seeming to neglect me, he managed to reassure her. He even coaxed a laugh or two out of her, and in the end convinced her that Pops would want her to get some rest.

Before we left the restaurant, she called the hospital and, when they reported no change in Pops's condition, agreed to go home for a few hours. We drove her back to pick up her car, and then, because she was so tired, Alex insisted on following her home to make sure she got there in one piece.

He just took hold of the situation. I felt

176

terribly proud of him.

We didn't talk on the way home. I sat close to him, drinking in the faint scent of his cologne, my fingers laced through his as he guided the car with one hand. Sometime that day, without being conscious of the moment of decision, I'd elected to quit worrying and enjoy the fairy tale.

We made love on the living room floor.

It was fast, almost violent. Red love, hot as a sun gone nova. And yet Alex managed to make luxurious even that frenzied bout of carnal friction: it seemed impossible to me that any man—especially one so young—could be so perfectly in tune with my every desire, but he was.

Later we climbed the stairs and made love again on my bed, surrounded by vase after vase of his roses. Afterward, flushed, exhausted, giddy, and drunk on each other as well as on the scent of impossibly pink roses, we lay caught up in a lazy tangle of arms and legs, smoking cigarettes while we tried to remember—for what reason, I can't recall—the lyrics to a particular Bob Dylan tune.

'How can you *know* that?' I demanded, laughing when he had it perfect right down to the *the pump don't work 'cause the vandal took the handle.*

He tweaked my nose. 'I may be a couple years younger than you, Sal—'

'A couple?'

'But that doesn't mean I have no sense of the

177

historical value of these things.'

I bopped him over the head with my pillow. He returned the favour. Thirty seconds later, laughing and shouting and swatting each other, we'd progressed from the bedroom to the hall.

'I'll show *you* "historical value," you—'

The doorbell.

We both stopped, pillows raised. Mine had burst open. Eiderdown drifted like snowflakes to the dark wood floor at our feet, filtered down through the banister's spindles toward the foyer.

Alex put one finger to his lips. 'Shhh,' he hissed, trying not to laugh. 'Maybe they'll go away. Who comes to see you at twelve-thirty on a Tuesday night, anyway? One of your other boyfriends, I suppose.'

The bell rang again, more insistently.

Alex stopped smiling. 'You don't think it's Chips, do you? You don't suppose Pops...?'

He dropped his pillow to the floor, stirring a small flurry of feathers, and started for the steps as if he fully intended to go down and answer the door stark naked.

'No!'

He paused on the top riser. 'Sal?' He came back to me and put his hand on my shoulder. 'You're white as a—'

I heard myself stutter, 'The drafting table. That's what the note was. I forgot about the plane.'

'What?'

'The airport. Mariah!'

'Who?'

My knees buckled, but Alex caught me before I slipped to the floor. 'Clothes,' I said as he helped me into the bedroom. 'Need clothes. Alex, you have to go, you have to go now!'

Ding ding ding.

She was really leaning on the button. I wanted to scream. I wanted to kick myself for forgetting. Alex tossed me a sweater and jeans from the laundry basket beside the bed. He was still nude.

'Get dressed!' I screamed it at him when I meant to whisper.

Dingdingdingdingdingding...

He grabbed my arm. 'My stuff's downstairs. What the hell's wrong with you?'

'It's Aunt Mariah, God, it's Mariah, I forgot they were coming!' I clamped my hands over my ears to shut out the sound of that frigging bell.

'Jesus, calm down!' He gave me a shake. It didn't help. I had already lost control of the situation, not to mention myself.

A fist—no doubt Norman's big, meaty one—thudded against the heavy oak door. A storey away, I heard him yelling. 'Wake up, Sally! Wake up, you ditz!'

'Who's Mariah? And who the hell's that guy?' Alex hissed through clenched teeth as I half-dragged him, a sheet tucked about his waist, down the stairs. I'd already broken out in a sweat. The top of my head began to lift off, and I couldn't catch my breath. I wished I had a handful of Chips's tranquilizers. Alex

179

went into the front parlour and, with one last confused and angry look, closed the pocket doors behind him. I stood alone in the dark foyer facing the door, feeling nine years old and terrified.

I made myself take three deep breaths—

—*You can do this, you can do this, you have to do this*—

—And then I turned the bolt and twisted the knob.

Norman—and I'd never have mistaken him for anyone else, even though I hadn't seen him in nearly twenty years—nearly fell in on me, fist raised mid-knock.

In the back of my head, I heard Richard Dawson's voice: *All right, everybody, it's time to play Family Feud!* Geraldo was on my team, and he was pulling a .357 Magnum on Norman. Phil Donahue, in a loud print wraparound skirt, cautioned him that violence never solved anything.

'Finally!' Aunt Mariah huffed, as she marched over the threshold, a white-haired Hessian. 'For heaven's sake, turn on a light!' Norman went back out to the porch to fetch their bags.

I fumbled for the rheostat, quickly twisted it to what I thought was the low position, and pushed it. The lights blazed on full blast.

'You don't have to blind us,' Mariah barked, shielding her eyes as Norman bumped into her from behind. She muttered, 'Be careful, dear,' before she turned back to me. 'We waited at the airport,' she said, blinking and drawing herself

180

up to her six-feet plus shoes, 'for two entire hours.'

I supposed this was my cue to pull out a ceremonial sword and impale myself, but I was so overwhelmed by the panic beating at the inner wall of my chest that I couldn't speak, let alone commit *hara-kiri*.

'Bet you even forgot we were coming, didn't you, Sal?' Norman sneered. The years had not been kind to him. The hard jaw of his youth had gone jowly, like the Aunts', and he looked thick and dissipated. His hair, once the typical jet black of all 'true' Frenches, had thinned and turned to salt and pepper. 'Same old Sally.'

Yes, same old Sally. Still scared of Norman. Still decidedly unfond of White Shoulders. The thick cloud of it surrounding Mariah mushroomed out to fill the foyer and clog my nostrils.

To my left, the pocket doors slid open. Alex, fully dressed, casually stepped into the foyer and put his arm about my shoulders. I sagged against him, grateful there was at least one person in the house who liked me, and wishing, at the same time, that he would just go away.

He said, 'Evening. Sally didn't tell me she was expecting company. Alex Langley.' He extended his hand toward Norman, who didn't take it.

Lips pursed, head canted back, Mariah stared down her nose at him for what seemed a very long time before she turned to me and sniffed, 'Still up to your old tricks, I see.'

181

13

Alex

As I pulled into my spot in Ardith's parking lot the next morning, I was still feeling guilty for leaving Sally alone with those people, despite the way she'd rushed me out the door. Aunt Mariah was one big scary old lady, but I didn't understand why her presence would reduce Sally to the mental level of a fifth-grader who's just been hauled to the principal's office for smoking in the john.

And then there was cousin Norman. He never did shake my hand. I was relieved, to tell you the truth. Something about that guy gave me the creeps. I could tell he had the same effect, if not worse, on Sally.

It occurred to me there was quite a bit about Sally—and her background—that I didn't know.

I had walked into the gallery, given Betty and Darryl each a good morning nod, and poured myself a cup of coffee before I got this really horrible sinking feeling. I'd totally spaced out the New York trip. I hadn't told Sally.

Swell, just swell. Well, how was I to know that half the Addams Family would show up on her stoop in the middle of the night? I'd thought there'd be plenty of time to break it to her.

I put my hand on the phone, then decided it was too early to call her. Then I picked it up anyway and phoned, instead, the hospital. Chips wasn't there yet, but I got the report on Pops: no change.

Darryl and Betty took down the painting I'd be babysitting on the plane and busied themselves, in the back room, constructing a crate. As lousy as Darryl was at most things, I had to give him credit for building the world's best custom shipping crates. Betty mostly passed him tools and kept him company. Mary was still out with the flu and Ardith was holed up in her office, which left me alone on the floor.

The gallery didn't get much midweek foot traffic. People dropped by, of course, but usually they were people we knew: clients or friends or both who stopped by for a cup of coffee and some gab. Occasionally a stranger would wander through the front door, and maybe one time out of a hundred they'd turn out to be client material. Pretty low odds.

So at about 10:30, when the guy walked in, I gave him a quick visual appraisal: small-town Midwesterner, I guessed, probably in the city for vacation, maybe a convention. He was middle-aged and jowly, with thick grey hair cut in a style ten years out of date, like those people on Christian TV. A bright red sportscoat strained across his stomach, and he wore loafers with tassles. Not expensive ones, either.

I pegged him for a realtor, or some other sort of salesman: the particular sort that had an 'appropriate' dirty story—gleaned from a

183

joke book—for every occasion. Definitely not a buyer.

I smiled at him anyway, and said, 'Morning. Can I help you?' He didn't look one bit like the type that browses art galleries. I figured he was probably just killing time. Maybe he wanted to use the restroom.

But he came straight over to my desk and stuck out his hand. I stood up and shook it.

'Morning' yourself,' he said. He was a little too happy. 'Bob Daws, from just outside Wichita. Kansas, that is.' He gave out with a big belly laugh, as if he'd just said something hilarious. It was loud enough that it brought Ardith out of her office and up the hall. She stopped at the edge of the main gallery floor, a cigarette in her hand and a disgusted look on her face.

'Alex Langley,' I said once he stopped laughing. 'What can I do for you?'

'Well, I'll tell you, Alex, I'm in town to see my sister and her kids. And Sunday morning we're all sitting round the—mind if I take a load off?'

I shook my head and motioned him toward the client chair, even though he was already halfway into it. I sat down, too. Just past his shoulder, I saw Ardith, still standing at the mouth of the hall. With one manicured finger, she made a little motion across her throat.

'You were saying, Mr Daws?'

Ardith glowered at me.

He pulled a clipping out of his pocket and began to unfold it. 'Call me Bobby. Anyway, we were all sitting around the breakfast table

184

when my sister—that's my baby sister Grace, her oldest boy just started college. Anyway, Grace looks up and says to me, "Bobby, didn't we go to high school with a girl named Sally French?" '

Well, he had my attention. Ardith's too. She took a couple of steps toward us, then stopped.

'And I said, "Well, yes, Grace, we sure did," and she handed me this paper.' He smoothed it out on my desk and jabbed a finger at the photograph of Sally with Peaches. 'That's her, all right. Little Sally French. Hasn't changed hardly a bit. I went with her in high school, y'know. I was a senior and she was a freshman. Good old Brigston High. Fight, fight, fight for the orange and white.'

He paused to sweep a glance across paintings on the far wall. 'These things hers?'

I nodded dumbly. This glob, this *jerk,* had been Sally's high school boyfriend? He looked old enough to be her father. Her uncle at the very least.

'People buy 'em?'

I nodded again. 'This is a sold-out show,' I heard myself say, by rote. 'It will be on display until a week from Friday.'

He stood up, turned in a slow circle, then scratched at his head. 'Goddamn! What for?'

I stood up, too. I didn't feel too well. 'Excuse me?' I managed.

'I mean, what do they buy 'em for? No offence, now, Alex, to either you or ol' Sally. But it's not like they're real pictures of anything,

185

is it? Back home, Sally used to paint real nice stuff. Had this little shack of a workroom out back of her aunt's house, and she had that whole thing full'a pictures of, well, you name it. Good stuff, too. But they were real paintings, you know, of kids or ducks or flowers or something, like a person'd want to put in their house. She gave me one, one time, of a hog. My mother's still got it.'

From across the gallery. Ardith snorted behind her hand. He didn't hear. He walked over to the wall and bent to squint at a title tag.

'*Sin and Sensibility?* What's that supposed to mean?'

I opened my mouth, ready to unenthusiastically deliver my little speech about artistic intentions and the evoking of emotion or mood, as opposed to illustration; but there was no need, because the painting had hooked him, just like that.

He slowly rose up and stood erect, hands at his sides, his mouth open slightly. His eyes flicked over the canvas, paused at the focal point, ranged out, moved back again.

His right hand started to stray towards his crotch, but he caught himself just in time.

He cleared his throat, then turned to me. 'I, uh, well, there's *somethin'* about it, isn't there?'

I heard a snicker and glanced toward the hall just in time to see Ardith disappear into its mouth. Her heels clicked away.

'Don't suppose you'd have Sally's address or phone?' he said. He shifted his weight from foot to foot. I almost felt sorry for him, but not quite. 'Like to look her up.' He gave the painting one last glance, then turned his back on it as if he didn't trust himself and wasn't sure why.

'Like to take her out,' he said, after he'd cleared his throat again. 'Talk about old times. Maybe even relive a few of 'em, if you know what I mean.' Then he poked me with his elbow and winked. It was all I could do not to slug him.

'I'm sorry.' I said it very politely, considering that my teeth were clenched. 'We're not allowed to give out personal information about our artists. But I'll be happy to tell Miss French that you were in,' I added, and thought, *Over my cold, dead body, Bubba.*

He scowled, then shook his head. 'Well, rules are rules. That's what I keep tellin' my nephews, anyway.' He pulled a business card from his wallet, scrawled something on the back, then handed it to me. 'You tell her I'd like to see her. I mean,' he added, leaning closer, 'I'd *really* like to see her, if you get my drift.'

He leaned closer still. I got sharp whiff of dimestore aftershave. He whispered. 'Say, is she as, you know, wild as she used to be? Me and her used to go at it like a couple'a—'

I took a step away. It was either that, or do something that would likely lose me my job and gain me a lawsuit. I said, 'I'm sure I wouldn't know.'

'Well, I ran off,' he said. He was looking at another French painting, one across the way. 'Might still be with her now, but I ran off to

San-Fran-Cisco. Was gonna be a rock 'n roll star. Sounded sexy, you know? But it didn't work out. Got back to Brigston a few years later, but ol' Sal was long gone and that goofy family of hers wouldn't—'

'I'll tell her you were in, Mr Daws.' I said, cutting him off.

'Bobby, just call me Bobby.'

'If you'll excuse me, Bobby?' I gestured toward the papers on my desk.

'Oh, sure, sure! No rest for the wicked, eh, Alex?' He laughed again. What a wit.

What a prick.

And he wasn't the only one. After he left and I sat on my desk, slowly shredding his business card, I decided I didn't know who I was more angry with: Bobby Daws, or myself.

That man, that jerk, that paunchy, middle-aged classless son of a bitch was not only Sally's contemporary, he was one of her ex-lovers. I told myself that he probably wasn't such a bad guy. I told myself that I might have liked him if he hadn't bragged on bagging my girlfriend.

I didn't believe myself, not for a second.

And then the word 'girlfriend' got to bothering me. That didn't seem right for Sally. I'd been practically certain there was something much deeper there, but now I didn't know. The woman I'd held and loved and lusted after and obsessed on for the past few days—the past two years, if you counted all the metaphysical lust I'd had over her paintings—suddenly seemed a complete stranger.

She told you, Alex. It wasn't like she tried to hide

188

it. She said she'd been around. Jesus, she said she'd lost count.

It actually dawned on me, at that moment, what 'lost count' meant. And she'd had plenty of time to do it in, hadn't she? Seventeen years between us, seventeen, almost eighteen years of balling her brains out with every Tom, Dick, and Bobby Daws that crossed her path.

I couldn't shake the picture out of my head—a long line of men, all sizes and shapes and ages, queued at a turnstile outside Sally's bedroom door, and a sign: *Please take a number and step to the rear of the line.* And below that, an LED readout: *Now serving Number 742.*

I'd been a prisoner of my hormones, and an idiot to ever get involved. All her little quirks—the way she had of phasing out and getting lost in thought, for instance, or those small, skittish movements when she was in a crowd—that before had seemed charming, now seemed to me to smack of instability,. Maybe she's crazy, I told myself. Her family was certainly over the edge. And my nasty little experience with Suzanne had taught me never to do 'crazy' again.

Of course, that was different. Suzanne had been obsessive. And vengeful. After we broke up and she'd sent me that smelly little present via parcel post, I found out that I'd got off easy; when my predecessor had broken up with her, she'd gone out and bought a live, six-foot boa constrictor, let herself into his apartment, and left it snoozing beneath the covers of his bed. When I heard about that, I was actually kind of happy she'd just sent me a dead perch. Whatever poor schmuck she was seeing now had my sympathies.

No, Sally wasn't in Suzanne's league, not anywhere near. But she was...well, I wasn't sure *what* she was. I mean, I didn't really think Sally would just snap one day and go ballistic in a convenience store, but she was sure carrying around a strange assortment of idiosyncracies.

And we were a generation apart. I'd been nuts to imagine that we could spend the rest of our lives together. What could we ever possibly have in common once we got all the balling out of our systems?

I sat there for maybe ten minutes after Bob Daws left, thinking every rotten thing in the book about Sally French, stuff I won't repeat here. It was that bad.

And then I hit some sort of mental wall and began to backtrack. Maybe it wasn't her fault. The other stuff, I mean; I knew she couldn't help when she was born or who she drew for relatives. I tried to imagine how it would have been to be young when she was fourteen or sixteen. It'd been a wholly different, less cynical and more hopeful world, with hippies and free love and walls covered in Peter Max art or posters that said *Clapton is God.*

Have another hit. *Make love, not war.*

Well, she had.

It wasn't fair to hold that against her. I couldn't blame her for it any more than I could blame my great-grandmother for singing white blues in a Chicago speakeasy and drinking

190

bathtub gin back in the 1920s.

But still, I did.

And again, there was the age thing.

I'd known it, been told it, practically had my nose ground into it. But it hadn't hit me, *really* hit me, until that morning. I supposed that in time I could rationalize my way through that stadium full of ex-lovers. I supposed I might eventually be able to talk myself, on a gut level, into ignoring it.

But combine the turnstile boys and the generation between us, then tack on all the eccentricities and the way she'd practically gone nuts when the aunt and cousin had showed up?

Too much. She was borderline crazy and old enough to be my mother, I told myself. And if she had been my mother, she'd likely have had no idea who my father was. It was a nasty thing to think, but I thought it. I wanted my life to be simple and uncomplicated, and this thing with Sally was neither. It was just too damn hard. And then I took it a step further into my old friend Heavy Rationalization. She'd be better off without me, wouldn't she? Hadn't she herself tried to break it off just the night before? Between her loony family and her career, she already had her hands full without me around to complicate things. And she was an experienced woman, to be kind about it; right now I was nothing more than a new toy for her. I'd save her the trouble of telling me to get lost.

Wouldn't she be happier with somebody who remembered the Nixon Years?

Wouldn't I be happier with somebody who didn't?

All right, call me a jerk.

The boot fits.

I decided it'd be light years past lousy to break it off over the phone, though I might have to do just that. I honestly didn't know if I could look her in the eye and say it. I finally decided I'd just tell her the part about the New York trip. By the time I came home, I might have either a better plan or more guts.

It was mid-afternoon before I mustered the nerve to phone her.

There was no answer.

I was relieved.

14

Sally

I'd had better days.

I woke to the sound of Aunt Mariah banging around downstairs. I knew it was Aunt Mariah down there because I could hear Norman upstairs. His baritone, unchanged since his days as a high school glee-club star, carried into my room along with the faint hiss of the shower. He was singing. 'Ragtime Cowboy Joe,' and he was in high spirits. I could tell because he was throwing in sound effects. 'Yee-ha!,' he yipped in the pauses, or, 'Ho, mule!'

With my bladder close to bursting, I threw on clothes and crept past the bathroom, through the office and studio, then down the back stairs, hoping I could sneak to the first floor powder room without crossing Mariah's path. Fortunately she'd vacated the kitchen. Scraping sounds came from the front room. Doubtless my furniture was in all the wrong places and she was making it right.

I made it to the powder room undetected. As I splashed water on my face to the muted roar of the toilet's flush, I took a look at myself in the mirror.

'Almost forty,' I whispered to that dripping, sleep-creased face. 'Almost forty, and you're sneaking around in your own house, afraid of an old lady and her pervert son.'

I stuck the corner of a washcloth under the tap, then rubbed at my teeth with it. *I am a grown person,* I thought, *and this is my house. I shouldn't be creeping around like a cat burglar. I shouldn't have had to throw my lover out into the street in the middle of the night. It's not logical. I should be having some sort of catharsis. I should march straight out there and tell them to quit moving my furniture and hogging my bathroom and go find themselves a hotel.*

But when Mariah knocked at the door and shouted, 'Finally out of bed, are we?' all I did was mumble 'Yes,' and dry my face.

Old habits die hard, I guess.

When I came out, I heard Norman overhead, thumping toward the front stairs. I went the

193

opposite way, toward the kitchen. Mariah was there, an apron tied around her waist. Since I didn't own one, she must have brought it with her. The kitchen was almost cloudy with the scent of her perfume.

She was dressed for the day, and I supposed she planned on going along on Norman's appointment, because she had on lipstick and heels. I wondered what the folks at Mr Chippy's would think when their ace inventor of cereal giveaway toys arrived for the big meeting with his 68-year-old Amazon mommy in tow.

She tucked her chins and stared down at me. 'Norman and I have already eaten,' she said. 'I saved you some eggs. Lord knows there wasn't much to work with.'

I flopped down into a chair, a child again. Maybe it was a good idea Norman was taking her along. With Mariah around, they'd be afraid *not* to buy his goofy invention.

She slid a plate in front of me. I picked up a fork and stared at it.

'I cleaned out your refrigerator. All that junk food! It's a wonder you don't have rickets or scurvy or something. You really ought to take better care of your health, Sally.' She picked up a dishrag and began to wipe the front of the refrigerator. 'That person—that boy who was here last night. You're sleeping with him, aren't you? Bad blood. I always said so. It's disgusting already, but couldn't you at least find someone your own age to...to do that with?'

'He's not a boy,' I said softly to my eggs, and pushed at them with my fork.

'I can't say I'm surprised it's come to this,' she went on. 'Don't think I didn't know what you were like at home, Sally French. Don't think for a moment I didn't know what went on out in that so-called studio of yours. Boys, boys, boys. Day and night, the boys. It was worse than having an unfixed cat.'

My hands were clenched into fists, and I was quaking on the inside: a familiar but highly unwelcome feeling.

'Norman was never any trouble. Always a good boy. Good in school and good to his mother. Things like that pay off, you know. God is always watching. And now, with this deal Norman's making with Mr Chippy's...' Smugly, she smiled past me and out the window. 'Norman's going to buy me a fur. A real ranch mink. I already picked it out of the Camellia's Tall Ladies' Fashions catalogue. I daresay it'll be the only one in Brigston, if not the whole county. You just have no idea how much money a thing like this invention of Norman's can make, Sally. Maybe as much as fifty thousand dollars!'

I made nearly three times that last Saturday night, you provincial old bat, I wanted to say. But I didn't. The thing between Mariah and me had nothing to do with money, it had to do with jealousy and anger, maybe even hate. I felt that I'd compress that fork in my fist into nothing, squeeze it into oblivion, kill it.

'I never knew what to do with you, you know,' she continued, and turned her attention and her dishcloth to the already sparkling

195

countertops. She let free a long, martyred sigh, her trademark.

'At least the neighbours didn't find out. Thank God for that. Well, I hope you'll have the decency to refrain from any more of that monkey business while Norman and I are here. I suppose you're taking drugs, too. Sex and drugs, hand in glove. I've read about that crack cocaine business. And AIDS. It's in all the magazines. You and that boy had better be careful, is all I can say. I tried hard with you, Sally. I won't let it be said that I didn't, but you never once—'

Just then Norman came in. For the first time in living memory, I was actually happy to see him. I wondered if he'd backed down the stairs, holding tight to the railing, like he used to at home. It was his old fear of heights. He could go upstairs just fine; coming down was the problem.

'I'm ready if you are, Mom,' he chirped, and bussed her on the cheek. 'Sally's driving us, right?'

I made myself lay down the fork. 'I am?'

He looked at me as if I were the town idiot. 'Duh,' he said, and made a face that might have been appropriate on a twelve-year-old boy, but not on a middle-aged man. 'How else? We flew in, remember? And took a cab from the airport.'

I cringed and muttered, 'Sorry.'

Mariah folded her apron and laid it on the countertop. 'I should think so.'

I drove them as far as the hospital, then got

196

out and handed Norman the keys. 'You've got a map,' I said, ignoring Mariah's insulted sputter. 'Where you're going is easy to find.'

They drove off and left me on the kerb. 'Don't worry,' I said to the ever-diminishing back end of my car. 'I'll take a cab home.'

So there I stood, without benefit of a shower or a real toothbrush, afraid to go into the hospital, afraid to go home, and pissed at the world. I finally walked across the street to a convenience store and stuck a quarter in the pay phone.

The nurse put Chips on the line, and five minutes later we were in her car.

It was nearly noon, so we went through the drive-through at a McDonalds, then pulled into a space in the back lot. Chips was looking more like herself. Her clothes matched and her hair was neat, but even an artful application of Estee Lauder hadn't managed to mask the worry on her face. She dug through the sack and handed me something wrapped in green paper.

'I think that's your fish,' she said. The car smelled of french fries.

She bit into her burger, chewed once, then scowled. 'Stinkin' pickles.' She slid half of one from her mouth and tossed it in the sack, then lifted the top bun to find the others.

'Left 'em standing at the airport, did you?' she said, once she had her sandwich back together. 'That's a pretty big thing to forget, Sal, even for you. 'Spose you had other stuff on your mind, though.' She smiled, then took a bit bite.

I mumbled, 'Yeah,' around a french fry.

'So Pops is awake? When are they going to move him?'

She shrugged, then looked out the window. 'Damn doctors won't say. Not that it matters much to Pops. He doesn't know where he is. Doesn't care, I guess. Doesn't know me at all, but then, that's nothing new. Which one of those is my shake?'

I handed it to her, and she sucked on the straw thoughtfully. 'What did Alex say? When they got there, I mean.'

'Not much. I didn't give him much chance, I guess. I just...I kind of freaked out, Chips. I don't think I was very nice to him. I practically hurled him out the front door. He probably thinks I'm crazy.'

She balanced her shake on the dashboard and, grinning, picked up her burger. 'Oh, I think he already knew that, Sal. How long are the Terrible Two staying?'

'Until tomorrow afternoon. Their plane leaves at three.'

'Just a little better than twenty-four hours,' she said. 'Stay at my place till they're gone, why don't you? I'd be glad to have you. I don't like the idea of you being under the same roof with that pig.'

I shook my head. 'It'll be all right. I mean, I don't think he'll try anything. Not with Mariah there.'

'You sure?'

'Yeah. It's just....they're—well, you know. We've discussed this before.'

Her mouth twisted before she said, 'I'd really

198

feel better if you'd stay at my place.'

I shook my head.

'Well, if you're gonna be stubborn...' She bent forward and felt along the floor, then brought up her purse. Out came the Valium. She handed me one. 'Take it.'

I did.

'That oughta loosen you up,' she continued. 'So stuff won't bother you so much. And if that Norman creep gives you a hard time, you won't freeze up. You'll just slug him. In fact, why don't you just go ahead and slug him anyway? For old times' sake. I'll help.'

I sorted through my fries with one finger. I didn't have much of an appetite. 'Don't think I haven't thought about it.'

We sat quietly for a few minutes, eating, sipping our shakes. It was nice, sitting in the back lot like that, facing the trees. A little breeze came through the car, on the chilly side, but not too cold. Just a little fall nip. It reminded me of when I was in high school, and the boyfriend of the moment would take me to the A & W in the next town over. It was about the only place to go on a date.

'—About Suzanne,' Chips was saying.

'Huh?'

She gave me a slow shake of her head and a very long-suffering look. 'You were off-planet again.'

'Sorry.'

'I said that you shouldn't worry about anything Suzanne said.'

'Suzanne who?'

199

'At Peaches' party.' She reached for my fries. 'You gonna eat these?' When I shook my head, she dumped them onto the smashed sack in her lap. 'She's a real bitch, and she's just mad because Alex dumped her. Carries a grudge, that one. It's been months and months.'

'That girl? She was beautiful. They went together?'

'About a year,' Chips mumbled around a mouthful of my fries. 'That's what I hear, anyhow. Grapevine. Okay, Peaches told me. He knows everything.'

'But she was so beautiful...'

'She's sharp, too, but those are about the only two things she's got going for her. Guess Alex finally figured that out.' She stuck the prescription bottle into my purse. 'For later,' she said.

'Chips, I don't know if it's such a good idea to—'

'Aw, crap. Won't hurt you. And don't worry about me. I've got plenty. Practically live on the stuff.'

'That's what I'm worried about.'

She took a huge bite of her burger. 'Finish your sandwich, Sal,' she mumbled.

She drove me home and I waved from the kerb as she drove away. It didn't seem fair, somehow. Friends are supposed to support each other in times of trouble. This gets complicated when they both have trouble at the same time.

My house key was on the ring I'd given Norman, so I had to let myself in through

200

one of the conservatory windows. Other than quick visits to pick off dead leaves and check the misters, I hadn't been in there for better than a week, and I sat down on the wrought iron loveseat for a few minutes, just to enjoy the room. The little fountain had never seemed so pretty, and the plants, with their little automatic, watering system making a faint *drip-drip-whoosh* in the background, had never seemed quite so lush.

I imagined Chips' Valium had something to do with this.

I finally dragged myself upstairs. The hall was still littered with eiderdown, spread out and scattered into fluffy islands from Norman tramping through it. I found the vacuum and got most of it up, and then I took a long shower and washed my hair.

I supposed I should go down to the front room and pick up Norman's bedding. That was where he'd slept the night before, since I'd given Aunt Mariah the only guest room. We'd hardly talked after Alex had left the house. I supposed Mariah thought she was punishing me with the old silent treatment, but I'd been grateful.

With a towel wrapped round my head, I went to the linen closet and pulled out two sets of fresh sheets, one for each of them. Aunt Mariah could be a little sloppy about some areas of housekeeping, but she was a maniac about fresh linens. Back home, she used to change the beds every day.

I went to her room first, and as I opened the door I was smiling just a little, thinking that she must have hated sleeping in there. Except for a few of the pictures, the room was done in period antiques or reproductions, and she hated antiques. She liked everything up to date. The date was, of course, 1955, but that was the date she liked.

As I dropped the folded sheets on the bureau, it struck me that something was wrong. At first I thought it was just the scent of the room, which had always smelled faintly of the lavender potpourri I kept on the bureau, but which now smelled of Mariah's perfume. I stood there a moment before I realized that the pictures had been taken down. Not all of them—there was still that big kitschy print of Victoria and Albert over the bed, and the watercolour ducks still bracketed the lowboy dresser—but one wall was bare. The important wall.

She had taken them down, taken down my mother's book covers. I found them in a stack under the bed, their frames turned toward the floor.

A tidal wave of dark red fury nearly staggered me. I gathered up the pictures, hugged them to me, heard myself repeating, 'You bitch, you rotten bitch,' through clenched teeth.

I carried them to my room, then found my purse. I took another one of Chips' little pills.

Forty minutes later, I was sound asleep.

It was dark when I woke up, and the house was quiet. I rolled over and looked at the clock. Two in the morning. I'd slept through Norman's triumphant return from Mister Chippy's. I bet that had ticked off Mariah: a happy thought.

I was wide awake, so I did what I usually did when I was wide awake in the hard, dark middle of the night: I painted.

Without music, of course. God forbid I should disturb the Medusa down the hall. I carried a vase of Alex's roses to the studio. That was the pink I wanted.

I wondered if he'd called, and almost hoped he hadn't. If he had, I was certain that talking to Mariah—or Norman—had been no picnic.

I began mixing paint. Oh, that pink. Rose madder is one of my favourite colours; I don't know why. It always makes me happy just to see it on my brush. I began to work, to slip faint ribbons and barely perceptible washes of it into and over the yellow: a translucent field here, a complicated network there. I missed Alex, but I'd see him tomorrow night, I knew. Once it got to be afternoon, I'd get Norman and Mariah on the plane, then call the gallery and explain to Alex, and everything would be fine again.

I loved him; I knew that now. Despite the years between us, despite what that Suzanne girl had said at the party or what anyone else might say, I loved him like I'd never loved anybody or anything except painting. And he cared for me. The years made no difference to him. My past made no difference. When I was with him, I was strong, I wasn't afraid.

I thought about the way he smelled, how warm and large his hands were, and how gently they touched me. I thought about the clear, forever blue of his eyes, and the soft resonance of his voice in the dark.

I thought about silly things, too, like the way his wallet was outlined in his back jeans pocket and how his pants cuff rode his boot just so; the unruly shock of wheat-coloured hair that never failed to tip over his forehead, no matter how many times he pushed it back; his warm, rumbling laugh; the way he'd casually rub my back or wink at me, like we'd known each other forever.

Maybe we had.

The painting began to grow, to take on life, to hum to me. Rose hovered over yellows turned to peach, faded, thrust forth, danced.

I was in love, really in love, for the first time. Everything would be all right. Everything would be perfect.

It had been light for several hours when Aunt Mariah banged on the studio door. 'Are you in there, Sally? Why is this door locked?'

I set aside my brush and wiped my hands on a paper towel. I could just imagine her out there: those little silver clips holding the pin curls in her hair, the ancient carpet slippers on her feet. The same dark green men's bathrobe she had worn all the time I was growing up would he hugged about her and cinched at the waist with a fortress-like finality.

I opened the door. I was almost shocked to see her in a coffee-brown robe and matching scuffies. The pin curls were there, though.

She glared past me into the studio. She didn't seem very chipper for somebody whose son was going to gift her with a mail-order mink to wear to the Safeway. 'Who's in here with you? I specifically asked if you couldn't control yourself for just the few days that we're—'

'Nobody's here, Aunt Mariah,' I said, and tried to remember where I'd left the tranquilizers. 'I was just working.'

Her gaze settled on the easel for perhaps a half-second before she dismissed it with a snort. 'Norman and I found a market on the way home yesterday. I'll be making oatmeal, if you want any.'

She turned to leave.

'Aunt Mariah?'

'What?'

'How'd it go? Norman's appointment, I mean.'

She stared at me a moment. I don't think I'd ever seen her look quite so odd. It was a combination of anger and frustration and something else. Humiliation, perhaps? 'As if you care,' she said at last. If Aunt Mariah had been anyone else, I would have sworn she was on the verge of tears.

She turned away, turned the corner. I heard her slippered feet clomp down the hall, then start down the stairs before she paused.

'Some man called for you last night,' she said.

My heart stuttered against my chest, caught.

'Allen or Alex somebody. He said to tell you he's going to New York.'

I ran after her and leaned over the railing. 'New York? When? For how long?'

She shrugged. 'Today. I think he said for a

few days. Is that the boy you were—the one who was here?'

I slumped down to my knees and leaned my forehead against the banister spindles. 'No, Aunt Mariah. It's a different one. I have thousands.'

I heard her cross the foyer, then slide open the pocket doors to the front parlour. 'Norman, sweetheart? Time to get up.'

15

Alex

Brick Lowell's driver met me at La Guardia and, with the help of two redcaps, we loaded the crated French painting into a rented truck. Darryl did a bang-up job of packing artwork, but those crates of his—especially for really big paintings like this one—weighed a ton.

Once we got free of the airport traffic snarl and eased out onto the Grand Central, the driver, whose name was Delbert King, dug into his pocket and pulled out a crumpled pack of Camels.

'Mind?' he asked, as he held the pack to his mouth and lipped out a cigarette.

I shook my head, then reached for my own. I'd been chain-smoking ever since Bobby Daws had darkened the gallery door, and the smokeless plane ride had seemed an eternity. I couldn't eat, couldn't keep anything down, and hadn't been able to since the afternoon before. Just a touch of the flu. That's what I told myself, anyway.

Delbert, it turned out, was a man of few words. Next to none, actually. By the time we'd made the silent two-hour drive down the Long Island Expressway, found East Hampton, and turned down Brick Lowell's winding drive, I'd sucked up the rest of the pack I had with me and was itching to get at my luggage so I could crack open a new one. I thought maybe I'd just stick the whole thing in my mouth and light it.

Brick, a brisk salt breeze snapping his jacket, came out to meet us. He was in a lousy mood, which was pretty normal for him, and chewed out the driver for taking so long. Delbert must have been used to it, because he just swung open the back of the truck, and slid the ramp into place without saying a word or even looking at Brick.

After a couple minutes of grouching, Brick finally turned to me and grinned, like somebody had flipped the switch for his facial muscles. He grabbed my hand and shook it, too hard.

'Alex! The man for the job! Nip in the air today, eh? Come on in the house while Delbert unloads the crate. Stephanie just got back from the club. I know you remember our Stephie. She certainly remembers you.' He gave me one of those man-to-man, I'd-love-to-welcome-you-to-the-family winks.

He steered me toward the house, which was a really pushy contemporary: tons of glass, very

207

stark, totally sterile. Out back, about a hundred yards away, choppy grey waves slapped the shore. It depressed the hell out of me.

'Of course I remember Stephanie,' I said, and stopped halfway up the path. 'But I'd better help Delbert. And I think we'd better unload the crate inside the truck. Took four of us to get it in there, and I don't think the three of us could get it out.'

I'd only said 'the three of us' to be polite. Brick Lowell would have been no more likely to sully his hands with manual labour than ladle out dinners at the Bethel Mission.

He scowled. 'Oh. I suppose you'll need tools or something.'

'Got 'em.' Delbert's voice echoed from inside the truck. I heard the first squealing complaint of crowbarred wood.

Brick gave a curt nod. 'I'll wait for you inside, then,' he said, and turned on his heel.

I climbed up inside the truck. Delbert, a Camel dangling from one corner of his mouth, already had one of the crate's corners loosened. He handed me his crowbar, picked up a hammer, said, 'Asshole, ain't he?' and pried out another nail.

Mindy Lowell, Brick's gaunt wife, held out a silver tray artfully arrayed with canapes. 'Have another, Alex. I had Cook make them just for you.'

I took one, popped it in my mouth, and hoped I wouldn't throw it up. I made myself say 'Um' and smile at her.

'We don't usually indulge,' she said. She put the tray down in front of me, then patted her stomach. 'Wouldn't want to get fatsy-watsy, would we, Stephie?'

Stephanie, still in her tennis clothes and slouched in a green suede chair across the room, looked up from the rug, said, 'God forbid,' and looked back at the rug again. There was nothing behind her but a glass wall full of grey sky.

Mindy pursed her lips, then just as quickly turned to me and smiled. The whole family had perfect teeth. 'It's such a lovely painting, isn't it?' She meant the French I'd just hung next to the fireplace.

'Beautiful,' I said. 'You made a good choice.'

Actually, I thought it was one of the weaker paintings in the show, but then, art is pretty subjective. If they liked it the best, then it was the best for them. The painting I couldn't take my eyes off, though, hung on the opposite side of the mantel; another French, titled *Repercussions in Red*. Brick had bought it at the first French show I'd worked. I had loved that painting then, still loved it; and it still ticked me off that a jerk like Brick owned it. It was the painting that had made me fall in love with Sally two years before I met her.

I didn't want to look at it, but I couldn't stop.

'.... Few friends over for dinner,' Brick, posing with an unlit pipe, was saying.

'To celebrate the new painting,' Mindy added. She eyed the canapes. 'I do hope you like veal.'

Stephanie looked up. 'Oh, Mama, not veal again!' I had to admit that Brick's money had managed to chisel Stephanie into a pretty girl: she was, in fact, right on the edge of beautiful. Perfect nose, perfect teeth, perfect chin, trim figure. I felt sorry for her.

I went back to staring at the painting.

'Now, Stephie,' her mother began.

'Well, I *showed* you those pictures of the way they keep them. Poor little baby calves.' She crossed her arms. 'We've talked about this before. You know I won't eat it.'

Brick stepped into my line of vision. His face went dark and he turned toward her, but before he had a chance to get nasty, I said, 'I'm afraid I don't eat veal, either. Besides, I really should be getting into town. I've got reservations at—'

'Nonsense!' Brick barked. And then, apparently, he remembered he was trying to court a potential son-in-law. He twisted his features into a vague semblance of joviality. It was pretty scary when he did that. I always imagined he was holding an axe behind his back. 'I'm certain we can come up with something else for you two kids to eat, can't we, Mindy?'

She nodded. 'Of course, dear.'

'And we can't have you running off so soon,' he added. 'We planned for you to spend the night. Give you and Stephanie some time to talk. I know how young people are.' Good old Brick. As tactful as a hammerhead shark, and just about as pleasant.

Stephanie stared at her knees. 'Oh, Daddy. Really.'

Somebody—Delbert, I supposed—had carried my luggage to the guest room, a gun-metal grey minimalist affair, obviously done by a decorator who'd designed it with a spread in *Architectural Digest* or *Metropolitan Home* in mind, rather than an actual guest. The bed looked like, and was roughly as hard as, a morgue slab.

By then it was almost dark. First thing, I found a pack of cigarettes, then went out on the balcony and lit up. About halfway through the second one, I heard car doors slam down on the driveway, around the side of the house.

Company. Hot dog.

The balcony, which jutted toward the water like the prow of some surrealist's ship, wrapped about half of the second floor. I walked down a few feet, just around the far corner, to get out of the wind. There was nothing to sit on. I slouched against the wall, then stuck out one leg and propped my foot against the railing.

The moon was rising, and the water had slowly eased from grey to silver. The tide was bringing it a little farther up the beach with every wave, and there was something comforting about the off-killer rhythm of it. I supposed it was a primal thing, being lulled by the sound of waves. I thought Sally would have loved this. Sally would have found a painting in it. Sally found paintings, and magic, in everything. I flicked my cigarette down into the gravel below, then lit a new one.

I'll never have to face her again, I thought, *because if I keep smoking like this I'll probably*

211

die of cancer before I get back to Minneapolis.

It occurred to me that all the way out here I hadn't been able to think of anything but Sally, and lately I'd been thinking about her as if she were dead. I'd started out angry and hurt, and admittedly, a little shocked, although that was my own fault and no one else's. But now it was like I'd buried her and was going through mourning.

Sally would have loved the light on the waves. Sally would have hated this house as much as I did. Sally would have adored the campy steward on the plane and laughed at his sick-bag jokes and got those little crinkles at the corners of her eyes. Sally would have sat next to me and dozed off under the crook of my arm. I would have stroked her hair, and it would have smelled sweet and tangy, like her shampoo.

If only.

Well, it was too late now. The note had been sent, mailed out yesterday evening at the post office. She probably already had it.

Dear Sally (I'd written),

I'm sorry. I'm a coward, and I was wrong. You were right all along. This won't work. Please forgive me.

Alex

I kept telling myself it was all for the best, that I'd done the right thing. Hadn't I saved us both from worse grief, sure disaster? Better to stop it now, stop it clean, before I got another fish in the mail.

Not so clean though, was it, Alex? Why didn't you just go over there and stab her?

I heard a little scraping sound behind me, then, 'Oh. Sorry. I didn't know you were out here.'

My head jerked up. 'Stephanie. No, don't go back in.' I stood up straight and brushed a few errant ashes off my jacket front.

She had changed out of her tennis gear and into a black dinner dress. Her dark, sleek hair was tied back with a silver-and-black bow. Sally would have looked prettier in it, except Sally should have had gold thread instead of silver.

Stephie said, 'You're sure I'm not disturbing you? You looked sort of, um, lost or something.'

I chucked my cigarette over the rail. 'No, it's fine. You look nice. Pretty dress.'

She smiled a little. 'I just wanted to apologize. For Daddy, I mean. He can be a little, uh...' She paused as if looking for just the right word. 'Overbearing,' she said finally. She was, it seemed, a generous girl. 'I know you didn't want to come.'

I shook my head. 'It's not that, Stephanie, it's nothing to do with—'

'Don't worry about hurting my feelings, Alex,' she said. She crossed her arms and hugged her elbows against the chill. 'I don't like you much, either. Not in that way, I mean. I mean, I think you're *nice* and everything, but, well, you know.'

I smiled back at her. 'Yeah,' I said, 'I know. I think your father just wants somebody around to catalogue his collection. Somebody he can get

213

for free.' I caught myself. 'Oh. That is, I don't mean he thinks you aren't—'

She waved a hand. It was a graceful motion, but it had nothing on the languid, liquid way Sally moved. Sally didn't walk or gesture so much as she floated. Flowed.

'I know what you're going to say,' Stephanie said. 'And you're right. Daddy thinks that's about all I'm worth, I guess. No offence to you, of course.'

We both grinned.

'He's got tons of things, you know,' she said. 'There's a whole room downstairs that you can't even walk into because it's stacked so solid with paintings. There are more at the apartment, in town. It's a sin, I think, doing that. Just you wait. A big old rat or something is going to get into one of his storerooms and make a million-dollar nest. He already ruined a gorgeous Frankenthaler. Put his foot right through it when he was trying to get back to another painting. I thought that'd teach him, but...'

I offered her a cigarette, but she made a face. 'Not me. Those things'll kill you, Alex.' I nodded in agreement then lit another. I figured I had three packs to go till the coronary.

I was thinking, too, how wonderful it might have been, in another life, to stand on a balcony like this with Sally, and to light her cigarette. No, two at once, like that guy in *Now, Voyager.*

You're a sap, Alex, I thought. *A total sap at twenty-two, not to mention a wimp. But it's too*

214

bad and it's too late. There's no one to be romantic with or for. There's no Sally, no affair, because you killed it. It would have died anyway, but you did it in. Keep on telling yourself it was a mercy killing. If you say it often enough, you might believe it one day.

'Who is she?' Stephie asked.

'Who? Helen Frankenthaler?' I wasn't sure how long I'd been standing there, staring out over the sea and clutching my lighter. I slid it back in my pocket.

'No, silly,' she said. 'The girl you were thinking about when you were out here by yourself. And again just now.'

Women. How do they *know* stuff like that? Well, I guess you can't fight it.

I said, 'Sally French.'

'The painter?'

I nodded.

'Must be personal, then, not professional. A man doesn't look like that over a business associate.'

'Yeah,' I said, and leaned my arms on the railing. It had gone dark. The stars were coming out. The moon's reflection was a long, pale, broken string on the water. 'Yeah, it's personal.'

'Do you love her?'

I studied my knuckles, then the ember on the end of my cigarette. I honestly couldn't make my mouth work. I guess I was afraid of what might come out of it.

Stephanie put her hand on my arm. 'Do you love her, Alex?'

215

'It's over. I ended it.'

'You don't look to me like it's over. Not anywhere near. How does she feel?'

I shrugged and looked away. This was the last conversation I wanted to be having, and one of the last people I wanted to be having it with.

'But do you still love her?'

I turned toward her. 'Yes, I said after a moment, and that word felt like a knife. 'Yes.'

There it was. All through the anger—anger Sally hadn't deserved, had she?—and the fine, lofty logic about what was best in the long run, best for both our futures, I still loved her. It had been there all the time, the thread that held together the fabric of whatever it was Sally and I had, the thread I couldn't unravel, no matter how I worried it with rhetoric, plucked at it with rationalization after rationalization, no matter how I tried to ignore it. It's one thing to realize you're a jerk, quite another to discover you're selfish and a coward.

If Stephie hadn't been standing there, I think I might have burst into tears.

She smiled: one of those *woman* smiles that man, so long as he lives, will never figure out. She said, 'Then you have to tell her.'

I stood up, shook my head. My eyes were burning, and I blinked them several times, fast. I heard voices, party sounds, coming from inside.

'It won't work. It's too late. There are too many...differences. Let's go down to dinner. It's cold out here, and you in that sleeveless dress. You'll freeze.' I turned toward the door, but

216

stopped when I felt her hand on my elbow.

'It's never too late, Alex. There's never an obstacle too great, not if you really love each other. Not if you both want it to work.'

I just stared at her. I couldn't believe this was little Stephie Lowell, daughter of Brick-the-Prick. I couldn't believe I was talking to her about my love life, either.

She said, 'Tell her you love her, Alex.'

I hadn't the heart to tell her that nothing was that simple. What I'd done to Sally couldn't be bandaged with a word and left to magically, scarlessly heal. I was no necromancer. I couldn't bring back the dead.

I tossed my smoke out toward the beach, then took her by the shoulders, held her at arm's length. I'd had enough of this conversation. I appreciated her concern and all that, but if she kept it up I was fairly sure I'd throw myself over the railing.

I made myself smile.

'You amaze me, Miss Lowell.' A burst of raucous, slightly mean laughter rolled toward us from downstairs. Brick nobody but Brick. 'Stephie, how on God's green earth did you get to be so smart?'

She smiled with her mouth sort of half-puckered, as though she had lots of secrets and no intention of telling any of them. 'Oh, you'd be surprised. I'm not around Daddy *all* the time, you know.'

She took my arm, and as we went inside and started down the hall toward the stairs and the lights and the people, she grinned up

217

at me, plainly satisfied that she'd just solved all my problems. Sweet kid. Funny, how you can spend two years avoiding somebody and then all of a sudden find out you like them.

I smiled back and said, 'I'm kind of hungry after all,' even though I wasn't. 'Let's go attack the side dishes.'

'Not too much, though,' she said in a perfect imitation of her mother's voice. 'Wouldn't want to get fatsy-watsy, would we?'

16

Sally

After Aunt Mariah's intrusion into the studio that morning, I'd skipped the oatmeal and gone back to bed; three hours later, when my alarm jolted me out of what had promised to be a lovely dream, I felt almost perversely cheery.

Alex was on his way to New York—maybe he was there already. Norman and Aunt Mariah were still in the house, but they'd be leaving within hours, and Alex would be back any day.

It was a fortunate and serendipitous trade. It'd been almost twenty years since I'd last seen Norman, seven since my last run-in with Mariah. With luck, it might be another seven or twenty before I saw either of them again. And Alex was coming home to me, maybe for forever.

The bedstand clock told me it was just past noon. I'd slept through breakfast and probably lunch, too, since Mariah liked her meals early. I decided I'd grab something on the way home, after I took them to the airport. Their plane wasn't due to take off until about three, but Mariah liked to be sure about these things. She'd probably want to get there and start checking in by two, which meant we should leave a little after one. When I was little, we always had to be everywhere—church, doctors' appointments, community barbecues at the Elks'—at least a half hour early.

'Just in case,' she always used to say, although I was never clear what this was just in case *of*.

They had found the cabineted TV in the parlour. I heard them talking down there, and soap opera sound—a little weeping, a little tragic music—floated up the stairs along with their voices. I was half-surprised the thing still worked. I hadn't turned it on in years. The portable in the studio was handier.

Confident that Norman and Mariah were both engrossed in somebody's fictional battles with infidelity, drink, stolen babies, or all of the above, I took a long, hot shower, blew my hair dry, dressed, and popped a pill. There was still the drive to the airport to contend with, after all. Best to go through in on a nice, floaty cloud.

They were still watching the tube when I went downstairs. Mariah, dressed in a green print dress and a dark green sweater with one of those little gold chains clamped to each side of the collar, sat primly in the big wingback chair, which she'd moved across the room to block the window. Norman was stretched out on the couch, one foot on the coffee table and an open briefcase in his lap. He was toying with a small object of brightly painted cardboard, holding it to the light and squinting into it. I wondered if it was the invention Mr Chippy's had turned down. The Cuber-Viewer thing.

As I stepped down into the foyer, I was so busy looking to see if Mariah, in her furniture-moving frenzy, had scratched my floors that I stumbled over their bags.

Mariah's head came up just as I caught myself.

'About time,' she said, and glanced at her watch.

Norman scowled, tossed his toy into the briefcase, and snapped it closed.

I straightened the luggage. 'Sorry. Have you had lunch?'

Norman said, 'It's almost one, Sally. What do you think?'

I didn't look at him. I'd managed to avoid any major altercations with Norman thus far, and I wasn't going to press my luck. 'When would you like to leave for the airport?' I asked Mariah. Out of habit, I stuck my hand into the bowl on the little table beside the front door, and it came up empty. I said, 'Where are my car keys?'

Norman sat up and dug in his pocket. 'Right here.' He tossed them to me. I missed, and they bounced off my breast, then hit the floor with a little jangling thud.

He muttered, 'Butter fingers,' then lay back down.

'No need for you to inconvenience yourself,' Mariah said archly. She was looking at the television, not me. 'I ordered a cab.'

'Really, Aunt Mariah,' I lied, 'I don't mind.'

Somebody was at the front door, a cab driver. His taxi, dingy yellow and dented, idled at the kerb.

Deliverance.

In the split second it took me to turn around and say 'Your ride's here, Aunt Mariah,' I had already planned to call Ardith for Alex's arrival time, order out for pizza and lay in a small field of alizarin crimson on the painting upstairs.

Joy!

The driver, with no help from Norman, carried out their bags. Mariah snugged her sweater about her shoulders, then started toward me. I was afraid she planned to do something totally out of character, like hug me, but instead she stopped two feet away and said, 'Have you seen my purse?'

I shook my head.

Norman said, 'Me neither, Mom.'

Grumbling, she started up the stairs, which left me alone in the foyer with Norman. I glanced out the open front door. The cabbie raised the trunk lid. The mailman turned up the walk. A kid rode by on a red bicycle and thumbed his bell in front of the house.

'I'm sorry it didn't go well with Mr Chippy's,' I said lamely, and wished I'd offered to fetch

Mariah's purse for her. 'I'm sorry they didn't buy.'

Norman scowled. 'Mama tell you that?'

I shrugged. 'Not in so many words.'

'Buncha jerks,' he said, under his breath.

'Don't feel too bad, Norman,' I said, and glanced toward the head of the stairs. *Hurry up, hurry up.* 'Mariah and the Aunts still love you.'

'Big deal.' He stared past me toward the Iris Lady on the landing. 'She looks kinda like you,' he said.

I watched the mailman drop the mail into my box. The taxi driver lifted the first suitcase into his trunk. I was thinking that taxis had awfully big trunks. Maybe even big enough for Norman and Aunt Mariah, if a person folded them up.

'Real blond.' He was staring at me. A horrible queasy feeling began to twist the pit of my stomach. I knew that stare.

'Missed you, Sally, ' he said, very softly. 'Still think about you sometimes.'

He fingered a strand of my hair. I backed up a step. The newel post dug into my back.

One corner of his mouth turned up cruelly. 'Still the same little mouse. You miss me, too, sometimes?'

I heard myself say, 'Never.'

He touched my jaw with his fingertips. I flinched and turned away. He said, 'Too bad we can't stay longer. I'll have to come again, without Mom.'

I didn't answer.

'No oak tree here for you to shinny up, just

that little lock on your bedroom door. Flimsy little thing.'

Chips had practically promised me those pills of hers would prevent me from freezing around Norman, but they weren't working. All I could do was whisper, 'Don't touch me.'

'You don't mean that, Orphan Annie, never did.'

I bit at my lip. 'I always meant it.'

'Coy,' he said. His fingers slid down the side of my throat. Vipers.

'Found it!' cried Mariah from above. Her footsteps clomped overhead.

Norman scowled at the ceiling then stepped back a few feet. I took a deep breath. *Just a few more minutes, God: just a few more minutes and they'll be gone.*

Outside, the cab driver slammed his trunk shut and started toward the house. Above, Mariah paused on the landing. 'Norman, are you sure you haven't forgotten anything? Did you use the potty?' She opened her purse and plucked out a tissue.

The cabbie stepped into the foyer, his hat in one hand and a thin, disorganized stack of envelopes in the other. 'Want your mail?'

I took it from him and glanced at the top envelope. Familiar handwriting.

'Yes, Mom, I did. And I've got everything,' Norman said before he whispered to me, 'Almost.'

Why did that handwriting seem so familiar? Neat and firm. It seemed I'd seen it hundreds of times.

Mariah started down toward us, purse in one hand, tissue in the other. She blew her nose.

The gallery, I thought. *All my statements have that hand, and I know it's not Ardith's.*

Just as I realized it had to be from Alex and made the first careful, happy tear at its corner, Mariah said, 'If you're sure you've got everything, dear,' and fell down the stairs.

Norman rode along with her in the ambulance. I followed in my car. I just kept praying it wasn't her hip. My motives were wholly selfish; I was terrified she'd have to be in traction or something for eons, which would keep her in the hospital, and Norman at home. With me.

I was reasonably certain that there was no internal damage, though. She'd been bitching and moaning and complaining too loudly for that. She'd even hit one of the paramedics with her purse. She was a pretty tough old bird.

By the time I pulled into the parking lot off the emergency entrance I'd convinced myself it was only a little sprain, and that tonight they'd be taking a plane for Kansas and I'd be alone, gloriously alone, to paint or sleep, or run naked through the house, if I wanted.

As I sat in the emergency waiting room thumbing through a year-old magazine, I was awfully glad I'd taken that tranquilizer. I took another one, though, just in case. It wasn't long before I was oblivious to the sirens and the moaning and the stench. And the taste of ancient potato chips and Twinkies from the vending machine.

It was almost six by the time Norman made an appearance. He looked haggard and pale and a little stooped. I jumped up and blurted, 'Jesus, is she dead or something?' and immediately felt like an idiot.

Norman just shook his head. 'She's all right. Thank God. She broke her...' He hesitated, then pointed to my lower leg.

'Tibia?' I asked. 'Fibula?' And wondered where on earth I'd remembered that from.

'Something like that.'

A man's voice called, 'Make way, coming through!' and we sat down just in time to avoid being knocked over by a speeding gurney and two orderlies. Somewhere a woman was crying. I couldn't see her.

'What did the doctor say?' I prompted.

'Said Mama has bones like iron. Clean break. They want to keep her a while. For observation. Because she's old, I guess.'

'How long is "a while"?'

He rubbed at his eyes, then tented his hands over his face for a moment before he dropped them to his lap. 'Few hours. Are you all right?'

'Yeah. Just worried.' Poor Norman. He was having a pretty rotten week, what with the cereal company turning him down, and now this. I didn't envy him the next few weeks. I couldn't think of anything much worse than being stuck in the same house with an invalid Mariah.

He said, 'Did you call the Aunts?'

I hadn't thought to. I shook my head.

'Figures.' He scowled abruptly, looking for a

225

moment like his mother in male drag. 'Never think of anybody but yourself. Well, I'll call them from upstairs. Why don't you go see about renting a hospital bed? And a wheelchair. You can pick us up out front at ten or so, I guess.'

'Rent a *what?* Can't she—'

'Jesus Christ!' he snarled, suddenly fierce. 'I never saw anybody so selfish! It was your damn staircase she fell down, you know. We ought to sue.' He got to his feet and glared down at me with tired, narrowed, bloodshot eyes. 'Just do it, Sally, and be back at ten. And don't forget this time.'

I sat there for a good ten minutes after he stalked off. And then, numbly, I got a number from a nurse at the desk, and, over the intermittent wail of sirens and the crackle of the intercom loudspeaker, phoned a medical supply company that would deliver at night. They were not cheap. I gave them a credit card number, and they promised to have everything there by eleven, including sheets for the bed and a sheepskin pad for the wheelchair.

I wandered upstairs to find Chips, but was told Pops had been moved out of Intensive Care to a semiprivate room. The other bed was vacant, so it was just her and Pops in there. All the lights were off except a little lamp beside his bed, turned down dim.

Chips, cowled by both the shadows and her long, dark hair, was softly singing to him, one of those nonsense songs he'd made up for her when she was little, and that she'd once sung for me in

226

a moment of inebriated nostalgia. I heard just a snatch of Chips' rumbling alto sing-song before she looked up. 'Sal?' she whispered. 'What you doin' here?'

I explained about Mariah, then nodded at Pops. 'He's a lot better, huh? For them to move him, I mean.'

'So they tell me. You're sure havin' a shitty day, aren't you? Sure you don't want to move over to my place for a while?'

I shook my head.

'Want some gum?'

'No thanks.'

Pops opened his eyes, stared vacantly around the room, right through Chips, then focused on me. 'Velda,' he said quite plainly, 'I can't find my good Coleman stove anywhere.'

He closed his eyes again and began to snore softly. He seemed another man from the one I'd first met ten years before, the man who'd taken Chips and me camping, who'd taught me how to fight and land a northern pike and hadn't laughed when I'd managed to fall out of the boat. Over a campfire in the Minnesota woods, he'd told us what I supposed were the Chippewa versions of ghost stories—familiar to Chips, but new and fascinating to me. He'd been a master carpenter before he'd retired, and back in the days when I'd first moved into my house and was renovating it, he'd drop by now and then to 'inspect' the work in progress, down a half-pot of coffee, and kid around with me and the workmen, most of whom he seemed to know.

I hadn't gone to visit him much since the

first illness had put him in the nursing home, and not at all in the last couple of years, my excuse being that he wouldn't have known me anyway. It crossed my mind at that moment that I should have gone anyway, for Chips' sake at least. It broke my heart to see him so changed.

I said, 'His colour's good. This one didn't affect his speech.'

She nodded. 'Lucked out. A little trouble with his right hand, but he's almost back to his old self. Jeez, you look stoned out of your mind.'

'Huh?'

'How much of that stuff of mine you taking, anyway?'

I slumped down on the empty bed. 'Not nearly enough.'

Norman and Mariah were late. Mariah, dopey from a shot they'd given her, sprawled in back with her newly plaster-casted leg stuck straight out and softly bumping the opposite door. Norman, in the passenger seat, twisted sideways to hold Mariah's hand and mutter, 'There, there, dear,' or 'Poor Mother.'

The truck from the hospital equipment place was waiting for us. They unloaded the bed in pieces, wheeled Mariah inside, moved my poor parlour furniture yet again, and turned the front room into a sick room.

Mariah was in her newly assembled bed and asleep by the time they collected my signature and their tip and drove off.

Norman flopped down on the sofa, which was

228

now pressed against the far wall. He yawned. 'I'll stay down here with her tonight,' he said wearily. 'In case she needs anything.'

I nodded. He looked too dragged out to be dangerous, but I still wished he'd handcuff himself to the sofa.

I said, 'Goodnight, then. I'm going up.'

Only after I'd closed the pocket doors between us did I remember the letter. I slid it into my pocket and took it upstairs. I didn't want to sully it by rereading it in such close proximity to Norman.

In my room, I sat cross-legged on Alex's side of the bed and balanced the envelope, one corner torn, on my knee. It was joy, pure joy, to see it, to touch it. Alex had touched it, had written my name. I'd savour his letter, and then I'd lock myself in the studio and paint until dawn.

I'd worry about Norman and Mariah tomorrow.

Carefully, I opened the envelope the rest of the way and slid out a single small piece of white notepaper. I sniffed it before I unfolded it. Was there just a whiff of his aftershave? I smiled and thought, *Oh Alex, hurry home, hurry home to me.*

And then I read it.

I'm not certain how long I sat there, reading it over and over again, telling myself it was a mistake, that this note was from some other Alex, written to some other Sally, and not believing, not believing.

Eventually, I believed.

At last I rose, feeling old and tired in my bones and weary beyond measure, and went to the studio. I flicked on the lights and stood before the painting.

This is a lie, I thought. *This is the fantasy, the mask. And now it's going to be the truth.*

I pushed aside all the jars of colour I'd mixed, pushed aside the joyous yellows and heady pinks and vibrant roses, and began to mix anew. Blues, but not the blues of wisdom, not the blues of infinity. Blues and violets and purples: a touch of cerulean in this jar, cerulean for faint hope; ultramarine and alizarin for the treachery to crush it; purple lake for surrender; caput mortuum, the mouldering violet of decay; indigo, deep indigo, for despair.

I saw it in my head: a dank matrix, a purpled web upon the rose and peach; and me—Mars black, dark and fetid—caught in the centre.

I began to paint, and as I painted, I wept.

17

Alex

Autumn in New York isn't all it's cracked up to be.

It's several hours from the Hamptons into town, and I wouldn't have minded taking the train. I figured the noise and the strangers might help me keep my mind off things I'd rather not think about. But Brick, who was still trying to butter me up, insisted that Delbert drive me in.

It was a rotten trip. Not the car, of course; I rode in Brick's limo, with a glass panel between me and Delbert, who wasn't talking anyway. There were a couple of nice deep virginal ashtrays to fill up, and a bar. I put a small dent in Brick's Scotch supply, smoked most of a pack of cigarettes, and tried not to think about Sally.

After I'd checked into the Plaza and grabbed some lunch to soak up the Scotch, I started the courtesy calls I'd promised Ardith I'd make. I began with the uptown galleries. Two of the establishments I was supposed to visit carried Sally French's work. One of those, plus three more, carried paintings by two of the other artists Ardith agented.

By 2:30 I'd visited the Madison Avenue galleries for six cups of coffee and a lot of handshaking and bullshitting, then walked down to 57th for three more coffees, one designer water, and more glad-handing. More bull, too.

I walked back up to the Plaza to relieve my bladder and check for messages, then took a cab down to SoHo. More of the same, except at one place I got espresso instead of coffee.

On the three other occasions Ardith had sent me to New York, I'd made a quickie vacation of it. Did a little sightseeing, took in a show or a museum or two, that sort of thing. Tried not to look too ga-ga or touristy (but probably did anyway) and had a good time.

Not this trip. I considered seeing if the hotel could find me a ticket for anything interesting. A musical, maybe. But the only thing I asked for at the desk were my messages. There were two: one from Ardith, telling me that Edgar Shulmann would be calling me, and one from Dr Shulmann.

When I returned his call, Shulmann invited me to dinner. I couldn't very well turn him down. He collected Sally French, and bought from us as well as from one of the uptown galleries. I'd only met him once, a year ago, briefly, and I was prepared for another interminable evening of polite (and boring) intellectualization on the subject of art. Or maybe he was the type who cared only how much his investments had appreciated. Either way, I didn't foresee a festive evening.

I figured that it'd at least get me away from the phone. I kept staring at it, putting my hand on it, almost calling Sally, then stepping away. What the hell could I say to her, anyhow? *Sally, I'm a jerk.* Well, she already knew that by now, didn't she? *Sally, I'm sorry.* Big deal. *Sally, please forgive me. Let's try again.*

But I wasn't sure about that last part, not by a long shot. On a gut level, there was nothing I wanted more. I missed her so badly that I could barely eat, barely sleep. I missed the sound of her, the look of her, the taste and scent and feel of her. I wanted her in my arms, in my bed. She was already in my heart.

But then my brain would kick in and override everything else. Despite Stephie's sincere, if

232

simplistic, counsel, I knew the gulf of years was too great. What would my mother say if I brought Sally home and introduced her as my wife?

'Mom,' I'd say, 'I want you to meet Sally. You have a lot in common. I mean, *really* a lot.'

And what about those relatives of hers? They didn't exactly look like party animals, and I'd be stuck with them, too. There were volumes about Sally I hadn't read, metaphysically speaking. I'd barely touched the Readers' Digest condensed version.

And what about that, about her past? Would I spend the rest of my life running into men who'd elbow me and wink at the mention of her name?

Edgar Shulmann sent a car for me. Not a limo, like Brick, but a cab. It deposited me in front of an older, understated apartment building, and after I signed in and the doorman waved me along, I rode up to the tenth floor.

'Dr Shulmann?' I said, when he met me at the elevator.

We shook hands. 'Call me Edgar,' he said. He was a little guy, and looked to be in his late sixties. He was balding on top, and what hair he had left was pulled into a tidy little ponytail, dark blond streaked with grey. Dark eyes, as sharp and sparkling as wet flint, smiled behind tortoisehell glasses. He was a psychoanalyst, if I remembered correctly.

'Nice of you to invite me, Edgar,' I said, as

he opened the door to his apartment. 'Ardith sends her regards.'

It was a great apartment: eight rooms, high ceilings, a big terrace with a view. The whole thing was decorated to the tits, but warm, with lots of wood and dark, rich, understated colours. Unlike Brick's sterile place by the sea, Edgar Shulmann's apartment looked like a nice place to kick off your shoes and sprawl out with the Sunday paper.

I was gratified to see a few ashtrays cluttering up the place. One of them even had ashes in it. I reached for my pack. 'Mind?'

'Not at all,' he said, and smiled.

He offered me a drink, then excused himself. 'Got to check dinner. It's my hobby. Cooking.' He disappeared then popped his head back around the corner. 'You're not allergic to shellfish, are you?'

I smiled and shook my head, and prayed he wouldn't bring out a tray of raw oysters. The way my stomach felt, I'd probably vomit just looking at them.

I lucked out. He'd made linguine with some sort of creamy sauce with lobster and scallops, and I surprised myself by wolfing down a plate of it and asking for seconds. There were soft, buttery bread sticks with garlic; a salad, too, and custard with raspberries for desert.

I pushed away from the table full as a tick, as my dad would say, but I felt fine. I wasn't certain what had come over my stomach. Maybe it was the good meal, maybe it was the company.

Edgar Shulmann was a really nice old guy. He was probably a good shrink, too, since he'd put me at ease right away and got me so relaxed that, by the time we finished dinner, I could have flopped out on his couch and gone to sleep with a smile on my face. When I thought about it later, I decided that the minute I'd stepped off that elevator he must have seen how tightly wound I was, and he just unwound me. That was all there was to it. I suppose some people would call that manipulative. I called it a godsend.

He took me—a cigarette in my right hand, an ashtray in my left—on a tour of the apartment, or rather, the art in it. His collection was eclectic, from really traditional to totally outrageous.

After an hour of chatter about where he'd bought this piece or that, combed with stories about artists and galleries and out-of-the-way dealers he liked to ferret out on his travels, he said, 'I hope I'm not boring you, Alex. I don't entertain much these days. Not since Johanna passed on.'

I started to offer condolences, but he waved them away. 'It's been six years. I still miss her, though. Friends keep trying to fix me up, but I suppose I'm just one of those one-women men. That's probably old-fashioned, but I can't seem to help it.'

I knew what he meant and wished I didn't.

He had three Frenches. One, dated five years back and new to me, hung in the dining room. Two more were in the library. One I recognized as a painting we'd shipped to the Madison

Avenue gallery a couple years ago. It was a beaut. The base colour was a deep, silky green, the same green as that blouse Sally had worn to Peaches' party, the blouse I'd slipped from her shoulders as the rain had softly drummed above us on the Caddy's roof. The moonlight, through rain-streaked and breath-fogged windows, had silvered our skins. I could almost hear her again, those little sighs she breathed next to my ear...

I lit another cigarette.

The second painting was from the previous year's show in Minneapolis. I remembered it, too.

It was a wonderful piece. All of Sally's paintings went for the groin, but they took different routes. Some were an immediate jolt to your adrenal system. Some enticed you slowly—romanced you—so that you didn't realize you'd been debauched until it was too late. This one performed an intellectual seduction: tones of amber and gold floated in that airy, almost supernatural haze she created, with swirls of pale blue that were visible only from certain angles. They seemed to pulse as the eye moved over them.

'I have two others,' Edgar said.

I was staring at the painting, following a thread of blue.

'They're quite...different from these. I don't believe Ardith knows I have them. Are you familiar with French's early work?'

I made myself look away from the painting. I was half-afraid I'd try to crawl inside it. *Sally, what have I done to you?*

236

I said, 'Her earlier work? I'm afraid not. I'd like to see them.'

We walked down the hall to a large bedroom that had been converted into an office. The wall switch he flicked as we entered turned on only a small, green-shaded lamp that cast a yellowish pool on the desk and its litter of papers. Dimly, I could see bookshelves, piled haphazardly with books and folders and journals, and the murky outline of a chair.

'This one,' he said, as he walked away into the gloom, 'I bought perhaps a dozen years ago in a St Louis gallery. Tiny nook of a place. I happened on it by accident when I was out there for a conference. Nice little gallery, but they didn't know what they had. I paid only five hundred for it.'

I heard a soft scraping sound, and then he switched on the light above the painting. He stepped back, out of the way. He said, 'Interesting, isn't it?'

Quite the one for understatements, was Dr Shulmann.

'This is French?' I said, then realized it couldn't be anything else. There was some of that subtle layering, a hint of the finesse to come, just a touch of the delicacy; but all of the yearning was there, and all the power. It just hadn't been fine-tuned yet. It was raw, almost dangerous.

The colours—the entire spectrum, as if she'd tried to use every last trace of pigment on her palette—swirled and collided, crashed into each other in something closer to frenzy than dance.

237

And this one contained a figure, something I'd never before seen in one of Sally's paintings. Usually the focus was an abstract nest of something like pearls or bubbles or a weave of colour that grew tighter and tighter until it seemed to fall away or swirl away, and disappear into infinity. Or suddenly loom out. The last kind I thought of as 'thrusters.' Ardith called them 'invisible dick' paintings...when there weren't any clients around, of course.

At the core of this one, though, was no such abstraction or trompe l'oeil effect. There was, instead, the figure of a woman, very small and almost crushed by the whirling chaos. Her body was formed by the ragged colours swirling into it. She was nude, and she was curled into a tight fetal position. Her face was hidden.

I whispered, 'Jesus.'

Edgar said, 'It's titled *Past the Scream.*'

We stood quietly for a moment. I think Edgar was just admiring the painting. I was in shock.

Then he said, 'There's another.' I didn't know if I could take another one, and slumped back against the desk. Edgar didn't see. He had walked off into the gloom again, toward the far end of the opposite wall. I could barely make out his figure as he reached up and fumbled with another painting light.

'This is the first French I ever saw,' he said. 'I'd never heard of her before that. Doubt anyone else had, either. I found it, oh, maybe eighteen years ago in this funny little gallery—well, more like the art version of a junk shop, really—in Elgin, Illinois, and I'm ashamed to tell you what

I paid for it. We were visiting Johanna's sister, and—damn. I hope this bulb isn't burnt out.'

I heard a faint scratch and squeak of metal on metal.

'I don't normally use these things. I usually work in here on the weekends, and I have the drapes open.' A small metallic complaint. 'Bulb's loose,' he said. 'Let's see if this works.'

The light came on. He stood in front of the painting, blocking it. I could tell it was smaller than the other Frenches he had, maybe 40 inches by 40 inches, and that the colours were dark. That was all I could tell.

'Johanna didn't like this one,' he said. 'Made me keep it here, in my study. I thought about hanging it down at the office, but she wouldn't let me. She said it would likely throw half my patients into crisis. As usual, she was right.'

He moved aside.

It was a portrait: a cruel self-portrait of a younger Sally that seemed to disregard her prettiness, exaggerate her faults. Her face, which took up a good third of the canvas, was downturned. Her eyes were lidded. The corners of her mouth turned down slightly in what seemed to be resignation. Her skin was so pale, so translucent, that she seemed lit from within, but with an unhealthy light. Wrapped tightly about the top of her head, in coil after coil that spilled down to drape across her shoulders and breasts, was a snake with pulsing scales of purpled cobalt.

The background was a murky eddy of deadened blacks and purples, and only after

I looked at it for nearly a minute did I realize there was a second figure in the painting. A black doorway yawned beside and behind her, and before it stood a man, thickly built and tall, and all but lost in the gloom. His arms were folded before him, and the attitude of his body suggested haughtiness, even cruelty. He appeared to be naked. There were no features to his shadowed face.

All the hair on my arms and the back of my neck stood up.

'Brilliant,' Edgar said softly, 'but such a hopeless thing. So terribly sad. The pain—' He stopped abruptly, as if he'd caught himself in the act of violating some strange, one-sided doctor-patient relationship. He cleared his throat. 'Well,' he said, 'it speaks volumes, doesn't it?'

I didn't answer. That painting made me want to cry or hit somebody, maybe both.

'I tried to find the artist,' he said, 'but the dealer—a total reprobate, I might add—said he'd taken it in trade for three frames, and he didn't know the artist's first name, let alone her address. He didn't even know if she was local. I was terribly pleased to find the other one, a few years later, in St Louis. Not only was I fascinated with the work, but it clearly proved she was still alive. Judging by this one, I was afraid she might have done something...rash. I've watched her career with great interest since then.'

I whispered, 'Oh God, Sally,' but I don't think he heard me.

He sat down on the edge of the desk, his back to me as we both faced the painting. He twisted to lift a pipe from the rack beside him, then dipped it into tobacco pouch he pulled from his pocket. 'There is a theory,' he said as he carefully tamped the pipe, 'that creativity and some forms of mental instability are intertwined; that the development of creativity stems from the attempt to stave off either one's own madness, or the madness of those around one. This is only a theory, of course.'

He struck a match. 'If that's true,' he said between puffs, 'then I would venture to say, judging from the evolution of Sally French's work, that she has to a great extent succeeded.'

He turned towards me. 'I would very much like to meet this woman one day. I had planned to come to this last show in Minneapolis, but...' He shrugged. 'A patient. These things happen. I was disappointed. I understand she was there this time.' With his pipe stem, he pointed toward the painting. 'I've often wondered. Is this a self-portrait?'

The snake wrapped round her head had red eyes. I said, 'Not a flattering one.'

'You know her, I suppose?'

I nodded. I tried to wrest my gaze from that painting, but couldn't.

'Know her well?'

'Not very.' There was more truth in those words than I'd ever imagined. I said, 'Does it have a title?'

Edgar puffed on his pipe, then nodded. 'It's called *The Prodigal*.'

241

18

Sally

When I was ten, my climbing tree died. I remember sitting in my room, crying as the too-near whine and sputter of the chainsaw assaulted my ears. I remember the last shivering scrapes and rustles of branches I imagined were clinging to the house, clutching at my window, begging me for help I couldn't give. I remember the crash, and the hopelessness, when it fell.

As some wag once said, *déjà-vu* all over again.

There was no place to run, no comforting oak to shinny up or climb out my window to, no storage shed in which to quake in the dark while my heart thudded in my chest and my pulse pounded in my ears. There was no safe room, no safe place. I was already in my last and best hiding place, and Norman was in it with me.

When I was a child, I prayed for a saviour. *Someone will come*, I had told myself while I shivered in that wood bin or trembled, hidden in my tree, my bladder ready to burst. *Someone will come and make it stop.*

Sometimes I'd fantasize that John Wayne was my father, and that he'd gallop up on his horse, shove Norman to the ground with a gruff, 'No

242

more'a that, Pilgrim,' and hug me the way he'd hugged Natalie Wood at the end of *The Searchers*. And then maybe he'd pull out his six-gun and shoot Norman through the heart. But no one came then, and no one was going to come now. Not God, not the Duke, not Chips, not Alex.

Especially not Alex.

How could I have been so foolish? Why had I let down my guard?

Because, for the first time, you truly loved someone. Because you wanted to believe he loved you. Because you wanted to believe that such a thing as hope existed in the world.

I would erase him. I'd already eradicated him from my painting. It loomed on the easel before me, its colours muddied by hopelessness, twisted by an anguish that overrode the bloom of love beneath; colours that knit, as they neared the spiralled focus, into a tighter and tighter web that sank in a dank miasma of grief and pain and corruption.

I thought, *Sally French Meets H.P Lovecraft*, and despite myself, I laughed. The harsh bark of it shocked me back into silence.

Downstairs, the front door banged: Norman, back from his errands. Mariah had sent him out. It seemed I hadn't the sense to own roughly one-half the necessities of life, the list of which included such must-haves as tea bags, chocolate mints, a heating pad, frozen fish sticks, and the current issues of three soap opera and two movie magazines.

And if I had the right thing, it was the wrong

brand. The wrong facial tissues, wrong coffee; wrong hand lotion, soap, and toilet paper. She was probably regretting that she couldn't send Norman out for a whole new niece, too.

I blew my nose and stood up. I'd finished the painting an hour before and had done nothing since but feel sorry for myself. Well, it was time to stop crying. Norman was home.

'Sally!' I wished Mariah had broken her vocal cords along with her leg. 'Sally!'

As I started for the front steps I heard her say, 'I'll bet she's gone to sleep again. For the life of me, I don't know what's wrong with that girl. Norman, go up and—'

I shouted, 'Coming, Aunt Mariah.' God forbid Norman should have an extra excuse to corner me alone.

Mariah sat throned in her wheelchair, angled in front of the television. Her broken leg was propped up on the edge of my coffee table. The office phone, which Norman had commandeered for her and brought downstairs, was at her side.

'How's Little Meg?' I asked, and wished I'd detoured to the bedroom for another pill.

Norman brushed past me on his way out to the car for another load. I stepped away and bumped into the wall. He smirked at me over his shoulder.

'As if you cared,' Mariah sniffed. She'd been on long distance with Millie and Mavis, then Little Meg, for the four hours since Norman had embarked on his shopping excursion. I'd heard her voice, a mostly unintelligible murmur in the background, from upstairs.

'Here I lay on my bed of pain—' She swept an arm toward that damn hospital bed, now pushed against the front wall. 'And you're upstairs, doing God-knows-what, and I'm down here all alone. I could have died and you wouldn't have noticed. Or cared.'

From the foyer, I said, 'You're not on the bed, Aunt Mariah, you're in the chair. Can I get you anything? A glass of water? Something to eat?'

Cup of hemlock?

She pursed her lips. 'Don't think you can just waltz down here and—'

Norman kicked at the front door, and I opened it. His arms were loaded with paper grocery bags, and as he crossed the threshold, he stumbled. He didn't fall, thank God—all I needed was another rental bed in my parlour—but he did drop a sack. It spilled oranges and cauliflower and canned fruit cocktail across the floor.

'Sonofabitch!' he snarled, before he looked toward the front room and added, 'Excuse me, Mother.'

She nodded, her lips tight, then flicked on the TV remote.

I started picking up produce.

'Damn thing,' he muttered.

'What damn thing?' The oranges went back in the sack.

'That cat,' he snarled, already halfway through the dining room. 'It could've killed me.'

I grabbed a head of cauliflower and followed him. 'The cat came in?' I glanced under the dining room table. It wasn't there.

Norman kicked open the kitchen door and dropped his burden on the counter. He peered around the side of the refrigerator. 'It's here someplace. Where's a broom?'

I started for the broom closet, then stopped. 'What for?'

'To chase the damn cat with, of course! God, you're dumb. You know Mama doesn't like cats.'

'Or dogs or parakeets or anybody but you,' I blurted.

He smiled. It made my flesh crawl. 'Well,' he said. 'The return of smart-mouth Sally. I wondered just how long this meek stuff was going to last.'

I backed up one step, toward the door. 'Don't let Mariah hear you, Norman. She'll wash out your mouth.' I hoped he hadn't noticed the quaver in my voice.

'That's it, Orphan Annie,' he said softly. 'I like you better when you're snotty.'

'Get screwed, Norman.' One more step back and I'd be able to put my hand on the door plate. I'd be able to run. But I stood my ground.

His smile widened into a lopsided leer. 'Is that an offer? I could give Mama her medication a little early. You'd like that, wouldn't you? It's been a while. A long while. Almost twenty years.'

'Since the last time you raped me?' My heart pounded so frantically against my ribs that I feared he could hear it. *Don't let him see you're afraid, Sally, or you're lost.* 'It's not going to happen again, Norman. I'm all grown up now. I'll hurt you if you try.'

He folded his arms across his chest. 'Sure you will. I can do anything I want to you, Sal. Anytime I want. Who the hell would believe you, anyway? Not Mama, that's for sure.'

'The police would believe me.'

He laughed. One soft, sarcastic bark. 'Bull. I know you, Sally. You never called the police before, not back home, not in Kansas City. You never called anybody. And you won't start now, because you know you want it. You always did, no matter how much you deny it. You'd just better get used to the idea, because Mama and I are going to be here for a long time.'

I swallowed hard. With a hoped-for bravado that failed miserably, I said, 'Do you still have to walk down the stairs backwards, Norman?'

He didn't seem to have heard me. Slowly, his eyes travelled down my body, then up again, and I was seized with a barely controllable urge to vomit. His eyes met mine again. He said, 'You're lookin' good, Orphan Annie. Can't wait.'

'Norman?' Mariah bellowed from the front room. 'Norman, come help me. My chair's stuck.'

'Coming,' he called. He stepped toward me. I wanted to move out of his path, but the fear had overtaken me again. I froze. He stood beside me, towered over me, our bodies not quite touching, and I felt myself shrinking, shrinking.

He leaned down, his lips next to my ear.

247

'By the way,' he whispered, his breath a foul, hot wind I imagined would erode my face, eat into it like acid. 'I couldn't find your screwdriver. So I bought one. You've played hard-to-get long enough, and that little lock's coming off your bedroom door this evening. You may think you're pretty smart now, but you'll end up squeaking like a mouse. Just like always.'

Aunt Mariah yelled again, and Norman answered, 'On my way, Mother!' before he whispered. 'I'll bet you're hot for me right now, Annie. I'll bet you're wet.'

Before I realized what he was doing, he'd already bent to jab his hand between my legs and knife it upward, against my crotch.

I staggered back. I think I made a small sound. The top of my head began to pound, to lift off.

'Yeah,' he said as he stood up straight and moved past me to open the door. 'You want it.'

The door swung closed behind him, and I heard him move through the dining room and into the parlour. 'What's the matter, Mom?' he said. 'Did this goofy thing get stuck again? Here, let me fix it for you. How about a nice cup of tea? I got the kind you like.'

I bolted up the back stairs, stumbled through the cluttered studio, knocked over a table. An ashtray crashed to the floor along with a jar of brushes. I didn't stop. I ran to my room, twisted the lock, and sobbing, threw myself on the bed.

It was the scratching that woke me.

Scritch scritch scratch at the door. A soft *thump thump* against the frame.

I thought, *Norman,* and hugged my pillow before I heard him, downstairs, talking to Mariah over the TV noise. I'd slept into the evening. It was dark outside the window.

Scratch scratch thump

I went to the door and pressed my hands and ear against it, whispering, 'Alex?' with one breath and, 'Get real, Sally,' with the next.

The door shivered against my hands. Something on the other side rubbed against it.

I guessed I shouldn't have made that crack about the painting, about H.P Lovecraft. Maybe I'd called up some enormous, suppurating, seaweed-dripping demon who was simply famished for the taste of human flesh. Softly, I said, 'If you're Cthulu, you'll want to go down the stairs and take a left. There's a couple of real big ones down there.'

Then I turned the latch, twisted the knob, and opened the door a few inches. The cat squeezed through and commenced a purring, rubbing serpentine around my ankles.

I carried it to the bed. It was either that or fall down a lot, since it wouldn't stop rubbing my ankles and tripped me with every step I tried to take.

I plopped down next to it on the rumpled sheets. 'How'd you manage to keep clear of Norman?' I asked. I held out my hand and it rubbed its head against my fingers, nibbled them gently, then rubbed again. I glanced at the clock. Almost eight. Still early, but hadn't Norman threatened to give Mariah her sleeping pills ahead of schedule?

That thought sent a pang through me. I had to do something, had to get out, get away from them, from Norman. I picked up the phone and dialled the hospital, but when the switchboard answered, I hung up without saying anything. Sure, Chips had offered to let me stay at her place. But I couldn't stay there forever. All I'd done since Norman and Mariah had arrived was avoid them and run away from them, even if it was only to the illusory safety of a locked door or the anaesthesia of pills or sleep. Or all three. It would have been four if the booze hadn't been down in the parlour cabinet, with them between me and it.

Something had to be done. Yet as much as I wanted nothing more than to put about five hundred miles between myself and good old Norman, the idea of running away from my own house made me feel a little less than proud of myself. What to do? I wasn't sure, but all of a sudden I knew of a way to buy myself some time to think. It was a little underhand, maybe, but considering who I was dealing with, it wasn't *too* sneaky.

First I took another of Chips' magic pills. I was already shaking from just the idea of what I was going to do. I needed to be calm. Calmer, at least.

I picked up the cat and went down to the kitchen, the back way. Quietly, I fixed the cat a bowl of food and another of water, then took them to the back porch. He followed me, and I shut him outside.

Then I took a deep breath and walked out to the front room.

Mariah was on her bed, which had been cranked up so that she was almost sitting. A box of Kleenex rode her lap, and the floor on both sides of her bed was scattered with crumpled tissues. Norman lay sprawled on the couch, an open can of cashews balanced on his belly. They were both engrossed in the television.

For some odd reason, this little scene irritated me almost more than what Norman had done to me in the kitchen. They'd invaded my world, taken over my household, thrown me off schedule. Because of them, I'd missed several days of my talk shows, and I was pretty certain that Oprah or somebody would have done one that'd have taught me how to get rid of unwanted house guests.

Mariah looked up first. She said, 'And to what do we owe this honour?'

I smiled as if she'd just said something clever. 'I was thinking, Aunt Mariah. You know how, when I was little, we always used to watch TV on Saturday and Sunday nights together? And you'd have a cake or something, and we'd all drink Pepsi in summer or cocoa in the winter?'

She lifted a brow. 'I remember. What of it?'

Norman remembered, too, because he sat up so quickly he almost dumped his cashews. I suppose he was remembering the way he'd wait

251

for Mariah to go into the kitchen so he could hold me down on the couch and shove his finger in me.

'Well, I know it isn't Saturday, Aunt Mariah,' I said, 'but I thought maybe, if you'd like, I could fix us all some hot chocolate and a snack. If Norman got milk, that is.' I knew he must've. Mariah couldn't bear to have less than a gallon in the fridge at all times, just in case. 'It'd be like old times,' I added hopefully.

Mariah blew her nose while she considered this. She wadded the tissue in her fist, dropped it to the floor next to the wastebasket, and plucked a fresh one from the box. 'Well,' she said at last, 'I did have Norman pick up a sweet. What did you get, Dear?'

'Sponge cake,' he said. He looked very smug.

Mariah sneezed and blew her nose again. 'If I didn't know better, I'd say there was a cat in this house.'

'Sally let one in,' Norman said in a bratty, sing-song tone.

'Actually, Norman,' I replied, 'you're the one who let it in. I'm the one who let it out again.'

Mariah tossed another tissue on the floor. 'I thought so. Well, don't you go letting it in again, Sally. You know perfectly well I can't stand cats. I think you do these things just to torment me, and after we go out of our way for you. Just this afternoon Norman fixed your kitchen faucet without being asked.'

'Dripped,' said Norman, staring at the television. 'Just needed a new washer was all.'

252

I closed my eyes and willed myself not to scream. 'Thank you, Norman. Do you want hot chocolate or not, Aunt Mariah?'

'Are you sure you know how to make it?' she asked. 'You know you were never any good in the kitchen. Remember the time you tried to bake that pineapple upside-down cake? I thought I'd *never* get the stink out of my kitchen. Of course, you did get it right on the second try, I'll say that...'

'If you don't like it, Aunt Mariah, I'll find you something else.'

By the time I got back to the kitchen, I was feeling better about things. I poured milk into a sauce pan and started it warming, cut three slices of cake and slid them onto plates, and then, smiling at Norman as I passed the front room, entered the downstairs powder room and closed the door behind me.

Mariah's sleeping capsules were on the lavatory. I tipped two out into my palm, and then, just to be sure, a third. I was fairly certain Norman would never taste them, not in hot chocolate, and I'd have the rest of the night to think of what to do.

I slipped the pills into my jeans pocket, then reached over and flushed the toilet.

'Sal,' Norman called just as I opened the door, 'bring me Mama's prescription, would you?'

I had a twinge of guilt, certain for a split second that he'd read my mind and was toying with me. Even if he was a jerk, Norman was intelligent, which is the worst kind of jerk. But that didn't make him psychic.

'Sure,' I said and, to buy myself a few seconds, added, 'Where is it?'

'On the sink. Duh. Didn't you see it?'

I took it to him.

Mariah looked up from the television screen. Her eyebrows worked into a knot. 'What's that?'

Norman held up the bottle. 'Sally brought your pills, Mama. Would you like one now?'

She shook her head. 'With my cocoa,' she said.

I said, 'Coming up,' and with the capsules practically burning a hole in my pocket, went back to the kitchen.

I dumped powdered Hershey's into the steaming milk, then divvied the end result into three mugs. Mine and Mariah's went at the right corner of the tray, handles out. Then I broke open the capsules—all three—and stirred their contents into Norman's cup. It went on the tray, too, along with forks, napkins, and three pieces of cake. I dropped the empty gel capsules down the drain.

I carried the tray out. Mariah took her cake and chocolate somewhat suspiciously. I handed Norman his. I sat down.

Norman said, 'Here's your pill, Mama,' and handed one to her.

She swallowed it with a drink of chocolate, then pursed her lips. 'I suppose it's all right,' she admitted. 'You made it with that packaged stuff, though, I can tell. You should use real—'

'I'm sorry,' I said, cutting her off. 'It's all I

have. I'll get the other tomorrow.'

Norman lifted his mug to his lips, and I held my breath. He took a small sip, then set it down. He made an odd face, then licked at his lips. 'Mine tastes funny.'

I felt as if all the blood in my body had suddenly drained out, through my feet.

'It's just not as good as what I make,' Mariah offered. 'It's all right, though. This cake could use icing. Sally, tomorrow I'll tell you how to make a lemon glaze, and you can put it on the rest of this.'

Numbly, I mouthed, 'Yes, Aunt Mariah.'

Norman stood up, mug in hand. 'I can't drink this. I'm gonna get a root beer.' He paused in the doorway, and without turning toward me, said, 'Sal, why don't you move over on the couch and sit by me? Be like old times.'

19

Alex

By eleven o'clock I was itching to get back to the hotel. Those last two paintings Dr Shulmann had shown me wouldn't let me alone, and I knew I had to call Sally or change my plane reservations—or both.

Maybe some of it was pity, even though Edgar had said—if not in so many words—that Sally had risen above whatever had caused her to paint those early paintings. Some of it was guilt. But most of it was wanting her, even if only to hear the sound of her voice, even if all she did was cuss me out I just had to hear her, had to know she was all right.

She probably hated me.

That made two of us.

Edgar Shulmann rode down to the lobby with me, then walked me outside. 'Thanks so much for coming, Alex,' he said, as the doorman flagged down a cab. 'I've enjoyed your company.'

We shook hands and I got in the taxi, but before it pulled out into traffic, Edgar rapped on the window. I rolled it down.

'It's none of my business, Alex, but you smoke far too much. Almost a pack just since you got here. If you're interested, my patients have had fairly good results with hypnotism.'

I said, 'Thanks, Edgar. Maybe next time I'm in town?'

He stepped back and I leaned forward, toward the holes in the plastic shield between me and the driver. 'The Plaza Hotel,' I said.

There was one message waiting for me. It was from Ardith, telling me I should phone another of her pet clients, Clark Pembroke, and give him her regards, maybe take him to lunch the next day, if I had time before I left for the airport.

In my room, I sat on the edge of the bed with my hand on the phone for a good five minutes before I picked up the handset. Even then, I didn't know what the hell I'd say once I got Sally on the phone.

It rang maybe ten times before she answered. 'Chips?' she said, in place of hello.

'No, Sally, it's me.'

'Alex.' She didn't sound exactly overwhelmed. She started to say something else, but only got as far as 'I—' Then there was a soft thud, and then a man's voice: 'Sally's busy right now.' There was a click, and then nothing but dial tone.

I stared at it for a second or two, and then I slammed it down into the cradle. I crumpled the message from Ardith and threw it on the floor. Fuck it.

Then I picked up the phonebook and found the listing for the airline.

'I want to change my reservation,' I said, when they finally picked up. 'When's your next flight for Minneapolis?'

20

Sally

'One of your boyfriends, I suppose,' Norman said, as he unplugged the telephone. He tossed it across the room. It hit the wall with a bang and a macabre half-jingle, then clattered to the floorboards. For some idiotic reason I thought, *a hard, yellow sound.*

I picked myself up off the studio floor, where I'd fallen when he'd pushed me, and edged away.

So much for plan B. As Mariah dozed off, I'd excused myself (to get Norman another soda, I'd said), all the while calculating how quickly I could run up the back stairs, grab my purse from my room, then sneak out the back way. So much for that feeble glint of courage, so much for holding my ground: I was going to take the coward's way out and run for it. I wouldn't have my car keys—not without Norman knowing it, since they were on the hall table—but I'd have money for a phone and a cab.

But the tiptoeing son of a bitch had followed me. My elbow and shoulder thudded from the fall I'd taken on the back stairs when he'd kicked my legs out from beneath me, and now red fire shot through my knee. The studio floor was hard.

Norman took a step forward. 'Quit playing around, Sal.' He was smiling, but it was a totally humourless, completely menacing expression.

'Leave me alone, Norman. I'll scream. Mariah'll hear.' I backed up again and felt the corner of the drafting table cut into my side.

'She just slept through the phone. Must've rung a dozen times. She won't hear anything.' He reached toward me. 'I gave her an extra pill. C'mon, Orphan Annie.' He said it the way you might speak to a less-than-favoured dog, a dog that's straining against the leash. 'Let's play doctor.'

I lurched away. The drafting table snagged by sweater and scraped a raw place on my side before I stumbled toward the easel and seized the first thing that came to hand: a clear glass vase stuffed with pink roses.

I don't think he actually expected me to throw them. He didn't even duck. He just said, 'Hey!' and raised his arm, but not quickly enough.

The vase caught him just above the temple, staggering him and sopping his shirt with water. His hand blocked only a few of the flowers, and when he dropped to his knees, three or four were still trapped in his fingers.

I didn't wait to see if he went all the way down. I didn't stop to find my purse. I ran from the studio, down the front stairs, past Aunt Mariah, snoring on her hospital bed, then out to the porch, where I promptly tripped over the cat.

Snarling, 'Jesus!' I caught myself on the porch rail. I thought about giving the cat a good swift kick, but instead I picked it up and ran—limped, really—to the car. It wasn't locked. I crawled in, the cat still in my arms, then locked the doors and slid down in the seat. And waited. I had a good view of the side and front of the house. All the downstairs lights were on, and the Iris Lady on the landing glowed. The house looked far too cheerful, considering what lurked inside it.

It wasn't long before a slow charcoal shadow—Norman, head bent, backing down the last few stairs—crossed the Iris Lady, and a few seconds more before he stepped out on the front porch. He stood beneath the light, his hands clenched into fists at his sides, his head turning slowly as he looked from one end of the street to the other. His breath came from his lips and nostrils in shallow clouds of grey vapour. More vapour rose in wisps from his soaked shirt. Then he twisted to the side and stared directly at the car.

I squirmed down farther into the seat and wished myself invisible, clear as glass with no glints to give me away. I held the cat too tightly to my chest, held my breath.

I saw him mouth the word 'Damn.' Then he turned and went back inside. The door slammed behind him. The outside light flicked off, leaving the porch in cold shadow.

I let myself breathe.

Just another night in the carefree life of the happy French family.

I wished I'd made friends with at least one of my neighbours. Too late for that, though. 'Hi, I'm your neighbour, Sally, and I hope you don't mind if I spend the night on your sofa, because my Cousin Norman's acting up just a teensy bit...'

Right.

There was a convenience store with a pay phone about four blocks away, and I poked through the glove compartment, then felt under the seats, hoping for spare change to make a phone call. I found nothing but a few grimy pennies and half pack of stale cigarettes. I pulled out one and lit it, then rolled down my window a crack and, wincing, stretched my legs across the opposite seat.

My knee ached, my shoulder thumped angrily, and my side, where the drafting table had scraped it, stung with a bright-orange intensity. The cat, at least, seemed comfortable. Purring raspily, he stretched out along the length of my thighs, then twisted sideways, kneading his paws against the seat back. I decided I'd wait until the house lights went out, and then sneak in the back window, get my keys and purse, and go over to Chips' house.

Norman had accomplished what I'd sworn, at least to myself, that he wouldn't. He'd driven me from my own home, chased me into hiding, and reduced me to a child once more.

But it wasn't exactly like old times, because this time I'd hurt him. I'd fought back before, certainly, but always with the knowledge that he'd eventually win; perhaps that was why he always had.

But this time I hadn't frozen. I hadn't choked. I'd not only got away, I'd got in a good lick beforehand. I hoped he had a lump on his head the size of a doorknob. A bright red throbbing one.

He was so cocksure he could do whatever he wanted because he always had. He was so sure I'd never tell because I never had. But this time he was wrong. Because this time, if it came to that, I *would* tell. I'd call the police and holler rape so bloody loud that the rest of the Aunts would hear me all the way back in Kansas and Little Meg and the others would be seized with apoplexy.

The only problem was that I couldn't report it unless it happened, and I'd take whatever measures were necessary to prevent it.

At the moment, I didn't suppose there was anything the police could do. *Officer, he pushed*

261

me around, see this bruise? No, he didn't exactly hit me. Yes, he's a relative, a house guest. No, there were no witnesses. But when I was little—no, it was never reported, there's no record. Yes, it's just my word against his. How long does it take to get a restraining order? That long? Yes, I'll be sure to call you if actually does rape me, and thank you so very fucking much...

I stubbed out my cigarette and lit a new one. It was just as harsh as the one before it; the first drag, too deep, burned the inside of my nose and brought water to my eyes, reminding me I'd once read that cigarettes contain cyanide gas and arsenic. It seemed a happy thought, and I sucked the smoke in greedily. I wondered what colour cyanide gas might be, if one could see it. A sickly yellowed green was what I imagined for the arsenic. Chartreuse.

The cat dozed off, stopping purring. The car windows were fogging over, and I wished I had a jacket. I wished I had a handgun, that was what I really wished. No, I didn't. I knew I couldn't shoot anybody, not really, not even to wound them. Not even Norman.

He'd looked so surprised when that vase, crammed with the last of Alex's roses, had come flying at him. If only it had been an anvil.

I pictured the vase in slow motion, spinning roses over glass, glass over roses, water streaming in loops, spraying droplets as it arced through the air against the backdrop of that purpled, diseased painting on my easel on its way toward Norman's skull. A lovely image: one I was certain I'd treasure forever. My only regret was that I hadn't had the stereo on, because the whole thing should have been choreographed to Wagner.

It had been an interesting way to dispose of the last of Alex. Earlier that day I'd shredded the rest of his roses, petal by petal, and wept while I'd done it. But I wasn't going to cry any more. No more of that maudlin garbage for me. He'd broken my heart, but only because I'd let him get close enough to do it. My fault. *Mea culpa.*

But why, oh why, had he done it?

And why had he called tonight? To gloat? To see how much damage he'd done? To explain why he'd thought it necessary to tell me he needed me, he wanted me, he cared for me, before he crushed me under his heel with that stupid, cruel note?

To tell me he was sorry?

'Doesn't matter,' I whispered to the drowsing cat. 'Too late. We're on our own.'

And then, just when I was absolutely certain I had no more tears left to give to Alex or to myself, they spilled again. I picked up the cat, rousing him from sleep and starting his purr anew, and hugged him to me. I buried my face in his warm fur, and thought how strange that a red cat should smell so sweetly, richly blue-green; pine trees and fresh earth.

'Forty years old,' I whispered against him, once I got my tears under control and could talk without choking. 'Almost forty goddamn years old. You'd think I'd have a handle on some of this crap by now, wouldn't you? But

263

here I sit, locked out of my house and freezing to death in my own driveway with a fleabitten no-name alleycat.'

Eyes slitted, the cat lifted his head and rubbed his face along my jaw. His rumbling purr vibrated against my cheek, my throat, my chest.

'Well, all right,' I added, scratching softly between his shoulder blades with one finger. 'Maybe you're not so fleabitten. If I ever get myself out of this mess, you want to move in?'

He didn't say no.

I settled back to watch the house, to wait until it was safe to go in.

21

Alex

The plane trip felt like it took forever, but it was still dark when I landed in Minneapolis, and not much past five when the taxi dumped me in front of my building.

I was too tired to think, too nerved-up to sleep. I didn't go upstairs. I left my stuff with the doorman and went straight to the parking garage. Twenty minutes later I turned onto Sally's quiet, tree-lined street, still wondering what the hell I was going to say to her at five-thirty in the morning. I didn't know that

264

I'd even have the balls to ring the bell. But I had to go there, even if all I did was sit in the driveway for a few minutes.

I was still disturbed by those early paintings, and by the phone call. I'm ashamed to admit it, but the first thing I thought when that guy hung up on me was that Sally had already replaced me: that she was up there in her bed—*our* bed—with some other guy. I was halfway to the airport before I realized it was only that jerky cousin of hers. She'd probably told him what an idiot I was. He probably thought he was protecting her from me.

I pulled into her driveway and sat in the Caddy, radio off and heater going full bore, while I smoked and looked up at the house and wondered if Cousin Norman was sitting up there in the dark with a shotgun across his knees. The windows, even the tilting wedge of skylight glass at the top of the house, were dark. That skylight would have glowed brightly had she been working in the studio. But there was no sign of life. Everybody was asleep.

I put my hand on the keys to turn off the engine, then hesitated. I doubted she was in any mood for a predawn caller, especially me. I pictured her answering the door, her robe pulled round her, her eyes half-lidded, her beautiful face soft and barely blushed with sleep; and how pissed she'd probably be when she saw it was me standing on her porch. I couldn't for the life of me think what I'd say to her, anyway. How do you begin to apologize to somebody for wounding them so deeply for so little reason?

But just thinking about her, the way she'd look when she came to the door, had me stiff. I scowled at my lap and said, 'Shut up. You're what got me into this mess in the first place.'

I was about to shift into reverse and get the hell out of there when I noticed something moving in the back window of her old Impala, just ahead in the drive. And then I noticed that in addition to being patched with thin veils of frost, the glass was fogged.

The thing in the back window moved again this time rubbing vapour from the glass. The cat.

I cut my motor and stepped out onto the drive. The cold slapped me in the face. Still September and it was already practically arctic at night. Good old Minnesota.

'How'd you get shut in there, cat?' I grumbled, as I reached for the Impala's door pull. I saw Sally at the same moment I realized the door was locked.

I tapped on the glass. 'Sal?' I rubbed frost from the glass with the side of my fist. It melted at my touch and trickled thinly downward. The fog on the inside made her appear a hazy mermaid, underwater, a pasted blur. She was sleeping. I tapped again.

She jerked forward, flailed slightly, and hit the steering wheel with her elbow before she seemed to realize where she was. She turned, pulling her legs off the passenger seat, then straightened to stare at me through the haze. It seemed like a long time before she lifted one hand and wiped at her side of the glass.

'What are you doing out here in the middle of the night, Sally? It's freezing! C'mon, get out. Let's get you warmed up.'

She didn't move.

'Look, I'm sorry. I mean, I'm really sorry about...about what I did. We have to talk. But we can't talk if you've got pneumonia.' Man, I couldn't believe it. I sounded like somebody's mother.

Behind the foggy, half-frosted window she folded her arms and glared at me. 'Go away.' Her voice was muffled, hollow. The cat stepped onto her lap and curled into a ball.

'I won't go away,' I said as evenly as I could, considering my teeth had begun to chatter. 'I'm staying right here until you come out of the damn car and go inside with me.'

Very calmly, she said, 'Go to hell,' and turned her head away.

I stuck my hands under my armpits. 'Sally, God damn it, either come out or let me in. I'm cold.'

She ignored me.

'I said I was sorry, okay? At least give me a chance to explain.'

'Go fuck yourself,' she said flatly, and didn't look at me.

I stamped my feet, and felt my shoes slither a little. The drive was slick with frost, and I thought, *Great, I'm going to slip and crack my skull open, and it's going to be Sally's fault because she won't get out of the frigging car; no, my fault she's locked in there to begin with; no, her fault for being so damn stubborn.*

267

I yanked one hand free of its nice warm berth beneath my armpit; raised it, clenched, over my head; pounded my fist, once, hard, on the roof of the car.

She jumped. The cat leapt off her lap and into the back seat. The *boom* bounced back at me off the dark houses, the night-black trees.

It felt good. I slammed my fist against the roof again, harder than before, and felt the cold, slick metal give, then spring back with an echoing thud.

'God damn it, Sally!' I was yelling then, and it felt good to yell. 'I flew back early because I needed to see you, to explain. But you're beginning to piss me off. I only want to talk—'

She twisted toward me then, her face flushed and hostile, almost wild. Her open hands, pink-palmed, slapped the inside of the glass as she shouted, 'Go away! Leave me some peace!'

I jumped back this time. Anger pushed at the inside of my skull, an anger based in my own impotence and fed by Sally's rage.

I grabbed the door pull and jerked it until the car rocked. 'Come out of there, damn it, or I'll haul you out!'

She turned her back on me. She crossed her arms.

It was as if the frustration and cold and sleeplessness and anger had conspired to shove me out of my body, out of my senses. With absolutely no inkling that I might be doing the wrong thing, or that I should—or could—stop myself, I marched back to the Caddy, opened the trunk, yanked out my jack, marched back to Sally's car, and bashed in her rear passenger window.

Her scream jerked me out of the trance. The jack suddenly seemed too hot to hold, and I threw it down. It clanged on the pavement just as the cat leapt through the hole. He hit my shoulder and used it for enough traction to bank ninety degrees and vault halfway down the drive. He landed running.

Sally was out of the car by then, too.

'Are you *crazy?*' she hissed across the Impala's roof, and glanced at the surrounding houses. Across the street, an upstairs light flicked on. 'Who the hell do you think you are to come over here and—'

'I'm sorry, I'm sorry,' I said, and held up my hands. 'Please, I didn't mean...I just...shit.' I lifted a hand toward the broken window. Little square bits of safety glass sparkled on the drive, made tiny pinpoint prisms across the car seat. 'I'll pay for it,' I added lamely. 'I don't know why—'

'Yes, you do.' She backed away, edged toward the break in the wall where steps led up to the side yard. 'You wanted to see how much damage you'd done. You wanted to see if you could do a little more. To me, to everything. To us. Well, there is no "us" anymore. You saw to that, didn't you? Go away.'

She made it to the steps and up onto the walk. She turned toward the house, so that the dim light from the street lamp touched her profile. She paused.

'Why?' she said, almost whispering. The word was a small perfect puff of vapour, rising from her lips. 'Why did you do it, Alex? Were you laughing at me all along?'

'Laugh at you?' I said softly, incredulously. 'God, Sally, I never meant to hurt you. I was an ass. I...we have to talk. We have to straighten this out. You don't know what I've been going through.'

Very slowly, she turned and looked down at me, her face expressionless. And then she laughed. It was like no laugh I'd heard come from her before. This had no music, no magic, no humour. It sounded dead, hollow.

'So I don't know what you've been through,' she said, her tone mocking, almost cruel. 'Been through a lot, have you, Alex? Has big old nasty Life been mean to you? What's the trauma? Did they give the poor baby regular peanuts instead of honey-roasted on the plane? Oh, Life is wicked to Alex, isn't it? Bad, bad Life! Shall we spank its hands?'

Before I could stop myself, I'd taken a step toward her. 'Bitch,' I spat, then hated myself. She had every right to be nasty to me just for that stupid note, and on top of that, I'd just caved in her car window and more than likely scared her to death. Nearly scared myself to death, too. But it was too late to apologize, because she turned on her heel and ran down the side yard, toward the back of the house.

'Sally, please!'

She didn't stop. All that remained were her footprints on the barely frosted lawn, melted dark into the silver by the friction of her passing.

I sat in the Caddy for several minutes before I started her up and backed out onto the street.

It was botched, totally botched. If I had deliberately set out to ruin everything, I couldn't have done a better job of it.

Congratulations, Alex, you've won our grand prize! Yes, that's right—a lifetime of remorse and self-recrimination, all expenses paid! And thank you for playing Wreck Your Life!

Cursing under my breath, hating myself, I lit another cigarette and drove aimlessly down the side streets. I didn't feel like going home. I was too sad to sleep, too tired to dream.

Maybe I *had* been better off with Colette or Nancy or even Suzanne: at least I'd never been this shook up—this totally messed up, screwed up, devastated—over any of them, not at the best times, not at the rock-bottom worst.

I must have driven for at least half an hour, because it was just coming dawn when I found myself in front of Peaches' house. I set the brake, then rubbed my hands over my face.

Well, what the hell.

This time I grabbed a jacket out of the back seat before I cut the motor and got out. The rising sun hadn't brought along any of the prettier hues of morning. The yellowing trees looked anaemic and sooty under a sky the colour of a dirty nickel. It fit my mood perfectly.

Collar up, shoes grating on the damp pavement, I walked up the drive.

It took Peaches almost five minutes to answer the door, and when he did, he didn't look very happy about it. 'Jesus Christ, Alex,' were his first words. 'Do you have any idea what *time* it is?'

I just said, 'Could I come in?'

He pursed his lips and arched a brow, then stepped back and swung the door wide.

'What ran over you, dear boy?' he said, not unkindly, as I followed him back to the kitchen. He snapped on the lights, plugged in the coffeemaker, and yawned. 'You look dreadful.'

I sank into a chair and propped my elbows on the kitchen table. Peaches' kitchen was far too bright and gleaming for somebody as tired and filled with self-loathing as I was. Everything was white or chrome or both. My head sank, and I ran my fingers through my hair.

Something beeped: the microwave, I guessed. A few seconds later Peaches slid a clear glass plate under my nose. There was a hot pastry on it.

'Cheese croissant,' he said. 'Eat it right now, young man. It'll keep your strength up until I can make you something a little more fortifying.'

'Sorry,' I said, staring at the plate. 'I'm not hungry. I shouldn't have bothered you. I'll go home, let you go back to bed. We can talk later.' I started to push myself away from the table, but felt Peaches' hand on my shoulder.

'Child, child, child,' he said, as he dropped into the chair beside me. 'What could possibly...? Dear Lord, that bitch Ardith didn't fire you,

272

did she? If that's what it is, don't you worry, because—'

'No, no, she... It's not that, it's—' I covered my face with my hands, because I didn't want him to see that I was crying like some little kid, and then I couldn't quit. I think Peaches rubbed my shoulders. I know he gave me a handkerchief after I'd used mine up. All it did was humiliate me that much more, and I could not, no matter how hard I tried, stop bawling.

Finally I got myself calmed down a little. I felt eviscerated, not to mention ridiculous. Gutless dolt, that's me. I couldn't look Peaches in the eye. I was supposed to be this big deal, hotshot professional, the boy wonder of the art biz; not some mixed-up, lovesick baby. And lovesick, I realized, was just what I was. For better or worse. Worse, at the moment.

'I think we'd better talk, son,' Peaches said quietly, as he handed me yet another handkerchief. God only knew where he was finding them. Each one was perfectly ironed and creased.

I heard approaching footsteps echoing through the dining room, and thought, *Great, just great, now Anthony's going to see me like this, too.* But Peaches must have read my mind, because he gave a tug to my sleeve.

'Come along. There's much too much glare in this kitchen for a heart-to-heart. *Mano a mano.* For that, we need natural light, cigarettes, and coffee. Possibly whiskey. You know, something incredibly butch. Too bad I don't have a stuffed moosehead somewhere...'

I followed him along a short hall to the little office he kept at the back of the house, and after I shoved aside the couch's clutter of papers and art books, I plopped down. I felt like I'd been dragged behind a truck for ten blocks.

'Don't move,' Peaches said sternly, as if I could have, then slipped back out the door. I heard the murmur of voices and the distant rattle of crockery, and then he reappeared with a carafe of coffee.

He poured out two cups and shoved one at me, along with an ashtray, before he reached into his robe's pocket and pulled out a pint bottle of Irish whiskey. 'Ran out of hands,' he explained, as he poured a dollop into my cup. Then he sat down behind his desk, leaned back in his chair, and quietly said, 'All right, son. Start at the beginning.'

About the time I finished, there was a small knuckly rap at the door. 'Baldwin?' It was Anthony.

He didn't come in, bless him. I suppose he figured I'd already filled to overflowing my humiliation quota for the day. All I saw of him were his arms as he handed Peaches a tray with two plates of scrambled eggs, a small rack of toast, and two tall glasses of orange juice. The door closed, and he scuffed away down the hall.

'Well,' Peaches said around a mouthful of eggs, 'I must say, you've fouled it up beautifully. As far as unnecessary theatrics go, you've brought it up to nearly my level. Although

274

mine, mind you, are *far* more entertaining. Poor Sally.' He shook his head. 'A jack through her car window. Really, Alex. It's so...blue collar.'

I laced my hands behind my neck and propped my elbows on my knees. I didn't feel worthy of ever again looking up from the floor.

'Oh, for God's sake,' Peaches mumbled. 'Quit feeling sorry for yourself and eat your eggs. You know very well that Anthony doesn't cook very often, and he is decidedly unamused by those who don't appreciate it when he does.'

I made myself pick up my fork and shove a bite of eggs into my mouth. They were pretty good, actually.

'So what are you going to do about it?'

Chewing, I shook my head. 'I don't know.'

'Well, you'd better think of something, dear heart. If you want her back, that is.' He laid his fork aside and folded his hands. 'Do you?'

'Want her back?'

'No,' he said frowning. 'Do you want to take up nude mud wrestling. What did you think?'

'I don't know. I mean, I do—God, yes, I do. More than anything. But there's the age thing. And we've led such different lives...' I hadn't mentioned the boyfriends, or that turnstile I'd imagined at her bedroom door, or Bob Daws with his red jacket and middle-aged paunch and wink-nudge.

'Well, pardon me all to hell, Alex, but bullshit.'

'Huh?' I hoped he wasn't going to give me one of those naive little goody-goody lectures about love conquering all, the way Stephie had.

'Alex, you really are incredibly dense. At the risk of sounding trite, dear boy, nothing worthwhile is easy. What do you expect from a relationship anyway. All Barry Manilow and flowers? There's something called depth, boy, and you have to fight for that. I don't mean depth of passion or feeling, I mean depth of understanding. And if you don't have that, about all you've got is a hot date for the prom.'

'But Peaches—'

He waved a hand. 'Don't "but" me, I'm on a roll. You've as much as said you love her. Do you?'

I looked away and heard myself answer, very quietly, 'Yes.'

'And what does that mean to you, Alex? Let's find out just how big a boy you really are. Does it mean that she'll look pretty on your arm and make you some brownie points with Ardith and our provincial little art crowd? Does it mean you've got the hots for her talent? Dear Lord, that's nothing so unusual. She's a fucking genius, if you'll pardon my Frog. It's a well-known fact that, romantically speaking, I've no time for persons of the female persuasion; but I'd crawl naked inside one of her paintings and live there forever if I could conjure my way in.'

He poured himself another cup of coffee and added a shot of whiskey. 'Or maybe this passion of yours is the kind of love with an eye to the future. Maybe twenty years from now you'd like to be mentioned in biographies as her onetime paramour. Perhaps you envision Sally as the new Georgia O'Keefe, and yourself in the role of Juan?'

He sipped his coffee, then gestured widely with one hand. 'What do you mean by love, anyway, Alex? Is it that the sex is so hot your cock spends more time up than down? That's not love, boy, that's being twenty-two! Does love mean you've got a romantic crush on the *idea* of her, and the scent of her perfume starts you thinking in snippets of Shelley or Keats? Does it mean you think of her every time you hear a certain song, or that you like her bone structure, or that she laughs at your jokes and you're grateful for the audience?' He paused. 'Or does it mean you'd die for her?'

I stared past him, out the window. The frost was gone. The sun was up. One of the trees in the back yard sported three scarlet leaves mixed with the green. I said, 'Maybe all of it.'

'Then what's the problem, other than this little fiasco of misunderstandings you've managed to create out of thin air? Honestly, David Copperfield couldn't have done it better, Alex.' He waved an imaginary wand over the desk top. 'Abracadabra! Disaster! Really, dear boy, don't you think a live elephant would have been easier? And less messy?'

I lit another cigarette. 'There's the age thing.' I barely had the smoke out through my nose before I sucked down the second drag. 'Almost eighteen years, Peaches. A generation.'

He crumpled his napkin and dropped it on his plate. 'Well, aren't you the little snob! *Merde!* I never would have imagined it. I suppose if you were forty and *she* was twenty-two, it'd be perfectly all right.'

I said, 'That's different,' and knew it was ridiculous even as the words escaped my mouth. 'No,' I backpedalled. 'I know. I just can't make it click in my head. I keep picturing myself introducing her to my mother...'

He nodded. 'I see. You're ashamed of Sally.'

'Of course not!'

'You're ashamed of your mother?'

'Aw jeez, Peaches, you're twisting it all—'

'No. *I'm* not the one who has it twisted. I never dreamt you were quite so conventional, Alex.'

I couldn't think of a thing to say. Conventional? Me? I supposed I was, looking back on my life so far. But I'd never, until just then, seen myself in that light. I wasn't sure I liked it. In fact, I found it offensive.

Peaches stood up. 'When was the last time you slept?'

I shook my head. 'Yesterday morning.'

'Got up early, I suppose, on New York time?'

I ignored the question. 'It's not the age thing,' I said slowly, and stubbed out my cigarette. 'Not really. You're right, I guess. I mean, I guess maybe I am sort of conventional. But that part was just...'

I shrugged. I had one of those overwhelming feelings of dread, the kind you get when you're

278

pretty certain the universe is going to hand you a revelation you're not sure you're ready for. It crawled up over me like static electricity. It scared me. It made me mad.

'That part was just what?' He was going to make me say it.

'An excuse.' I felt my hand, all on its own, curl up into a fist.

He perched on the edge of his desk. 'Keep going.' When I didn't say anything, he added, 'You know, dear heart, it's not nearly so much fun for me if you don't say it out.'

'Damn it!' I shouted, at the same moment I realized I was on my feet and that I'd balled my hands into fists. 'Enough. Knock it off. I don't want to talk about it anymore, okay?'

He just sat there. He looked pretty calm, but his face had changed. The softness and joviality drained away, leaving him hard-looking, almost steely, and he suddenly seemed less like a surrogate mother and more like somebody who might just slug me back. Hard.

'What's the matter, Alex, are we getting too close to it? We're not talking about Sally here at all, are we? We're talking about how sorry you feel for yourself. Got yourself tangled up with a real live grownup this time, didn't you? Other end of the scale from that petty little flake Suzanne, or the one before, what's-her-name. You've always been the mature one before, haven't you, Alex? You've always been the guiding force, the one with the experience, the one with the polish, the one with a history. Well, surprise!'

279

'Peaches—'

'Shut up. I suspect there's more to this than you're telling me. I suspect you think you're being a gentleman about it. Fine, be that way.' He laced his fingers together and tapped the thumbs. 'The whole point is that you got scared and you panicked and you took it out on her. And now you're all sorry and pathetic. Get over it, Alex. Either fix it or don't, but take a goddamn stand and quit whining. It's boring.'

His eyes flicked down to my fists, then back up. 'What are you going to do, hit me? Seems rather pointless, doesn't it, when I'm not the one you really want to hit?'

I made myself relax my hands. As much as I hated to admit it, he was right: right about everything. And I guess if I went around punching myself every time I did something stupid or annoying, I'd spend most of my time unconscious.

I walked to the window, took a deep breath. 'Sorry.'

'I should hope so. You broke one of Anthony's mother's cups.'

It lay behind me on the floor, shattered. I hadn't heard it, hadn't noticed. 'Sorry,' I said numbly, and bent down.

'Leave it,' he said and waved me away. 'They're ugly cups, anyway. Go back to your excuse.'

I combed my hair back with my fingers. 'Look, I'm tired. You made your point. I don't want to talk about this any more.'

'Alex...' He said it like a schoolteacher who's

about to give you detention if you don't immediately cough up the capital of Rhode Island.

'All right, damn it. The age thing, the years between us. You're right. That—and yes, there was other stuff, too—was an excuse to...to avoid putting everything on the line. I wimped out.'

Peaches leaned forward slightly, his brows raised in impatience. He made a little 'hurry up' sign with his hand. For a second I wished I really had slugged him.

'It scared me, okay?' I announced suddenly, too loudly. 'You happy? I fell so damn hard for her that it scared the crap out of me. And yes, I still love her. I want to see her and hold her and breathe the same air she's breathed. I want to walk through rooms she's walked through. I want to hear her voice in the dark and wake up beside her every goddamn morning for the rest of my life. I never felt that way about anybody before, not even close, and it terrified me. Still does. And yes, self-pity is exactly what I've been wallowing in, and the whole time I've been disgusted with myself. And yeah, yeah: you're brilliant. Satisfied?'

The son of a bitch grinned at me. 'Oh, that's *much* better! Especially the "brilliant" part. Alex, today you are a man. My God, I think there's a painting title in this! *Epiphany at Peaches'*. You like? Fabulous alliterative ring, hasn't it? I must ask Sally if she can come up with something wonderful...'

I slumped back on the couch and lit another cigarette. I grumbled, 'How have you lived this

281

long without somebody murdering you?'

'Because I only pounce upon my unsuspecting prey when they are emotionally exhausted and suffering from sleep deprivation. Speaking of which...' He hopped off the desk, then picked up my dirty dishes and stacked them with his own. 'I insist,' he said as he bent to gather up pieces of broken cup, 'that you stretch out on that couch and go to sleep. Immediately.'

'But what am I going to do about—'

'No arguments. I've got nothing planned for today but puttering. I can call you at about noon, if you want, or later. You can sleep there all day, as far as I'm concerned. Do you need to check in with Ardith?'

'Noon's fine,' I said, moving the last of the papers and books so I could put my feet up. Something was still bothering me, something other than the contents of Peaches' lecture or my own embarrassing epiphany. Something we'd both glossed over, something I should be taking care of or looking into. I just couldn't think what it was.

'I can call Ardith later,' I said. My bones seemed to weigh a thousand pounds, almost as much as my eyelids. 'Thanks, Peaches. For everything.'

'You don't mean that now,' he said kindly, as he slipped out the door, 'but you will later, after you have a chance to think about it.'

I bunched up the throw pillows beneath my head, and as I gratefully closed my eyes, I heard Peaches, down the hall.

'Honestly, Anthony, you're not going off to

282

class like that! Go up and get the dark blue tie with the little black figures—the Ralph Lauren I got you for your birthday. And for God's sake, let *me* tie it this time!'

22

Sally

The window was balky from the chill, but finally it slid up almost soundlessly and let me slip inside the conservatory. Surrounded by the walls of my little Victorian hothouse, I flicked the switch for the hidden spotlights, turned the dimmer down low, then sat sideways on the wrought-iron loveseat and pulled my knees up under my chin.

Water trickled in the fountain. Ferns, ficus, rubber trees; arrowheads, pothos, the big fiddleleaf fig, the queen palms: all spread green, pampered leaves, moist with the artificial dew of misters, lush from applications of organic fertilizers and scientifically calculated water allotments. No plague of grasshoppers, no drought or flood or frost would intrude upon them here. Perfect warmth, nourishment, and humidity was theirs behind a prison of insulated glass.

I didn't suppose they cared.

I did, though. It was time to break free of my own prison.

If only I could figure out how to do it. It seemed I kept making my jails smaller and smaller, always thinking I'd locked the world out, that I was safe. But I was no longer certain what constituted safety. At any rate, if such a condition existed, I couldn't seem to find it.

Something had happened to me when Alex bashed in my car window. I'd been startled, then scared, then furious; now, as I sat in the warmth, arms wrapped round my legs, I began to see that act as a symbol. He'd been angry at something bigger than my refusal to come out of the car. That violent tantrum, I had just realized, was not so much *at* me as *because* of me.

There was a world of difference.

You don't know what I've been through, he'd said. And that had shocked me more than the broken window, angered me almost more than his note had wounded me.

Just what the hell could he possibly have been through?

I didn't know.

I had no way of knowing, because I hadn't let him tell me, any more than I'd confided in him about Norman and Mariah and the tangled mess I'd allowed them to make of my life.

I had no moral right to detest him for not understanding my situation, because I hadn't made the slightest attempt to find out about, or understand, his.

He had betrayed me, yes. Perhaps, in a much more devious and passive way, I'd done the same to him.

284

Too late to fix it.

I tucked my chin, balanced my forehead on my knees, and willed myself not to cry while I tried to think what to do next. I heard movements coming from the front room and froze, then relaxed; it was nothing more than the rustle of bedclothes and the creak of the hospital bed. Mariah must be awake, which would temporarily solve the problem of Norman. He'd never tried anything within her immediate sight or earshot, and I doubted he'd start now.

'Norman!' she called a moment later. 'What was all that noise a few minutes ago? What time is it?' Those sleeping pills might have knocked her out in a hurry, but judging from her voice, they'd worn off clean and clear.

When he didn't answer directly, she shouted, 'Norman, get up! I need you to help me to the potty!'

Overhead, a muffled thud, then the creak of a floorboard, followed by Norman's sleepy voice. 'Coming Mom.'

He'd slept upstairs then, instead of on the couch. I wondered if he'd slept in my room, if he'd laid in wait for me. The thought of him touching my sheets made me want to vomit.

A few moments later, the upstairs toilet flushed. I stood slowly, favouring the knee I'd banged on the stairs the night before, and turned off the lights. When I heard Norman start backing heavily down the front staircase, I slipped through the dining room and kitchen, then up the back steps to the studio.

The floor was scattered with broken glass and roses, interspersed with small puddles of water. Biting my lip, I edged around the mess and went to my bedroom.

Norman had been busy. My bed didn't look mussed—he must have slept in the guest room, after all—but the little lock was gone from my bedroom door. There was nothing left above the knob but two raw screw holes and the faint shadow, edged with newer varnish of the place the lock plate had been.

Damn him, anyway.

I grabbed a change of clothes, found my purse, pulled out Chips' pills, then tipped one into my palm. I stared at it for a few seconds, then put it back in the bottle.

What good were they doing me, anyway? Just another illusion of safety.

The bathroom door, at least, still had its lock firmly attached. I latched it behind me, piled the clean clothes on the hamper, ran a bath, and stripped. I found a nice big bruise, pinkish-blue and darkening, on my knee. The scrape I'd taken from the drafting table stung my side when I settled down into the water. I leaned back, gazed upward through the shower ring toward the ceiling, and let my vision slip comfortably out of focus.

It wasn't long before Norman banged on the door. I'd been expecting him.

'Where've you been?' he demanded from the other side.

'Out,' I said, and lifted one hand from the water long enough to shoot him the bird. He couldn't see it, but it made me feel better.

'Been to your room yet?'

I closed my eyes. 'Go away.

Thinly, I heard Mariah. 'Who are you talking to? Is Sally up? I'm hungry.'

Softly, as if his face was pressed to the door, Norman said, 'I won't go far, Orphan Annie. You can count on that. And I'm sorry about last night, Sal. I just figured you felt the same way I did. You didn't have to throw that vase at me, all you had to say was *no*. I left you a present. In your underwear drawer.' As my arms broke out in gooseflesh, he added more loudly, 'She's up, Mama. I'll come fix you some oatmeal.'

A few seconds later I heard him slowly clumping—backward, no doubt, and holding tight to the banister—down the front stairs.

I got out of the tub, gave myself a rough towelling, and dressed hurriedly. He'd been in my things. How much damage had he done?

In my room, I yanked open my underwear drawer. Earlier, I'd barely opened it far enough to snag a fresh bra and panties. Now I began to sort through it gingerly. My fingers touched something alien, and I lifted it from beneath several layers of lingerie.

And dropped it.

And stepped away quickly, hugging myself as through clenched teeth I repeated, 'Jesus, Jesus...'

It was a mousetrap, and there was a dead mouse caught in it.

Below, Norman called, 'Bacon or sausage, Mama?'

Mariah opted for sausage.

'Poor mouse, poor mouse,' I whispered, and made myself lift the trap from its cushion of underthings. In the bathroom, I carefully pried back the spring and let the tiny carcass—sleek, silver, and broken—drop into the toilet. I flushed it down. A burial at sea.

Slowly, I walked to the studio, the trap still dangling from my fingers. I dropped it in the wastebasket and began mechanically to clear the rubble from the floor.

Broken roses, broken glass.

Poor mouse.

I supposed I could just move in with Chips, or maybe into a hotel, until they left. Provided they *ever* left.

I swept up the last of the glass, blotted the last of the water, plugged the phone back in.

Poor mouse.

I wished I had a big rat trap. Big enough for a big fat rat, just Norman's size.

The phone rang.

'Sal?' It was Chips. She was crying. She sounded very small, not like herself at all.

'Chips, are you all right?'

A muffled brush of something against the receiver. 'Sal, I...' She stopped, choking slightly.

'Chips, where are you? What is it?'

I heard her suck in air: a strangled sound. Then, 'Oh, Sally, my papa's dead.'

Chips didn't live far from Lake of the Isles, and after I'd hugged her—and briefly explained how most of my car window had come to be strewn across on my back seat in small fragments—we drove several blocks, then walked down to the thin, grassy strip of park along the shore.

Despite the depressing qualities others may ascribe to it, blue has always been to me a wise but cheerful colour, clear-thinking and infinite. It is the colour of thought and air and infinity, or so I had always imagined. But on this morning there was no hopeful blue above or below. The sky, and the lake reflecting it, were a dingy, clouded grey, shading from dirty pearl to gunmetal with not the slightest relief that might have been provided by a patch of azure or cerulean.

The deep chill of early morning was for the most part gone, but we both wore pullovers: hers navy, mine beige. There were no children or dogs bounding along the sidewalk as there would have been in summer, and the park was for the most part deserted. A light breeze played across the shore and water, but only one sailor rode the lake. His sail was bright crimson. Against the pewter distance it seemed a bobbing, mobile wound.

'Sorry,' Chips said again, and pulled a fresh tissue from her pocket. 'I'll stop crying any time now, promise.'

I steered her toward a bench, then brushed away the fallen leaves. Three brown and crackly; two yellow, still soft. 'Let's sit down for a while.'

Chips blew her nose. Her face was drawn, bloodless. She'd lost weight over the past few days, I suddenly realized. Her cheeks were hollow, her reddened eyes sunken, her brow lined where lines had never been. Even her strong sculptor's hands seemed bony and frail, not her hands at all.

'I don't understand why they didn't see it coming,' she said thickly, and not for the first time. 'They had him hooked to all those machines and tubes. What good are they? Why did they have to put him through that when it didn't matter a damn anyway? Just last night they said he was better. Better than what? He died, damn it. Screw doctors.'

She slouched down on the bench, stuck her legs out straight, then let her head flop all the way back, exposing the whole of her long, slender throat to the grey heavens as if she were daring God to cut it and end her misery. Eyes closed, she added, 'Screw 'em all.'

'Chips, I'm so sorry.' I'd said it so many times in the past half hour that it had ceased to have meaning, but I didn't know what else to say.

She didn't move, didn't open her eyes. 'Yeah. We're all sorry. All but Pops. I don't suppose he cares, now.' She sat up suddenly, startling me. 'He hasn't cared—hadn't known what to care about, anyway—for years.' She turned toward me. 'You suppose he's with Mom? Do you believe in any of that?'

I looked away. She was too needy; I was wrung out, with nothing more to give than what I'd already offered. I said, 'I don't know.'

She sat back again. 'Nobody knows shit. We all just walk around down here, stumbling and bumping into each other and trying to do the least possible damage, and then they stick tubes into us and we're gone.' She stopped, then barked out one soft, sharp, hollow laugh. 'Life's pointless, and then you linger.'

I took a deep breath. 'Chips, I'm sorry Pops died. I feel really bad for you, and I know you're hurting right now. But you're not having such a bad life, you know? You have good times to remember. You had years and years with Pops that were great. You ought to be grateful for that. You ought to remember the happy stuff. Some people don't have it so great, you know. I—I mean, some people—'

I stopped myself. I couldn't believe what had just come out of my mouth, and the time I'd picked to say it. I'd have given anything to take those words back.

Chips' lips pressed together. She sat forward slowly. I held my breath. The tissue dropped from her hand to the yellowing grass before the breeze took it down over the sidewalk, across the narrow strip of beach, to the water's edge. She stared at her hands. I couldn't see her face.

'Poor Sally,' she said softly, at last. 'Poor little Sally, the perpetual victim.' She twisted her head to stare at me, her eyes narrowed. 'My father just died, damn it. I'm allowed to be maudlin. I'm allowed to grieve. I'm allowed to feel sorry for myself, okay? Life, or God, or Fate—whatever you want to call it—just up and did this to me and to Pops, and there's not a damn thing I can do to fix it. You think I don't know your life has been crap?'

'Chips, I—'

'Sally, *everybody's* life is crap. Everybody's lousy family is dysfunctional. I don't care if they beat you or raped you or ignored you or didn't put enough goddamn whipped cream on your goddamn hot fudge Sunday. I'm not saying that what happened to you wasn't despicable. What I *am* saying is that everybody's got *something.* Jesus, you watch those talk shows like they were Holy Scripture. Haven't you learned anything? What am I gonna to have to do, have Oprah phone your *personally?'*

I started to stand up, to run away, but she grabbed my wrist and hauled me back down on the bench. 'You gonna hide from me now, too, Sal?' she shouted. 'You're so goddamn smart, but you just can't get this figured out, can you?'

'Chips, stop!' I tried to pull away again, but her fingers dug more deeply into my wrist and I fell from the bench, landing on my knees in damp grass.

'You can't spend the rest of your life expecting somebody to save you or protect you or shelter you from the crap, because it happens all the time. There's an unending *rain* of it, a friggin' deluge, and it falls on everybody. The difference is that most people just smack it out of the way and keep on going, but all your life you've just hid under your desk, like that old "duck and cover" movie they used to show us in grade school. Well, that little hiding place isn't any more shelter from life than from nuclear attack, baby. And you've been under there for what, three decades? The crap's piled so high you can't see past it.'

I twisted against her grip; her nails cut into my wrist. Cold wet earth soaked the knees of my jeans. 'Chips! Please...'

She didn't seem to hear me. She leaned forward, her eyes dilated and locked on mine, her voice low again, almost eerie in its evenness. 'You gotta dig your own way out, Sal. You've got to do it yourself. Everybody else is too busy with their own shovel. OK, bad stuff happened to you when you were a kid. You couldn't do anything about it then. You were scared. Nobody believed you. And it wasn't your fault. I know that; you know it, too. But damn it, you're not a kid now, you're a grown woman, and you're letting those assholes from Kansas run you out of your house. Would have served you right if Norman *had* caught you last night.'

I gasped, and she stopped, immediately losing my wrist and grasping my hand with both of hers.

'Oh, Sally.' Horror twisted her features. 'I didn't mean that last part. I really, really didn't meant it.'

I looked away, leaned back on my heels, and rubbed my wrist. One tear spattered on my thigh and soaked an irregular blotch, small and dark, into my jeans. I hadn't realized I was crying. I said, 'I know, Chips. It's okay.'

'No, it's not.' She sat back, rooting in her pocket until she produced more tissues. 'Why are you on the ground?' She handed a couple to me, then blew her nose on another as I got to my feet and brushed muddy grass from my knees. 'I wish that just once you'd get mad, Sally,' she said softly, after I sat beside her again. 'All right, maybe not at me, but at *them*. Mad enough to actually *do* something about it, I mean.'

I wiped my eyes. 'Do what? Nothing I can do.'

'See?' she half-shouted, and I cringed. 'There you go again! Of course there's something you can do. Outside of acts of God, there's *always* something you can do. You can't talk a flood out of happening, you can't take an earth quake to court, you can't keep an old man from—' She stopped, biting at her lips. 'You can't keep an old man from dying. But you can, by God, get those people out of your house!'

'She has a broken leg,' I began, feebly.

'Big deal. She's not in traction, is she?'

'Well, no, but—'

'So why the hell can't she get on an airplane?'

I shrugged. 'Norman said that the doctor said—'

Her snort cut me off. 'Norman. Bah. Probably a lie, but we'll give him the benefit of the doubt. She rode in a car to get from the hospital to your place, didn't she?'

I nodded.

'All right. That establishes that the bitch can travel by land. Send them to a motel. Change your locks. Unplug your phone. Get rid of them. Get a restraining order to keep them away, if you have to, but get them the hell out of there.

294

You can work on the other stuff later. Like Alex, for instance.'

I wadded my tissues into a ball and made a fist around them. 'That's over.'

She glanced past me, up toward the parking lot and my car. 'He flew back from New York in the middle of the night, drove to your house at the crack of dawn, and then did that—' she waved at the broken window, '—because you wouldn't talk to him. Doesn't sound real resolved to me.'

She leaned back again, pursing her lips before she spoke again, this time more softly. 'I'll tell you the truth, kiddo. When you took up with that guy I gave you a bad time, but I really thought it was the best thing I'd ever known you to do for yourself. You took a chance. You put your butt out there. So he screwed up. You probably did, too. Maybe it's fixable, maybe not. But you won't know unless you give it a chance, right?'

We sat quietly for several minutes. I lit a cigarette, took one puff, then ground it out. Chips watched the sailboat. I said, 'Has Eric been around?'

She snorted softly. 'I suppose you could say that. He was around long enough to decide I wasn't any fun anymore. The creep swiped the emergency money—two hundred bucks and change—out of my cookie jar. You know, the Salvador Dali thingie shaped like a drippy clock? And I haven't seen him since.'

'Oh, Chips...' I touched her arm, but she shrugged my hand away.

'Just more crapola. Well, there wasn't much emotion invested there, at least. More like entertainment, as if all of a sudden you couldn't get HBO anymore and you'd just got used to it. The money pisses me off, though.'

She stood up and stretched. 'Take me home, would you, Sal? I'm lousy company, and you've got stuff to do. Besides, I wanna go out to the studio and beat up some clay or something.'

As we started up the slope to the car, she said gently, 'I was there with him. When he died, you know? I was holding his hand. And right before he went, he knew who I was. First time in years. He looked at me, and he smiled, just like his old smile, and he said my name. Just once.'

A small sob escaped her. We stopped walking, and I put my arm around her shoulders. 'I'm glad, Chips.'

'Just once was enough, you know?'

'I know.'

She wiped her eyes with the back of her hand, then found her cigarettes.

'Chips?' I asked after she'd lit one. 'I always wondered...what's your real name, anyhow?'

A small smile flickered at the corners of her mouth. 'Promise you won't tell?'

'Scout's honour.'

'Not anyone?'

I made an X over my heart.

She let out a long stream of smoke and stared off into the distance, toward that little red sail wobbling slowly across the lake. 'It's Alice. Alice Abigail Quincannon. Repeat it and die, White Eyes.'

I didn't go straight home. I drove to one of those windshield glass places, thinking I'd make an appointment to get the car window replaced; but they were having a slow day and took me right away.

The man who came to the desk had *Steve* embroidered on his breast pocket. 'Prob'ly 'bout an hour,' he said, as he typed something into his computer. The keyboard had one of those plastic skins on it, and it was filthy. He stared at the screen. 'Maybe an hour and a half. We got 'er in stock at the warehouse, but somebody's gotta find 'er and run 'er over here before we can install 'er.'

'Fine,' I said. 'I'll wait.'

I made myself as comfortable as I could in what passed for their customer lounge, and wondered why anyone would think of glass as 'her.'

That wasn't all I thought about, though. Chips had said some pretty harsh things to me, but she was right. As much as it had hurt me to hear it, I wished she'd said it years before. I should have been smart enough, or gathered enough perspective, to see it all on my own. I supposed my only excuse was that I'd started out as a victim and got used to it. It was a stupid excuse, but it was the only one I had handy.

And I'd been edging toward the light, I supposed, one tiny, hesitant, shambling step at a time, for a while already. After all, I hadn't let Norman run me completely away the night before. I'd stayed in my own driveway.

I laughed out loud, then covered my mouth, even though nobody was there to hear me. I'd slept in my car, frozen half to death, and thought it was an improvement? All right, it wasn't the height of bravery. But at least I hadn't sat out there waiting for Alex or John Wayne or Chips to save me. I'd known then that it was up to me to save myself. I just hadn't known how to do it.

Chips was right. I *could* get rid of them. The question was, how could I do it in the least traumatic way?

I turned this over in my head for a half hour or so, concocting plans, shelving them, thinking up new ones. And then I hit on a strategy that was beautiful in it's simplicity. A wonderful idea. The kind that Hayley Mills, in *The Trouble with Angels,* always called 'a scathing brilliant idea.'

I stuck my head out into the service bay. Steve still hadn't got to my car. He was working on a Buick, tamping the chromed guard around a newly installed rear window with a big mallet. The other workman—a huge-bellied, ponytailed guy who looked like a retired Hell's Angel—had hold of some machine that made a terrible racket and vibrated the walls as well as the tatoos on his enormous bare arms.

Why doesn't Norman ever piss off somebody like that? I thought, before I called, 'Excuse me?' over the noise.

Steve put down his mallet and came toward

298

me. He pulled his safety glasses off 'Ma'am?'

'I see you have a pay phone out here, but there aren't any books. Do you have a Yellow Pages I could borrow?'

23

Alex

Somebody was running a vacuum upstairs. I sat up awkwardly, then twisted my head in a stiff circle before I stretched my arms and worked my knee back and forth. It didn't want to bend all the way.

A short couch isn't the best place for a long person to sleep.

The digital clock on the shelf behind the desk read 11.05. Terrific. Three hours' sleep. Or was it only two? I wasn't certain what time Peaches had stopped playing Dr Freud and let me doze off. Well, a nap was better than nothing at all.

Pausing with every other step to alternately shake out my right knee and swivel my left shoulder in its socket, I hobbled to the desk and picked up the phone, then put it back down. What was I going to say to her? *Sorry I broke your window. Sorry I broke your life. Wanna kiss and make up, baby?*

Yeah, right.

But I had to hear her voice and know she was all right. It didn't matter if she cussed me out. It didn't matter if she hung up on me. Why the hell had she been sleeping in her car last night? What could have possibly chased her out of her house?

I grabbed the phone again and hurriedly dialled Sally's number, messed up on the sixth digit, and had to redial, and all the time I was thinking, *Answer, answer, answer...*

The phone didn't pick up until the ninth ring, and by then I'd been pacing on my knee enough that the kink was gone.

'Hello?' A man's voice. The guy who'd slammed the phone down on me before. Cousin Norman the Watchdog, no doubt.

'Good morning,' I said it as politely as I could, which was not very. 'I'd like to speak to Sally, please.'

'Not here.'

My free hand balled into a fist. It was getting to be a habit. 'Would you know when she might be back, or where I could reach her? This is her gallery calling. It's important.' When he didn't answer right away, I said, 'Hello? Are you there? This is the Ardith Crawford Gallery calling.'

'Yeah,' he said finally. 'I heard you. She's not—'

Peaches' phone beeped.

'You've got a call,' Norman said.

'This is more important. I need to speak to Miss French.' The other line beeped again.

'She's not here. I don't where she is or when she's going to be back. You'll have to take your chances like the rest of us, Sunny Jim.' He didn't say goodbye, just broke the connection.

I slid the handset into its cradle and it immediately jangled under my hand. I sat down behind the desk and rubbed at my face. My head seemed stuffed with soggy felt, my neck ached, and I don't want to tell you what my mouth tasted like. I would have given almost anything for a shower, and more than that for a toothbrush.

The phone rang again, then stopped. I supposed Peaches had picked it up.

With my footsteps clicking on the polished wood and echoing down the wainscoted hallway, I wandered toward the front of the house. I wanted to go home and take a shower, but not until I'd thanked Peaches and said goodbye. The vacuum hadn't started up again. He was probably still on the phone. Maybe Sally was at Chips' place. Maybe, after I'd got cleaned up, I'd give Chips a call.

Instead of going straight to the foyer and the front stairs, I made a right into the dining room. The long antique mahogany table, barren of even a covering cloth, was waxed to a high sheen. A dark mirror, it reflected the paintings that hung down the long walls on either side. I found myself staring at Sally's.

Where was she?

'God, I'm so sorry,' I whispered to the painting before I realized I'd spoken.

Behind me, a tennis shoe squeaked on the floor. I turned.

'Alex,' Peaches said. His face was pale.

'What is it?'

'That was Ardith on the phone. Chips

301

Quincannon's father died early this morning.'

At Peaches' suggestion, I went home. He'd told Ardith I was back, and while I wasn't exactly certain what else he'd told her, it was enough that she'd said I wasn't to worry about coming in.

I phoned Sally's house first thing, but once again got Norman, who told me she wasn't there, damn it, before he hung up on me.

I took a shower, found fresh clothes and a jacket, and then phoned Chips at home. She answered on the third or fourth ring and sounded breathless.

'Jesus, Frank, I told you I'm in no mood for this,' she said, instead of hello.

'Chips, it's Alex.'

'Oh. Hi.' She didn't seem all that pleased to hear from me, either. I supposed Sally had told her everything. 'I thought you were my ex,' she added, after a pause. 'The sonofabitch picked today to call and ask for more money.'

'I...I'm sorry about Pops, Chips. I just heard a little while ago. Do you need anything?' All right, it wasn't exactly brilliant, but it was all I could think to say. And even though I truly was sorry about Pops and sorry that Frank was a bum, the uppermost thing in my mind trying to figure a polite way to ask if she'd seen Sally.

'No, I don't need anything, unless...can you come over here?'

That took me by surprise, but I said, 'Sure, when?'

'Right now. I need somebody stronger than

me to help bend a section of this friggin' armature. New piece. Really big. It'll never fit through Ardith's door.'

I parked in front of Chips' house, and then, as per her instructions, walked down the drive, past her car, and back to the old carriage house. The doors were propped open, and I could hear Chips cursing before I was halfway there.

I called her name.

Something metal hit the cement floor inside, and bounced a couple of times with a loud *ding ding.* ' 'Bout time,' she yelled.

I walked in. The carriage house was two storeys tall, and she'd gutted it so it was one big open space, clear up to the old hayloft's rafters. She stood on a low platform in the centre of it, a pipe wrench in one gloved hand, the beginnings of an armature climbing into the air beside her. Her long hair was snagged up into a lopsided bun on top of her head, and she wore an old, torn sweater dotted with flecks of dried clay, solder, and tiny clots of brownish sculptor's wax. Her eyes were red, and crumpled tissues were scattered over the slab floor.

'Gonna be for Pops,' she said, as she climbed down.

'Has it got a name?' I couldn't make sense of the metalwork. At that stage, it's like looking at a neat row of three stars in the night sky, and having not a clue that it's Orion's Belt and there's supposed to be a whole guy up there.

'Not yet,' she said, and had me follow her to the far corner, where one end of a five-foot

303

pipe was clamped into a vice. 'I need to bend this sucker about twenty-five degrees,' she said. 'Push up. Or down. I don't care, so long as it gets bent.'

It wasn't all that difficult. I said, 'You could have done that yourself, Chips.'

She cocked a brow. 'You're pretty damn smart for somebody who's practically a professional horse's ass.' She pulled off her gloves and tossed them on top of a beat-up welder's mask on the workbench. 'Want a cup of coffee?'

'No, thanks.'

'Well, I do.' A small table, one of those 1950's dinette numbers, hugged the west wall between an industrial sink and a battered antique refrigerator. There was a coffeemaker on the table, and she poured herself a cup. 'How 'bout a Coke? Or a Vernor's? There's some in the fridge.'

I got myself a can.

'Sit down.'

I did, and found a place in her crowded ashtray to stub out my cigarette.

She leaned back in her chair, fingered her cup for a moment, then folded her hands in her lap. She looked me in the eye. 'At the risk of sounding like somebody's over-bearing father in some goddamn nineteenth-century melodrama, what are your intentions with Sally?'

Intentions? Slowly, I said, 'I'm not sure how to answer that.'

She glared at me. 'Try.'

I studied the red-and-white can in my hand. 'I love her, that's all.'

304

Chips shook her head. 'Big deal. That's a statement, not a plan. She told me about that letter you sent her.'

'Oh.'

She just stared at me, her face as blank as a slab of granite. I hated it when she did that. It made me feel guilty or inadequate or stupid. In this case, I was all three.

'Okay, I admit it, I'm a jerk. A moron. I made a mistake. I went over this morning and tried—'

'Yeah, I heard. Real slick, Alex. Captain Finesse.'

I sat up straight. 'You talked to her this morning? Did you see her? Is she all right?'

She took a sip of her coffee. 'She's fine. Stop squirming. The question is, are you serious about this? I mean, really serious?'

'Yes.'

'Then do something about it.'

'I'm trying! Either she's disappeared, or she just plain won't talk to me. Every time I call, that jerk of a cousin says she isn't there and hangs up. Chips, I *do* love her. I want to spend the rest of my life with her. If she'll have me.'

I slouched back in my chair and exhaled through my mouth. 'She's close to crazy, I think. I don't understand half the things she does or why she does them, but I love her. If I can't patch up this mess I've made, I think both Sally and I will be sorry for a very long time. Forever, maybe.'

She studied her fingernails for a few seconds before she looked up. 'All right. I believe you,

kiddo. But Sally's not crazy. It's just...' She
stopped and studied her coffee cup.

I knew then that Chips had the key. Gently, I
said, 'When I was in New York, I saw these old
paintings of hers. They... My God, Chips, they
made me want to weep. What happened to her?
Has she ever said anything? Do you know?'

'Yeah,' she said softly, not looking at me. 'I
know.'

I touched her arm. 'Please.'

She shrugged away my hand and, after a
moment, said, 'Okay. I'm gonna tell you
something. It's...it's not my place to tell you,
and I once promised Sally I'd never—'

She turned her head and, mouth twisting,
stared at the wall. 'I think it's important though.
If you want to understand her. She...she had it
rough. When she was a kid. She got past most
of it, but—'

'Past most of *what*? Chips?

Her mouth twisted again. 'It's Norman.' She
didn't look at me.

'The cousin?'

Her lips tightened, relaxed, tightened again
before she said, 'He raped her when she was
nine, and he kept on doing it for five years,
until he went away to college.'

All the air left my lungs; it seemed I couldn't
get it back.

'When he came home from college she was
just out of high school, and she moved out
and left town, moved to Kansas City, I think;
someplace like that. Two years later he showed
up at her apartment, out of the blue. She said

306

nobody paid any attention to the screaming—it was a rough neighbourhood. He stayed for three days. Jesus, Alex!' She suddenly leaned forward and grabbed at my arm.

Soda coursed over my hand and pooled on the tabletop. What was left of the Coke can was crumpled inside my fist.

Chips grabbed a rag and mopped at my cuff.

I jerked away, shoved the chair back, stood up. 'Why didn't you do something? You knew, and you didn't get her out of there. You should have told me, you should have told somebody! He's in her *house,* damn it!'

She jumped up, too. 'You think I don't know that?' she shouted. 'Fuck you, Alex! I love Sally, but I'm her best friend, not her keeper. She's a grownup. She's got this thing under control, even if she's sleeping in her car to do it. That's her choice. And I've been just a little busy, thank you. I'm not the one who led her on and made her fall in love with me, and then sent her a stinking Dear Jane letter and left town, am I?'

Images flooded into my head, too fast, all in the wrong order: the terror on Sally's face when the doorbell rang and she knew it was Norman and the aunt down there, feathers, white down from the pillows, drifting to our feet on the upstairs landing; Sally, standing with Chips on the gallery floor, with that yellow handprint on her backside; Sally shrinking away from outstretched hands at the opening, her posture pleading. 'Don't touch me, don't touch me';

307

Sally in her studio, that first night, her back to me as she gripped the sides of the sink, whispering, 'Do it here, Alex, do it now'; the condescending disapproval of her aunt's face, the barely disguised leer on Norman's; Bobby Daws in his red jacket, whispering, 'She still as wild as she used to be?'; the Iris Lady on the landing, so cool and aloof, untouchable, perfect in her isolation.

All those things and more suddenly went *click* in my head, like jigsaw pieces snapping together, all at once. Quietly, I said, 'Chips, I'm sorry.'

'I didn't tell you that stuff so you'd feel sorry for her or make excuses for her. I told you so that maybe you'd understand why she does some of what she does. Why she lives in that big old house like a hermit. Why she acts scared sometimes for no apparent reason. Why she doesn't like people to touch her. And I also told you because I...because I was a little rough on her earlier today. Sally's tough, Alex. If she wasn't she wouldn't have made it this far. But at the same time, she's...'

'Fragile. I know.'

She sat again and slumped in her chair, elbows on her knees, face tipped down. She rubbed at her eyes. 'It's just that people you love, they don't stay around forever. You've gotta cherish them, be with them, let them know you care.'

She sniffed, then blew her nose into the rag she'd been mopping my sleeve with.

I sat down across from her.

'Try and fix it, Alex, if you love her. But only

308

if you mean it, really mean it, and only if it's not out of some weird sort of pity. If you're not sure, if you've got one single doubt, then just leave her the hell alone, okay?'

I took her hands in mine. 'I don't have any doubts, Chips. And it wasn't what you said—about Norman, I mean, though I'm grateful you told me. It has nothing to do with pity. I'd already decided. I don't know if she'll have me back, but I have to try. And Chips? About Pops, I...'

She pulled her hands away and sat up straight. 'I don't want to talk about it right now, OK? Tell you what. Why don't you hang around here for a while? I'll try Sally at home for you. El Creepo's more likely to put through a call from a woman than a man, I bet. Once we know she's home, you can go do your thing. Till then, you can help me with this.' She tipped her head back toward the armature.

I nodded. My first urge had been to drive straight over to Sally's and strangle Norman, or rope and throw and castrate him, like a range calf. Maybe all of it. But I had to admit, grudgingly, that Chips was right. No matter how badly I wanted to knock old Norman into the week after next, Sally was handling it; unless the situation came to a crisis point, it was, perhaps, better—for her, if not for me—to let her deal with it in her own way.

'Okay,' I said, and pushed the phone toward her. 'But try now, would you?'

She dialled Sally's number, but got Norman. 'I'll try back in a hour or so,' she muttered, after she put the receiver down. 'Maybe she went to get her window fixed or something.'

Pulling her gloves on, she climbed up on the platform and pointed at a length of pipe. I handed it up to her, and fervently wished I was in my car, on my way to Sally's.

I pictured again Sally's self-portrait: the snake constricting about her skull; her face downturned, luminous and hopeless all at once; the dark, featureless figure looming in the background; the despair. I sorted the numbers quickly in my head. She would have painted it not long after Norman had locked her in her apartment for three days and...

The scum-sucking bastard. Fury coursed through me again, and I forced myself to push it back, unclench my teeth, relax my fists.

The Prodigal. A wave of gooseflesh covered me when I remembered that title.

Chips was staring at me. 'You okay?'

'No. I won't be okay until that guy's gone. Preferably in his grave.'

She scowled. 'Yeah. Get in line for that one.' She angled the pipe out over the armature and let one end drop, with a clang, to rest along another bit of metalwork.

'Chips, I don't know what this thing is going to end up being, but you'll never get it out of here.'

She shrugged. 'Gotta cut it into sections before it goes to the foundry, anyway. But if it still won't fit the doors, I'll tear down a wall. So tell me about these paintings you saw in New York. I've never seen any of Sally's older stuff.'

24

Sally

'It's about time you got here. Mama ran out of tissues.' Hands on his hips, Norman planted himself between me and the Iris Lady to block the downstairs landing.

I tried to go around him, but he stuck his arm in front of me and grabbed the newel post.

Mariah's wheelchair, one legrest jacked up into place, creaked toward me from the parlour, and it crossed my mind that, considering the amount of money they'd charged me for that stupid chair, they should have oiled it or something. She wheeled so close that she bumped my leg with her cast.

'Finally,' she said, and then she sneezed. Gone were the invalid's nightgown and robe. She had on a mauve print housedress and a little makeup, and she'd done her hair. Or maybe Norman had. Over the now-constant odour of White Shoulders, the foyer smelled faintly of hairspray. She yanked a crumpled wad of pink toilet paper from her pocket and blew her nose loudly.

'That cat's been in this house again. And just where have you been all this time? Off someplace with that *person*, I'll wager. That young hoodlum who keeps calling. Oh, he says

311

he's with some gallery or other, but we're not fooled, are we, Norman?'

The television remote was in her lap. She worried at it unconsciously, trailing her knobbly fingers over the buttons. She had painted her short, square nails, too, one of those pale iridescent pinks. She had left the moons white.

I said, 'Who called? Was it Alex Langley?'

She ignored the question. 'You missed lunch.' Her expression altered abruptly. Her lips pressed into a tight line before she licked at them with the very tip of her tongue. 'Mmm-mmm! Norman made fried ham sandwiches. With cole slaw from the store. It was almost as good as your Aunt Mavis's, once I told Norman how to doctor it up.'

'Gee,' I said dryly. 'Wish I'd been here.'

The smile disappeared, and she scowled again. 'Don't go taking that tone with me. God is always watching. I was only trying to tell you that Norman made extra. There's a sandwich for you in the refrigerator, some slaw, too. Unless you feel it's beneath you to eat something *we* made.'

Norman tapped his foot. 'The car?'

I held out the keys. He grabbed my hand when he took them, and wouldn't let go.

'Get some lemons, too, Norman,' Mariah continued, oblivious to our little wrestling match. 'I'll tell Sally how to make a nice glaze for that store cake you got yesterday.'

'Yes, Norman,' I hissed, and wrenched my fingers free with a jerk. 'Do get some lemons, by all means.'

He smirked at me, one eyebrow raised. I knew he'd aged, but I hadn't realized until just then how many wrinkles he had, and how the bags, a purplish cast, drooped beneath his eyes. He looked far older than 44. And with that dirty little fourteen-year-old boy's leer twisting his features, he looked moronic. A middle-aged man, afraid to leave his mother; a pathetic creature so mean and so unsure that he had resorted to the lowest crime of all, preying upon a captive child: the ogre I'd feared for so many years was unmasked, and found a buffoon.

It was a stellar moment.

He pulled on his jacket.

'Be back by three,' I said, as he circumnavigated Mariah's wheelchair and opened the front door.

'Why?'

I smiled. 'I have a surprise for you.'

'Oh, goody,' he said sarcastically. Closing the door behind him, he clomped across the porch. Through the frosted glass I watched his blurry shape turn around to back down the front steps, then walk out of sight.

See you later, perpetrator.

'And nothing for me, I suppose,' Mariah muttered after another sneeze and a snuffling blow into the toilet paper. She turned her chair toward my poor dishevelled front room, her broken leg jutting out before her like the prow of a ship.

I heard a muffled rumble as Norman started my car and backed out of the driveway.

After while, paedophile.

'The surprise is for you, too, Aunt Mariah.'

I was sorely tempted to ask if Alex had left a message, but I doubted she'd tell me either way. Besides, Alex had nothing to do with my plans for this afternoon. I'd talk to him later.

Maybe.

'What kind of surprise?' Mariah cocked her head slightly. The memory of ham sandwiches had mined far more enthusiasm from her.

I said, 'That would be telling.'

I took a good look at her, a really good look at what she was, and what she had become. I forced myself to strip away the psychic scars that through the years had distorted the lens through which I viewed her.

And what was left? An old woman who'd never had the fortune to be pretty or even handsome, even in her youth, and whose only remaining vanity was in her self-righteousness. An old woman, six feet tall in her stocking feet, who still said 'potty' when she wanted to use the bathroom. A woman to whom a ham sandwich was the high point of the week, and who had been denied the one pathetic prize she most valued in life: a mail-order mink.

She'd had one short marriage, probably to the only man who'd ever got up the nerve to kiss her, and no other liaisons. She'd lived all her life in the same strangled little town, and her energies, without exception, had been focused upon her son and a clique of siblings that prided itself in drawing no nurture from the spectrum of the outside world, preferring to cannibalize the single, safe, shadowed dot of self-absorbed

314

grey that was The Family.

How could the Aunts' dark, suffocating orb help but shrink to a pinpoint when they distrusted and feared anything new, anything bigger than they were, anything different from 'us'?

Mariah had known about Norman. But she'd been so mortified by what her son was doing all those years ago that she simply refused to admit such a thing could exist.

She'd become blind, deaf, and dumb, and busied herself with canasta and church work and resenting me, because I was the different one, the horrifying one. Her brother had created Frankenstein's monster, then dumped it on her. I was the freak and the aberration, and I was to blame.

If it's true that fear runs in families, and I believe it does, I hereby cast my ballot for nurture over nature. I'd brought myself to the point of fearing everything, and why? Because I'd been fostered in a house that stank of it.

I'd been afraid of life, of Alex. Of myself.

We all create our refuges, though. The Aunts had each other; I had my work. Was I so different from Mariah? From Norman? I wondered if my grandparents had been the same, and instilled these fears in the Aunts and my father. How deep into the core of my family tree did the decay run? How many generations had been poisoned, crippled?

Oh, how terrified they all must have been of my mother—my fair-haired, laughing mother —who was from a faraway, exotic-sounding place and painted pictures and wrote stories, and who'd stolen my father from their sad little circle. Perhaps she'd even taught him the unforgivable crime of courage.

I was her child more than his. They must have been scared of me, too, right from the start.

Imagine that.

Afraid of me.

Clear blue, clear blue, clear blue.

If Chips had been there, I would have bathed her feet with my hair.

Oh, I'd already made the first few limping steps when I'd let myself love Alex; maybe even before that, in smaller, barely perceptible ways. And I'd known about Norman and Mariah and me for a long time, I suppose, but Chips had made me *realize* it.

Maybe I'd write Oprah a letter, too.

'Sally!'

How long had I stood there, staring? Perhaps only a few seconds. It seemed an eternity. 'I said, 'Sorry, Aunt Mariah. I have some stuff to do. Do you need anything before I go upstairs?'

She eyed me suspiciously. 'Cheese and crackers would be nice. Saltines.'

'Okay.' I turned toward the kitchen.

'With some of that Cracker Barrel cheddar,' she added. 'And a root beer. And maybe some of those little hard candies Norman got. In the red wrappers, not the orange ones. I don't like those.'

I nodded. 'Sure, Aunt Mariah.'

I was almost to the dining room when she said my name again.

316

'Yes?'

She fussed at her skirt with old fingers capped in pearly, little-girl pink. 'I...Sally, what do you think about?'

'Beg pardon?'

'Ever since you were a child, you... What do you think about, when you go away like that?'

I had known her for almost forty years, and she had never asked. I said, 'Colours, mostly.'

She looked down at her lap, and then she gave a little snort. 'Foolishness,' she said softly before she turned away, the remote in her outstretched hand, and snapped on the television. 'Don't slice the cheese too thick.'

I didn't mean to scare you, old woman.

I fixed her snack, and while I was at it, chopped up half my ham sandwich for the cat. It came right away when I called *'Kitty-kitty'* from the backporch, and trotted inside, chattering and purring, when I held the door open. I stood a moment watching it eat, before I announced, 'From now on, your name is Vermeer. You should be honoured. He did primo glazes, the best.'

His ears cocked backward, toward my voice, but he didn't stop eating. I heard a muffled *ah-choo!* from the front room.

Scooping up Aunt Mariah's plate and candy and soda, I added, 'When you're finished here, Vermeer, old bean, there's a nice lady in the front room who *loves* pussycats. Just stay back about ten feet and you'll be fine.'

I heard Geraldo in my head: *Passive/Aggressive Behaviour. What is it, and how harmful can it be? Are you guilty of it? Our Focus for Today: We're Not Going to Tell You.*

Well, I thought, smiling as I carried Mariah's goodies into the dining room, then propped open the kitchen door just wide enough for a cat to get through, *I suppose a person can't fix* everything *right off the bat...*

By a quarter to three, I'd taken care of most everything I'd needed to do upstairs, including flushing the rest of Chips' pills down the john. I was in my room, emptying my underwear drawer of anything Norman or the dead mouse might possibly have touched—which meant everything—when the phone rang.

Downstairs, over soap opera music, Mariah called, 'Sally! Telephone!' before she blew her nose with a resounding honk.

'I'll get it up here.' I flopped across the bed on my stomach and put my hand on the receiver, but I couldn't muster the nerve to lift it from the cradle. What on earth would I say to him? What would he say to me?

I thought maybe I should just let it ring. Let him think no one was home. *Oh, aren't we big and brave?*

'Sally! Are you going to answer that?'

Well, as Doris Day used to sing, whatever will be will be. Amen; the end. I picked it up. 'Hello?'

318

'Sally?'

'Oh, Chips, it's you. How's it going?'

'Okay.' There was a slight pause and a muffled sound, like a hand pressing close to the receiver, and then she said, 'Well, Frank called. I don't know whatever possessed me to marry such a card-carrying prick. But I'm okay. About Pops, I mean. And I'm working. It's gonna be huge, the biggest ever. I'm gonna call it *Buffalo Dancer*. I'm not even doing a model first, I'm goin' straight for the glory. Gonna take a billion tons of wax. Anyway, it's gonna cost a friggin' fortune to cast it. Are you all right, Sal? I called earlier and got you-know-who.'

I twisted on the mattress until I could see out the front window and down to the street, and then I lit a cigarette. It tasted pretty damn good for something that's supposed to take seven minutes off your life.

'I'm fine,' I said, and exhaled, a blue-white plume toward the curtains. 'Everything's fine.'

'You sure?'

'Yeah.' I glanced at the clock, then out the window. Ten minutes till three, and nobody on the street. Yet. 'Chips?'

'Yes?'

'I named the cat.'

Another pause. 'What cat?'

25

Alex

Chips was still on the phone when I took off down the driveway. Fifteen minutes later, I was in Sally's neighbourhood. I didn't drive to her house. I parked about a block over, sat in the car for another five minutes, smoked a cigarette, and then got out and walked.

The sun had burned out most of the darker grey overhead, leaving the sky silver-white. It was still chilly. I turned my collar up against the light wind and rehearsed what I'd say to Sally, if she let me say anything at all.

'I'm sorry' sounded so damn lame.

The sidewalk was damp in patches and scattered with discarded, wind-skipped leaves turned yellow or brown or red. The breeze had come up a little, reminding me it wouldn't be long before sleet and snow season. I found the thought profoundly depressing.

By the time I turned Sally's corner, I still hadn't come up with the definitive apology, but I *had* decided to slug Norman if he gave me the slightest excuse. I mean, I couldn't just walk up and hit him, not without Sally figuring out that somebody—namely Chips—had told me something they weren't supposed to. But if he gave me an opening...

At first, because of the truck parked out front, I thought one of her neighbours must be moving. But then, as I neared, I realized her front door was propped open and there were people going in and out. I broke into a jog.

I didn't see the ambulance in the driveway until I cut up the corner of her lawn, and I thought, *If he's hurt her, I'll kill him.*

I stopped in the middle of the front lawn, though, because just then Sally stepped out the front door, the cat at her heels and a large green suitcase in her hand. She put it down, then took a step back to make way for two men, carrying a mattress between them.

The mattress blocked my view of her for just a second, and when she reappeared, she was staring right at me.

I couldn't do anything but stare back. She looked so beautiful, and I felt so far away and, well, small.

Another man, this one burdened with two long metal bed railings, passed between us; still, I couldn't move.

A guy in a white uniform shoved a wheel chair out onto the porch, bounced it down the steps, rolled it down the walk to the drive, and deftly folded it up. The last I only caught peripherally. I couldn't take my eyes from Sally's.

I thought of all the things I wanted to say, arguments and persuasions that were much more convincing in the abstract than they could possibly be if articulated.

I started toward her.

She waited there on the porch, the cat rubbing

321

serpentines around her legs.

I walked up the steps. My legs felt like they weighed six hundred pounds each. It wasn't until I stopped, facing her, that I realized I'd never before seen her in the full light of day.

She looked glorious.

She said, 'Hello, Alex.' She hadn't said it with much enthusiasm.

Two of the guys from the truck, followed immediately by the ambulance attendant, passed between us and went inside the house, bootsteps thudding.

'Hi.' *Well, that was brilliant, Alex.* 'Is somebody hurt?'

'No,' she said. 'Just leaving.'

I tried again. 'Sally, can we talk? I've got so much to say to you. I don't know how to start. I know that saying I'm sorry doesn't begin to cover it, but—'

'Heads up!' somebody called from inside, and the two guys who'd just passed us came back out, this time carrying between them the naked frame of a bed.

Both Sally and I, on our respective sides of the porch, took a step back to let them pass.

'I'm a little busy right now,' she said, when I could see her again.

Don't screw this up, Alex.

'I know. I just...let me stay, Sally, please? Let me talk with you?' I held my breath.

She bit at her lower lip thoughtfully and folded her arms. She had on a pale eggshell cableknit, and the chill had turned her cheeks a soft peach. She looked up at me, her grey eyes level, her expression inscrutable, and said, 'I suppose that if you—'

'You sacrifice your life for a child, and this is what you get!'

We both turned toward the door. The guy in the white uniform backed out, guiding the end of one of those collapsible gurneys. The aunt was on it, coming headfirst, the safety strap a bright blue stripe across her sheeted chest. Another attendant brought up the rear.

Sally bent to scoop up the cat.

The aunt pointed a finger at Sally. 'So you were going to give us a surprise, were you? This should've come as no surprise to me, young lady; I should have expected it from the likes of you.' She sneezed and blew her nose loudly. 'A cat! I knew there was a cat in this house, I knew it!'

Sally signalled for the attendants to stop. She let the cat jump down, then took the woman's hand. 'Mariah,' she said gently but firmly, 'you'll be much more comfortable at home, and this way you won't have to fly. I wrapped up all your snack things and put them in a cooler.'

She glanced at one of the attendants, who nodded. 'There, you see, Aunt Mariah? They're already waiting for you. And I bought the wheelchair, my gift to you, so you'll have it when you get home. Don't you miss Mavis and Millie and Little Meg? I know they miss you.'

Down on the street, one of the truck's back gates banged shut.

Sally patted the older woman's hand, then

smoothed the sheet and tucked it in.

'But why do I have to be...to be *carried* like this?'

The first attendant cleared his throat. 'Regulations, ma'am. We've got to follow the rules, just like everybody else.' He looked at Sally, and she nodded.

The stretcher on wheels began to move again.

'I talked to Aunt Millie,' Sally said, as the attendants eased Mariah down the steps to the sidewalk. 'They expect you. She said not to worry, she'd air out the house and put in fresh groceries.'

With her arms crossed again, she watched the gurney wobble down the walk. I watched her. The pervading sense of dewiness was still there, but it seemed to me there was something new. Did she stand a little straighter, hold her head a fraction higher?

Norman stepped out on the porch, a suitcase in each hand. He let them drop with a double *thud.* His back was to me, and he blotted out my view of Sally. He said, 'You little sneak.'

I heard her say, 'Like the man said, Norman, it takes one to know one.'

His shoulders tensed. His right hand clenched into a fist. 'I oughta—'

I grabbed his arm. I couldn't exactly spin him around—he outweighed me by at least fifty pounds—but I got his attention. 'Knock it off.'

He turned toward me, snorting. 'Oh—*you* again. What'd she do, call to let you know

324

the coast was clear? Or did you come sniffing around all on your own?'

That's right, you prick. Give me a reason. I'll hit you so hard your grandkids'll be born dizzy. I pulled back my right, ready for him. 'Listen, you son of a bitch, I—'

Sally stepped between us, put one hand on my chest and the other on Norman's, and pushed—hard. She knocked us both off balance. Norman stumbled over a suitcase and caught himself on the porch rail.

'Enough!' she barked, suddenly a small blond drill sergeant. 'Norman, get your bags. Your mother's waiting. Alex, go in the house and sit down. And take Vermeer with you before somebody trips over him.'

Numbly, Norman picked up his suitcases, then backed down the steps. Very strange. I said, 'Vermeer?'

She picked up the cat and handed him to me. 'Here,' she said, and turned to take a clipboard and pen from one of the ambulance guys. She signed her name, at the same time thumping the last suitcase with her toe. 'Don't forget this one.' And then she called, 'Norman?'

He was halfway down the sidewalk. He turned around, scowling. 'Now what?'

'I just wondered. Is Clive Lightfoot still police chief in Brigston?'

'No, stupid. He died ten years ago. His son Jimmy is chief now. Why?'

I'd never seen such a snotty expression on a grown man. As ticked as I was at him for talking to Sally that way (on top of everything else), I was kind of embarrassed for him.

A small smile crept across Sally's face. 'Jimmy? Really. I remember Jimmy Lightfoot. He was in my class.'

All of a sudden Norman didn't look so smug, although he still looked a little infantile. 'Why'd you ask me that?'

She shrugged—a tiny gesture, as tiny but as confident as her smile. 'Gee, no reason, Norman. No reason at all.'

He blanched, but she wasn't looking at him anymore.

One of the men from the hospital supply truck started up the steps. He had a clipboard, too.

Slowly, Norman turned and picked up his bags again.

I went inside.

The front parlour was a shambles. Furniture was moved every which way. A plastic waste-basket overflowed with crumpled tissues, pink and white. Plates, dirtied with crumbs and candy wrappers, sat stacked haphazardly on the coffee table. Movie and soap opera magazines littered the sofa, and a long white scratch marred the parquet floor.

The place smelled of perfume and hairspray and something else—ham and cold cream, maybe.

I shoved aside a few magazines and sat down. The cat flopped out next to me and began to wash behind his ear.

Outside, Sally was arguing with the hospital bed guy. She said she wouldn't sign anything until they agreed to have her floor refinished.

He said the scratch was already there. She said it wasn't, and she had witnesses.

A new voice joined in. 'You call for a locksmith, lady?'

'Yeah. I need these changed on the front door, and two more on the back door. I want both deadbolts to use the same key, ditto for the ones with the buttons.'

I heard the boxy clank of a tool kit hitting the front porch at about the time she started back in arguing with the bed guy.

I was too nervous to just sit there, waiting. I went out to the landing to visit the Iris Lady and then, although I had no business up there, not now and maybe not ever again, I started up the stairs.

Her bedroom door was closed. I didn't open it. I just stood there, staring at it. No matter how badly I wanted to, I had no right to go in there, even if only to stand in the centre of it one last time.

I'd wait in the studio.

I was almost there when I stopped stock still. It had just hit me. Sally, my Sally—my shy, quiet, neither seen nor heard Sally—was *arguing* with that guy. And I mean, she was giving him a hard time. She wasn't backing up one inch.

Alex, you are truly in deep guano.

And then I realized I was smiling. She was about to tell me to take my apology and shove it, and I was smiling.

Life is strange, huh?

But the smile left my face at the exact

327

moment I opened the studio door. That painting couldn't have staggered me any worse if she'd thrown it at me.

It was the canvas she'd started that first night. I could tell by the size, and by the yellow underpainting that showed at the edges of the stretchers. But dear God, what she'd done to it.

The compositional fields were the same—not in colour, but in density. Only a tiny hint of yellow showed through here or there, but it had been muddied, corrupted. Snaking ribbons of peach and rose surfaced, too, but they were incidental to the thrust of the piece. Deep black-blues and bottomless purples swirled and pulsed over the linen, sent out skeletal fingers of darkest indigo or purple lake or purpled thalo that interconnected into a subtle web of something I can only describe as despair.

Downward it spiralled, twisting deeper and deeper like otherworldly, blackened water taking a mad, warped path down a drainpipe to hell; and at the centre, the deepest point, it just went dead. Flat. No plummet to infinity. It just stopped in a matte dot, no bigger than a dime, of dull, dead black.

It made me sick to my stomach to look at it, but it wasn't the opticals so much as the pain that roared out of it and sank into it at the same time. It was horrible.

It was brilliant.

I realized my eyes were wet. I grabbed a paper towel off one of the paint tables, and when I did, something small and pink flicked up into the air, then settled to the floor. I picked it up.

It was a rose petal, mostly wilted. Pink.

Sonia pink.

26

Sally

'Fine, then. Have your supervisor call me.'

He opened his mouth again, as if he thought just one more argument might convince me, and then he seemed to think better of it. 'All right, Miz French,' he growled, and walked off toward his truck, slapping the clipboard against his thigh.

The locksmith, screwdriver in hand, looked up from the front door deadbolt. 'Givin' you a hard time, huh, Lady?'

I said, 'I've had worse.'

The equipment rental truck pulled away from the kerb just as the ambulance driver started his engine. I watched him carefully back down the narrow, walled drive and into the street. Norman sat in the rear, his back to me.

I'd seen enough talk shows to know you're supposed to confront the ones who have harmed you. You're supposed to tell them what they did was wrong, and that you're angry. Maybe that's what you're *supposed* to do, but I didn't feel the need. Norman knew what he'd done, and no

329

amount of rhetoric from me would convince him he hadn't been perfectly justified. That was just the way he was when it came to me.

To be honest, I had few fears that he'd go out and do it to somebody else. His crimes had been targeted at me and me alone: the bad one, the wrong one, the out-of-place one. No other person had ever, or would ever, fit into that narrow category again.

For Norman, it had never been the sex; it had been the humiliation. It had been putting me in my place, and trying to make me less frightening.

But I was going to give Jimmy Lightfoot, Police Chief, a call, anyway. I was fairly sure Jimmy would remember me with a certain fondness. And I was fairly sure he'd believe me, and that he'd keep an eye on Norman. Unofficially, of course.

And Mariah? What good would come of confronting her? Denial was her major gift. She hadn't believed me when I was nine, and she was no more likely to believe me now. And even if she did—even if, for one second, her heart recognized the truth—she'd never admit it. Not even to herself.

I knew I'd never see them again. There'd be no cards at birthdays or Christmases, no family reunion picnics, no funerals attended. They were my family only because of an accident of genetics. I was my only real family. And Chips, of course. What on earth would I ever do without Chips? Pops had wanted to be cremated, his ashes scattered over the lake up at Bemidji. I'd told her I'd be with her in the helicopter.

I supposed I was going a little overboard, what with changing the locks and all. I didn't *really* think Norman would come all the way back to Minneapolis and break in. It was more of a symbol than anything else, I guess.

The locksmith was staring at me. 'You okay, lady?'

I nodded. 'Give me a yell when you're finished.'

And now for Alex.

I had no idea what I'd say to him, but I wasn't frightened. I'd be all right.

He hadn't heard me coming up the stairs.

He was in the studio, crouched and rocking on his heels, his back to me as he stared up at the painting. He tossed a crumpled paper towel toward the waste can, and then he took his head in his hands. A single rose petal was clamped between the index and middle finger of his left.

He moaned, very softly, my name.

I came up behind him and touched his shoulder.

'Alex?'

He stood slowly before he turned toward me. His face was ashen. He said, 'Oh, Sally,' and then he looked away, the muscles in his jaw working.

I knew just how he felt.

It's amazing, after all the hurt other people do to us, that we pile so much more on ourselves.

331

I admit I was still drunk enough on power from the little farewell scene downstairs that for a fraction of a second, I considered slapping him. But I didn't, mainly because I had an equal and opposite urge to throw my arms around him.

I took the middle ground. I said, 'You wanted to talk.'

He combed his fingers through his loose, unruly hair. 'Sal, I...Jesus, there's so much. I don't know where to begin. About that note I sent, I was completely out of line. I know it hurt you, and I'd give anything—I mean *anything*—if I could take it back, just erase it. I guess the thing was that I fell so hard for you. I thought and thought and thought, and it still didn't make sense, and then this morning...'

He put a hand to his forehead and closed his eyes, tightly, for half a second. 'I didn't mean to get so angry. I just, I mean, I still—Christ. I'm babbling, I know, but damn it, Sal, I love you. I never loved anybody like this before, and it...it—'

'Scared you?'

He sighed, then nodded. 'It terrified me.'

Well, he was one step ahead of most of the planet. He already knew the monsters are real, and they are us. On him, the truth would not be wasted.

I said, 'Alex, I won't lie to you. You hurt me. You hurt me so badly that I wanted to die, and then I wanted to hurt you back. I wrecked your roses and I wrecked my painting. But you know what? A person can't go through life destroying because they feel destroyed. Or

332

hurting other people because they've been hurt. Or hiding from everything hoping it will all go away.'

'Sally, I—'

'Let me finish. Half the people in this world realize they're screwed up and that they've been had, and spend all their time crying over it or running away. The other half are so messed up that they don't *realize* it, and spend their time avenging themselves, without knowing why, on whoever's handy. And why? Because they're scared. We're all scared, Alex. Scared of the dark or scared of pain, scared of thunder or of being alone or of being with someone; scared that any sort of joy is just an illusion. Scared is something I understand inside-out.'

He was listening, all right, listening to every word, and he was hearing it, really hearing it. His eyes, those ancient, wonderful eyes, never moved from mine, never wavered; and I knew he was strong, that he had learned the truth about himself, and that he could take whatever decision I gave him and survive.

And only then, in that moment, did I know what my answer would be.

'I can forgive you, Alex,' I said softly. 'I already forgave you. I guess the question is, can you forgive me?'

'Forgive you? For what?'

'For not understanding. For pushing you away at first, and holding back. For not being younger. For not listening. For scaring you.'

He held out his arms to me, and I moved into them, into their comfort, melding my fledgling strength with his. His breath was warm and quiet against my temple; the soft pressure of his kiss upon my forehead was sweet.

He whispered, 'There's nothing to forgive. I did it to myself.' He slipped his hand beneath my hair to cradle my neck. 'I love you, Sally. I love you so much.'

Beyond him, past his encircling arm, sat my easel-bound painting. It was not so bad as I'd thought; it was in fact, good. But it wasn't finished yet. It was not yet the truth, because I hadn't known all the truth when I'd put away my brushes.

The place it ended, where it swirled down and stopped dead, was not the end. That little speck of hopelessness was what needed fixing, because there was hope. After the pain, after the hurt and despair, came faith, came understanding, came clear, clear blue. Just a little dab of it, one tiny window to make the rest bearable.

He said, 'I've thought about us, thought hard about everything about us. I want to marry you.'

I looked up at him. Yes, he would do, this golden boy. He would do for a good long time.

A shock of wheaten hair had fallen over his forehead. I brushed it back with two fingers, then slowly ran them across his lips.

I said, 'I won't marry you, Alex. I'm different now than I was before. You might not like what I'm becoming. I don't even know what I'll be when I'm finished. And I'm still too old for you, that won't change. But for now, anyway, I'll be with you.'

He cupped my head between his hands, his thumbs lightly stroking my cheeks. His smile was soft, still tinged with sadness, but there was hope there, too, and a burgeoning joy. He said, 'I'll love you whatever you decide to be, old woman. And I'll ask again, you know.'

I touched his chin and smiled. 'I know. Kiss me, you little whippersnapper.'

This Large Print Book for the Partially sighted, who cannot read normal print, is published under the auspices of

THE ULVERSCROFT FOUNDATION